Praise for

I started Naturally, Charlie and finis[...]
contemporary story about friendship and lovah's is an absolute pleasure in the
RomCom category.

The character development is spot on. Each supporting character has a purpose
and they are used for just the right amount of time. In fact, SL could, if she hasn't
already thought about it, spin-off with the characters of Justin and Rachel, and
maybe give Connor a story.

Heidi ~ www.thereadiacs.com

The book is easy to read, the pages flying by at an alarming rate the deeper you get
into the story (and by alarming, I mean "OMG! NO! I can't be almost done, I need
more, more, more!").

SL Scott's writing is fluid, the dialogue and banter between the characters
believable and charming, and not once did the humor feel forced. There was never
a single moment where I felt it got cheesy or that it made me roll my eyes from
overkill. It was just... natural. They felt like real people, every single one of them.

I give it a straight five stars. I leaned toward 4.5 a few times, because there were
some moments where it had me really wanting to yell at someone for their
reactions (mainly the females in the story... Rachel made my head spin once and
Charlie Barrow is an extremely stubborn ass woman) but at the end of the day, it
only added to the story in a positive way.

I highly recommend Naturally, Charlie and hope you love the charming Mr.
Adams as much as I do.

J.M. Darhower ~ author of *Sempre*

I was quickly drawn into the story as the writing and the characters had this reader
laughing and crying throughout. Although, both main characters share the same
name, the author has done a fantastic job of never confusing the reader. Alternating
the narrators captured my attention as we slowly learn just how intertwined their
pasts were, how important their present is, and how solid their futures can be.

For the lover of romance, interesting and charismatic characters, and for the
lover of someone who wants to read a tale where the twists and turns will lead you
through a timely story of finding yourself again, I highly recommend "Naturally,
Charlie".

A love story of friendship and trust, truth and faith, interspersed between funerals
and fun, this reader thoroughly enjoyed Scott's first, and hopefully not her last,
novel.

Cejsmom ~ southernfictionreview.com

Naturally, Charlie

To Jennifer & Louis (handwritten)

My Everything (handwritten)

S.L. Scott (handwritten)

11-16-12 (handwritten)

By
S.L. Scott

The Writer's Coffee Shop
Publishing House

First published by The Writer's Coffee Shop, 2012

The Writer's Coffee Shop
(Australia)   PO Box 447 Cherrybrook NSW 2126
(USA)   PO Box 2116 Waxahachie TX 75168

Paperback ISBN- 978-1-61213-131-3
E-book ISBN- 978-1-61213-132-0

A CIP catalogue record for this book is available from the US Congress
Library.

Cover image licensed by www.depositphotos.com / © Igor Mojzes
Cover design by: Jada D'Lee

www.thewriterscoffeeshop.com/sscott

About the Author

S.L. Scott is a former high-tech account manager with a journalism degree pursuing her passion for telling stories. She spends her days escaping into her characters and letting them lead her on their adventures.

Live music shows, harvesting jalapenos and eating homemade guacamole are her obsessions she calls hobbies.

Scott lives in the beautiful Texas Hill Country of Austin with her husband, two young sons, two Papillons and a bowl full of Sea Monkeys.

Visit her at www.slscottauthor.com.

Acknowledgments

My family means the world to me, so I want to give thanks to my sweet boys for their patience when Mama needed to write and for the kisses, hugs, *I lub you's* and *love you's* I received while writing this story. My husband, you are my heart.

I want to send a special thank you to my inspiring and amazing Mom, my stubborn and fiercely loyal sister, Stephanie, and my beautiful and smart niece, Andrea.

Thank you to the following:

To Kirsten who encouraged me to write and to pursue my dreams. To Jennifer who had to suffer through many early manuscripts as I found my legs in the writing world. And to Kerri who had to listen to my endless yammering about my stories on our live music nights.

I can't give enough love back to the women who have supported me with their insight and hard work on this book. Many hugs and a personal thank you to an amazing team: Jada D'Lee, Irene, LemmieJenn, and Susi. Your words of support are as invaluable as you are to me. Thank you for making this journey fun and educational. Who knew Guinness has less calories than a Budweiser? Well, I do now.

To a group of friends who I cherish and must mention: Suzanne, Mary, Flavia, Laura, Sonia, Jaime, Ruth, Erin, Shauna, Tanya, Marie and my online community of friends. You are appreciated more than you know.

To Jada D'Lee again for so much, including this wonderful book cover.

To the lovely and hardworking team at The Writer's Coffee Shop, thank you. Heartfelt thanks to Amanda, Janine, Kathie, Wyndy Dee, Elyse, and Andrea.

Dreams come in many forms and this book was one of mine. Thank you for reading and making my dream come true.

To my forever and a day

Chapter 1
Charlie Barrow

♀

"Damn it!"

My day starts with an irritation that some might see as an omen of things to come. Others might see it as a minor speed bump. I see it as another hassle in a gigantic series of hassles, but a hassle all the same. My life seems to be filled with agitations these days.

The toothbrush drops, and I watch as it bounces off the sink and straight into the toilet. With a frustrated sigh, I lean forward and spit the toothpaste out, realizing now that I only got to my bottom left molars before my grip slipped and the toothbrush went down.

I look at the blue stick floating in the middle of the toilet, mocking me as it drifts around. Pinching it between my fingers, I rescue the toothbrush from the cold porcelain bowl. My life isn't *that* bad to argue whether I should keep it or not. I toss the brush without a second thought and finish getting dressed for work.

I spill my coffee—er, I mean when a guy running into the Coffee Hut hits me with his shoulder, thus causing the coffee to bubble through the little spout on the lid and land on my shirt, I chalk it up to another annoying mishap in this stage of my life. After the coffee incident and ToothGate this morning, I need to pay closer attention to the world around me. These tedious little occurrences are still new to me, but they all add up to a large amount of unnecessary aggravation. I've always believed that it's the little things that make up your life. The bigger events just connect them. This is a philosophy I live by now.

I arrive at Smith & Allen, an auction house representing property from private estates and corporate collections. It's regarded as "preeminent in the marketplace of quality masterpieces, antiques, and antiquities." That's what's written in the brochure. I've been known to believe in such greatness before, but today won't be one of those days.

I make my way through the maze of cubicles to my own little sectioned-off grey area and find a large manila envelope crowding my tiny, tidy desk. I set my coffee down and toss my purse in the bottom right drawer, kicking the cabinet closed.

"Red or green?" Rachel Russo asks. She's my friend, coworker, and all around party girl.

"Green." I keep my voice flat, trying to maintain a straight face while I tease since I'm clueless to why she's asking me about colors.

I slide my jacket down my arms. Catching it in my hand, I hang it on the hook attached to the half wall that divides our two cubicles. When I sit, my chair does a slow bounce, adjusting to the weight it's now holding, and I slide my body forward.

"You don't even know why I'm asking."

I don't have to look at her to know she's pouting. I can hear it in her tone. I give in and play along. "What's it for?"

"Tonight. We're going out. So, my va-va-va-voom red dress, or my green-means-go-home-with-me dress?"

I can't hold back the laughter no matter how hard I try. "You're ridiculous."

"And on the market. So, which one?"

"*On the market?* What happened to Paolo?" I stand, leaning forward so no one overhears our personal conversation.

"He went back to Rome."

"Since when? Weren't you supposed to see him last night?"

"Yes, and I did, right before he left for the airport. I gave him his going away gift."

"Do I even entertain the question?"

"Yes." Her response is laced with giddiness.

"What was his gift?"

"Me, him, naked on his balcony with a bottle of red wine."

My mouth drops open. Okay, I didn't expect that. "Rachel! He has a second floor walk-up that overlooks the street."

She shrugs as if public nudity is common. Well, maybe it is in New York, but still. "It was a fantasy of his, and I enjoyed it. I look good in the nude. Remember when I modeled for a sculpting class? I got asked out by three of the students."

"That doesn't count." I roll my eyes. "One was the teacher—the very *female* teacher—one wore bifocals and was older than your grandfather—"

"And the other was Paolo."

I plop back down in my seat. "Point taken. Are you going to miss him?"

"I gave him the best night of his life so *he* misses *me*. See how that works? I predict no more than a month before he's knocking on my New York City door again."

"And by door, I'm guessing you mean your va-j? You know, you'd do well as a call girl."

"Jealous much?" She jokes with me as she sits back on her side of the divider.

"All the time." I always enjoy a good morning-time exchange.

With the envelope in hand, I scan the address label that's typed on the front:

Ms. Charlotte Barrow
Smith & Allen
584 Madison Avenue
New York, New York
10022

I blow a harsh breath as if I've been punched in the gut. My heart aches as I read the return address:

Mrs. James Bennett Sr.
12 Sutton Place
Penthouse
New York, New York
10021

I drop the package to the floor, the smooth paper like acid on my skin. At least that's what it feels like to me. Mrs. James Bennett Sr., also known as Jim's mother, has a knack for the low blow covered in a superficial camouflage of tact. And she doesn't disappoint today.

Tears fill my eyes as I search for anything to distract me, to make me not think about Jim. I look at my calendar and focus on the inspirational phrase below the picture, needing support, any support, I can get. I read, digesting the quote word by word. *When you have confidence, you can have a lot of fun, and when you have fun you can do amazing things – Joe Namath.*

Okay, a sports personality giving me life advice might seem strange, but I can deal with that. I mean, he is an icon—even if I don't know what for. I have confidence. I can do this. I take a deep breath then slowly exhale. *I am a strong, confident woman! I am a strong, confident woman!*

I pick the envelope back up and run my finger along the return address, touching the package and being careful not to be burned again—metaphorically. Turning it sideways, I open it as if it's anything else that comes across my desk needing my attention. Some papers and a three-inch-square box spill out before me. Proper etiquette dictates opening the card before the present, so I reach for that first.

The card isn't a card, though—it's an invitation to his funeral. I can't believe his mother is turning her own son's funeral into a social event. One of the main reasons Jim and I were never meant to be—our upbringings were just too different.

I knew the funeral was coming, although I didn't know if I'd be invited. My original plan was to crash . . . for Jim, in remembrance of the good times. As I turn the card over in my hand, I can't stop the roll of my stomach seeing it in print. He's gone, deceased, dead. Tears fill my eyes when I realize I'll never see him again.

Can I do this right now? I drop my face into my hands, my elbows supporting its weight, and I stare at the box. Memories flood from the last time I saw him—saw him alive. Maybe if I'd taken him back, he'd still be alive now. Maybe if I had pushed the hurt, the pain away that day he came to my apartment, he'd still be here. I'm tired of wondering if I'd taken him back whether I could have saved him.

I'm just tired.

Squeezing my eyes shut, I replay my mother's words, letting them in, and hope they give me the strength I need. *"You didn't cause his accident, just like you didn't cause him to make the decisions he made. He alone chose those."*

He alone.

Alone.

Alone, like I am now.

Jim's gone forever and I'm alone.

I wipe away the tears before they fall. I'm at work, and though some of my coworkers are aware of his death, I try very hard to keep my personal life out of the workplace. I think I'm strong enough to be here today, to deal with this, but not if it comes with the added pressure of smiling to reassure sympathetic coworkers. I can't do that.

But I can do this, I reason with myself. Not that I have much choice. I set the card down and pick up the box, hesitating as I lift the brown lid to peek inside. There in the fluffy white filler lies a simple white-gold ring with little diamonds sparkling like tiny stars randomly embedded in the band. I hold it between my index finger and thumb, remembering the life to which this ring once belonged.

I shake off those memories, not wanting to travel down that lane again, especially not at work.

The three days prior, I called in sick to mourn his loss, my loss, everyone's loss. It wasn't enough time to come to grips with his death. The sadness sits like a rock in the center of my chest. It was more like a small hole before I found out he died. My heart was healing, enough time had passed, and I was moving on. When his sister called me, the hole gaped open once again. Today, it's more like a hard mass. Maybe that's my heart. I can't tell these days, so I try not to think about it.

I put the ring, with care, back into the box and close the lid. I rummage through the papers included and find two letters and a poem that Jim wrote for me. I close my eyes, rubbing my temples, as my annoyance flairs. It's a photocopy of the poem, a private moment we once shared. I should have the original, but in my hurry to leave, it was left behind. Now that Jim's gone, I assume the original remains in the tight grip of his mother.

I'm quite surprised she sent my engagement ring, but I'm sure the reminder of the rift it caused is insignificant compared to the disappointment she felt toward me for loving it so much. I'm sure she wanted to rid herself of it—rid herself of me—once and for all. The other ring wasn't returned to me. I bet she kept it—or sold it. Either of those scenarios wouldn't surprise me, because that ring was really hers all along.

I pile the papers back into the envelope and slide the invitation and box on top of them before placing it inside the large drawer where I keep my purse. Once more, I kick the drawer shut.

"I'm in for tonight."

"Great! I discovered this cool place downtown—not too trendy—but it's got a great, hip vibe."

"Fantastic!" I feign enthusiasm, because although I'm not excited about going out, I need to go and try to start living again.

It's Friday, and standard for our business, I get a large amount of tedious paperwork piled in my inbox regarding this weekend's auctions. The day seems to flow by without any major interruptions, apart from the unexpected visit from Mr. Smith. He's our auction house's founding leaders' grandson and is a descendent of the original, blue-blooded families in this city.

Frederick J. Smith III provides an endless source of enjoyment among the staff. He's older than the States and less animated than a sponge. He's a character unlike anyone else I know—other than Jim's mother. They're very similar, more similar than I recognized before today.

"Ms. Barrow, I'm still not able to place your ancestry. You can fill me in when I have more time. It has bothered me so."

"It's Scottish, sir."

"No, no, Charlotte. I said when I have time." He walks off with strong intentions for the coffee room, accompanied by his assistant. "Oh, how I do love those foamy lattes you make, Teresa." She follows him down the corridor to make him that special treat.

I swivel back to my desk and notice it's almost five. Rachel pops her head up over my cubicle wall, all smiles and excitement.

"You ready?"

I pause to shut down my computer. "Yeah, I'm ready." Grabbing my jacket off the hook, I swing it on while pulling my purse out of the drawer. That's when I see the package again. I had managed to forget about it most of the day, getting lost in my work. But I can't avoid it now. I remove the papers and box, and toss the envelope in the trash.

Stuffing it all into my oversized purse, I make my way toward the elevators. Rachel keeps pace as the doors open like they know how desperate we are to leave. We glance over the crowd then squeeze in. As soon as the door opens, we race each other to the exit. That brings a smile to my face—a welcome reprieve from the heavy of today. After a quick good-bye at the corner, we separate, having already settled our plans to meet up later.

I walk to the closest subway and straight onto a train. My mind wanders, as it always does when I'm on the train, the tunnel whizzing by. It's how I decompress from the day.

As the subway approaches the next stop, I notice a man—an attractive man—standing on the platform. Dressed casually, he's wearing worn jeans, a light-blue, button-down shirt, and sneakers. A large group pushes in behind him when he steps on. His face is handsome and his eyes are kind. He's really good-looking, and for the first time in forever, I kind of want to flirt. Maybe I should talk to him? I probably shouldn't. He'll think I'm a weirdo. This is New York City. People don't like strangers talking to them on the subway. I watch as he lets everyone around him take the available seats, while he remains standing. His politeness is refreshing.

I'm staring too long, realizing a few seconds too late that this is my stop. I jump up from my seat and right into him. Since this is New York, no pardons are needed, but I still say, "Excuse me." I like to be polite, too.

"No, I'm sorry," he replies, maneuvering out of my way. Our eyes meet for a solid second before I turn back toward the exit doors.

I get stuck between a pole and a woman a foot shorter than me who refuses to budge. I look down at her and repeat, "Excuse me, please." I push forward without trampling anyone, but the doors close before I can reach them.

Deflated, I stand there, once again reminded that this is my life now—a series of hassles and a distinct difference from the one I once led. Life used to be sunshine. Life used to be easy before . . .

When I turn around to grab a pole, I notice the handsome man already entering the next train car. I continue watching until the door slides closed behind him.

The next stop comes, and I work my way through the crowd and up to street level, choosing to walk the five blocks back to my apartment. This is the second time this week I've had to backtrack like this. Sometimes I think I should give up the subway altogether and try the bus. It seems more natural for a person with my lack of aggression. I left my feistier side with Jim six months earlier. I still haven't mastered this new me yet.

A long bath eases some of the tension in my shoulders, but my mind is still left to flounder. The black dress I slip on is always flattering, but gives me the ability to blend into the background. Rachel can garner all the attention. It makes it easier since I'm not in a dating mode at this point in my life.

I stock my clutch and notice the invitation lying on the counter where I dumped my bag out when I got home. I pick it up, contemplating once again if I'm ready to read it. It will upset me, so I choose to walk away, leaving all the memories that come with it behind for the night.

Waving at me with enthusiasm when I walk in, Rachel looks like her confidence is soaring as she gets some much-desired attention at the swanky bar she's chosen to prowl tonight. She introduces me to the two guys she just met, Bob and John, who seem to be enamored by her charms. Their names make me question if they're using aliases tonight. Just like the guys themselves, they are generic.

I'm welcomed, and John even rushes to the bar to get me a drink. When he returns, he hands me a gimlet, and I graciously accept, though it's not a cocktail I normally drink.

I need this night more than I let on to Rachel. I can't be depressed anymore. It's too . . . *depressing*. I will enjoy tonight.

After a few minutes of talking about himself and his law firm, John winks at me then leans over. "You want to get out of here?"

Is he for real? Shocked by his arrogance, the answer is easy. "No. I just met you!"

He starts backtracking. "Just one drink back at my place. You know, and see where it goes from there." He touches my hair, looking at it between his fingers. "I've always heard redheads were fun."

Is that a perverted challenge of some sort? I don't smile. His rudeness doesn't deserve my niceties. I smack his hand away before backing up. "Well, you won't be finding out with me tonight."

I turn to walk away, giving Rachel a get-rid-of-them look before I head to the bathroom.

"You all right, Charlie?" Rachel asks.

"Just gonna powder my nose." I let my tone indicate how I'm feeling.

I've learned there are a lot of misconceptions about me and my fellow crimson comrades. Most men are predictable and make unwarranted assumptions. I fall into a stereotype of fiery-tempered sexpots. I'm passionate about my work and the ones I care about, but hot-tempered, no.

The other common belief is that we reds sleep around. I'm not easy, despite what people assume based on my follicles. My natural hair color is rare, so it draws men in like a moth to a flame. But I often see the disappointment in their eyes when they discover I'm more what is considered the girl-next-door type than a vixen. At least it's a good way to weed out the jerks like the one tonight.

Escaping, I make my way through the barflies flocking to this club's light.

One thing I've learned living in Manhattan is that a man who takes you home to do the deed earlier in the night has no intention of staying home. He'll be right back on the prowl before midnight. I don't mind a one-night stand if needed. I had one once, although it turned into a relationship, so I guess it doesn't count. I do mind, however, being one of several for a guy who gets greedy and abuses his good looks. At twenty-five, I've already learned it's hard to find a meaningful relationship in this city. Most are too self-centered to make the effort, and the others . . . well, are like me, just not that into the hunt.

I check my lipstick in the bathroom mirror before squeezing past a gaggle of girls celebrating a pending marriage. I don't think about what could have been my life. I try to convince myself I should feel lucky I found out the bad stuff when I did—*before* the marriage.

Rachel waves at me. A different man is standing with her at the bar. I'm not surprised she's receiving so much attention; she's gorgeous with her long, dark, wavy hair, brown eyes, and Italian heritage.

Not that I'm bad-looking or anything like that. I receive my fair share of attention. It's just more an acceptance that I'm not the typical sexy type, not like Rachel. I'm average height for a woman, but heels put me right at five-six. My body isn't athletic, but I exercise, so I'm fit . . . enough.

I look to her right just as her next conquest turns. Our eyes meet, but not for the first time. My mind flashes to the subway when Rachel introduces him. "Charlie, this is *Charlie*. How funny is that?"

"Very," I say, distracted by the sweetness of his smile and his handsome face. His brown hair is tousled, kind of wind-blown, but definitely not styled like most of the men in this city. I like that. His hair looks touchable, but I resist the temptation. A small laugh escapes me, and my real smile reveals itself before slipping away.

"You made it off the subway?" he asks.

"What?" The music is louder now, and the bar area is noisy.

"The subway?" He leans closer, and his warm breath hits my cheek. I detect a hint of whiskey. "I see you made it off the subway earlier today?"

"Oh, yes. Barely." I smile, wanting to blush and giggle like a schoolgirl, but I'm too intrigued that he remembers me. I look into his kind eyes, recalling the color from the train. They're light bluish-gray. His pupils are dilated in the darkness of the bar, but I can see the sincerity in them. "I got blocked, and had to jump off at the next stop and walk home."

"Sorry that happened. People can be rude sometimes."

"No worries. I'm getting used to it."

"The rude people or walking home?"

"Both." I laugh.

He laughs, too. "That's a pity. You're not from New Yo—"

"I'm ready for that drink you mentioned. Are you, Charlie?" Rachel interrupts, redirecting his attention back to her.

"Yes," we reply in unison then look at each other and burst out laughing.

"Jinx! You owe me a martini." I state this as if everyone knows this game.

He smirks, waving over the bartender. "I thought on jinx it was always a Coke?"

"I don't drink Coke."

He chuckles just as the bartender signals he'll be over in a minute. Without missing a beat, he says, "Martini it is, then. So, your name really is Charlie?"

"It's Charlotte, but I prefer Charlie. It's what I'm used to. Is your full name Charles?" Did I just ask that stupid question? I blush this time, the alcohol not helping. This doesn't faze Rachel, but doesn't go unnoticed by Charlie.

He smiles again, tilting his head as if trying to figure me out. "Yes, but I don't feel old enough to be called that."

Rachel laughs too hard to sound natural, and she leans toward him, putting her hand on his thigh. "Charlie here tells me he's interested in *dogs*." She makes it sound as if a dog is some rare animal found in Siberia.

He nods, giving her his attention again before turning back to me. I also nod to show a courteous interest in the topic, though I have none. Looking at her, I finally clue into what all of her odd expressions and bulging eyes mean.

I'm enjoying myself for the first time in what seems like forever, but I'm reminded that she met him first. I'm the one who interrupted, so I should go. I should go before I get invested in a guy who has already been marked by my friend, because I don't screw over my friends. "As much as I'd love to stay and chat more about dogs, I'm really tired after the day I've had. I think I'm outty."

"*Audi*, like the car?" he asks.

Rachel is rolling her eyes behind his back, so he can't see. She hates my lingo. It's a bad habit left over from my more frivolous college days. I look at Charlie and smile again. "No, outty. It's just a stupid way of saying 'out of here.' My college roommates and I used to say it."

"I've never heard the word before."

Rachel steps forward and laughs nervously. I've embarrassed her. She rests her hand on his shoulder, staking claim. "She always says the silliest things."

"I think it's cute," he says with a gentle smile on his face.

I look away quickly, thinking there is more to his words than the basic meaning.

"Silliest, as in adorable," Rachel says, her tone overly dramatic. "I meant she always says the most adorable things. I don't know how she comes up with them." She tilts her head toward the door, signaling me to leave.

"Well, I really should get going—"

Rachel's hugging me before I finish my sentence. "Yes. I'll see you Monday."

"Yeah, Monday," I mumble. The sudden and rapid good-bye is disorienting.

Charlie takes my hand and says, "It was really nice to meet you, Charlie."

"You too, *Charlie*." I emphasize his name for fun. What am I doing? I start to back up, now embarrassed by my own ridiculousness. He doesn't release my hand right away. Just when our arms are stretched as far as they can go, he tugs me forward again, both of us enjoying the moment. After another dirty look from Rachel, I drop my hand to my side and walk away. One more glimpse back, and I see him shift his hand to his lap.

Is this what a real connection feels like? It's been so long, I'm not certain anymore. As much as I want to stay and get to know him better, Rachel looks pleased with my imminent departure. Just as I'm about exit, I glance back, my eyes meeting his one final time.

I catch a cab, abiding by one of my golden rules: No subways after nine o'clock. Settling into the back seat, I reminisce about tonight. It was a good time, which was a nice change.

Thinking of Charlie, I'm glad Rachel found someone interesting this time. To most men, she's the epitome of a single city girl—if she sleeps with a guy too soon, she won't be considered wife material, and if she doesn't have sex with him soon enough, he won't want her as a girlfriend. I know under her optimistic enthusiasm she gets lonely. Hell! We all do. Right now, I'm just trying to enjoy the fact that I had a great time with a fascinating man . . . oh yeah, and Rachel, too.

I push down the pang of jealousy surging through me because she met him first. I take a deep breath and chant, "I will not fall for Charlie. I will not fall for Charlie." After I repeat the phrase several times, I rationalize that walking away was the right thing to do. Rachel has staked her claim, so I can't dwell on him, although I want to.

I crawl into bed later that night feeling hopeful, which is a nice reprieve from my usual sadness. I smile thinking that maybe, just maybe, I can find someone as charming as Charlie one day, too.

Chapter 2
Charlie Adams

♂

"I don't think I need it—"

"Dude, take it, just in case. If it brings you lady love, mm-hmm," Conner clears his throat, "then I've done my job."

I roll my eyes, but also laugh at the gesture. "I haven't seen a rabbit's foot in years. I think since I was eight." The orange foot is really creepy, but I don't want to hurt his feelings. I loop the chain onto my key ring anyway. "I'll give it back to you next week."

"No hurry. Just take care of it."

I'm caught between being creeped out and amused that he thinks this thing can do anything other than scare women away, but I humor him. "Yeah, okay. I'll keep it safe." I walk to the door and yell, "Rip it up in Aspen."

He shouts from the back bedroom, "Yeah, no doubt, dude!"

Leaving his apartment, I gallop down the stairs. I can barely remember the last time I snowboarded. It's been a few years. The last time was three years ago when I spent Christmas with Conner and his family in Park City. My family was still holding their grudge against me for dropping out of university and thought it best if I didn't come home for the holiday. They thought I'd come begging my way back into their good graces, return to college, and step in line to run the family business, but I didn't. I just hopped on the private jet with Conner and took off. My parents didn't call me on Christmas or New Year's like they had every other year of my life when we were apart. That hurt, especially since I called them on both days, and was sent to voice mail both times.

Most people, including all of my childhood friends, would have caved at that point, but my parents' wealth and status was not my concern at the time —just like it's not now. I had goals and my own dreams to pursue, and their cutting off my allowance and living expenses wasn't going to deter me.

The rift between us has continued to this day, but it's softened. I see my parents occasionally now. My mom reads my articles that make the paper, but that's all. I'm the prodigal son who let them down. I get their disappointment, but I don't understand the treatment. I'm their only son, their only child. Aren't they supposed to love and support me, no matter what? I work hard and don't need their money. Shouldn't they be proud I'm making my own way? *I am.* I hope one day, they will be, too.

As I approach The Bagelry, the smell of fresh dough and coffee permeates the air—my version of heaven in the morning. I turn and go inside. Tony leans forward on the counter and in his thick Bronx accent asks, "Your usual, Charlie?"

"The usual." I set my money down, taking my coffee and bag from him. As I back out the door onto the street, I call out, "Keep the change." Walking down the remaining two blocks to my apartment, I appreciate the new, warmer air that covers the city.

As I press the code to get in my building, Mrs. Lackey walks by, greeting me warmly. "Good morning, Charlie."

"Morning, Mrs. L." I return the kindness. She smiles to herself almost as if she's blushing from the interaction. She's eighty-three and always makes me smile, too.

I take my first sip of coffee as I unlock the door, always using the walk home to let it cool. Their basic house coffee is my standard. The rich but simple taste reminds me why I don't like the frou-frou fancy coffee drinks. Just a good ole cup of Joe for this guy will do just fine. It's that good.

After hanging my keys on the hook, I remove my bagel from its brown bag. My breakfast gets dropped on my desk, which I pushed to face the sliding glass door a few days ago, needing a new perspective. I open the door to the balcony and lean against it to people watch. We don't get many people in this area sightseeing, so the attractive girls I spy down below must be lost.

There are several clues that tell me they're not from around here. First off, they're too tan for a New Yorker emerging from a cold winter. They also wear bright colors—too bright for my taste. And finally, there is the most obvious giveaway—the map that they can't seem to figure out how to read. I laugh at my easy deductions when they ask a guy for assistance.

Our spring season kicks into high gear when New Yorkers leave and the tourists start arriving in droves. Inspired to write, I sit down in my desk chair. The antics playing out on the street below, coupled with Conner escaping the city in hopes of catching that last elusive snow storm of the season, give me plenty of material to work with, so I start typing.

When I finish the piece, I read through it again and do a quick edit. It's in keeping with my collection of articles on life in New York, and I know my agent will like it.

It's ironic that when I was growing up in Manhattan, I used to wish to be anywhere else in the world. And yet here I am at twenty-seven, still in Manhattan and now being paid to write about it. Crazy ridiculous! But being paid to write about the city I now appreciate is nothing to sniff at, and I don't. I love what I do for a living. I've worked hard and sacrificed a lot to get where I am.

I didn't luck into my life. I created the life I wanted to live. When I left college at the end of my junior year, my parents used every threat they could think of, but nothing could change my mind. I hated the life I was living. It was how they chose to live, not how I would. So I took off on my own and worked hard, earning and deserving everything I have despite what my parents predicted. I also know that I'm very fortunate, and I don't take it for granted, not like the life I led before. That all feels like a lifetime ago, like my memories are of a different person entirely now. I guess, in a way, they are.

I take an afternoon nap, knowing I'll need some energy for hitting the bars with Justin tonight. He's an animal, and even though I'm still in my twenties, that doesn't guarantee the stamina to play in his league of partying. I met him through Conner about three years ago. Justin's cool and loves the thrill of the hunt. It's always interesting to go out on the town with him.

After waking, I take a break from my apartment and go downstairs to check my mail. As I stand in front of the wall of mailboxes, I flip through the uninteresting bills, pausing at a large heavy cardstock envelope. I tab through my mind, hoping I haven't forgotten about a friend's upcoming nuptial or a younger cousin's graduation, but I come up empty on both fronts. I head back upstairs and rip it open after the other mail gets tossed onto a small table to my left.

A sigh escapes when I realize it's a funeral announcement for my great-aunt Grace. She died on Tuesday, but I wasn't called until Thursday, which still bothers me. I read the information relevant to her funeral taking place next Wednesday at three o'clock. The thought of a family reunion, especially one of bad tidings, is unsettling.

Dropping down onto the couch, I turn on the local news as a distraction until my stomach reminds me I forgot to eat lunch. I grab my jacket and walk to the closest subway station. Craving Chinese food, I head to the best in town which is two train stops away and worth the hassle of getting there.

While waiting on the platform, the crowd bunches around me just as the train arrives. The doors open, and I walk on with the herd. As I make my way to the center of the car, letting everyone else claim the seats, I hear a quiet voice.

"Excuse me."

I follow the voice and find a pretty, blue-eyed redhead attempting to work her way off the car without much luck. I stare into the innocence of her eyes for a second longer than what's considered polite before I scoot out of her way and apologize for blocking her. "No, I'm sorry."

I hope removing myself from her path assists in creating an opening for her to exit, although all of my instincts direct me to do the opposite, to keep her here. After hesitating for a second, I continue on my mission to find a seat and let her go. There's nowhere to sit back here, so I decide to move to another train car. I head toward the front, hoping to find a seat up there.

I make it home with food intact and eat while flicking through the television stations. Nothing's on, though, and I'm supposed to meet Justin in thirty. I turn the television off and get ready. A fresh shave and a change of clothes later, I grab my keys and am out the door right on time.

Walking in just past eight, I head straight to the back where Justin always reserves a table. I'm greeted with the usual round of handshakes and hollers from the regulars.

"Grab a glass, my friend. The pitcher's over there." Justin points to the corner shelf as I search through the rows of sticks on the wall, looking for Lynda. "Who's the lucky lady tonight?" Justin asks.

I find my favorite pool stick and chalk the tip. "Gentlemen, behold Lynda." I laugh, holding up the cue, knowing how they eat up the dramatics. I jokingly name the sticks after ladies I've spent time with.

"Now which one was Lynda again?" Bruce asks.

"I've got this one." Justin steps in to explain. "Lynda was the one in those little hot pants who strolled in one evening asking if we'd seen her friend." He makes a sad face. "Her friend stood her up, but Chuck here lent a shoulder to cry on all night—figuratively speaking." He looks at me and asks, "Did I do her justice?"

I don't like to brag about my *dates*, but he was a witness and loves to boast, even if it's for me. "We went out a few times until—"

"She went nuts over the boy," Bruce spews out. "I remember now. Dark hair, hot body, and big boobs."

"Well, to be clear, she didn't go nuts over me. She was already deemed clinically insane before we met." I correct his take on the situation, ignoring the rest.

I walk back over to the wall and grab any old stick, not quite feeling the same desire to use Lucky Lynda anymore. Was I seriously that much of a pig back then? Some of my old habits tagged along into my new life, but have since been kicked to the curb.

"You can break," Bruce announces. Justin grabs a stool to watch our game.

After a few pitchers, Bruce takes off and Justin stands, ready to leave. "Let's go. There's a bar around the corner that gets some good-looking girls in there." I follow without question. I'm tired of playing pool anyway.

We walk in, and I search to figure out the vibe in here. It's part professionals still partying after happy hour and part locals. I dig the relaxed atmosphere. I buy the first round and pay more for those two whiskeys than three pitchers of beer cost at the pool hall.

Justin is already working his charms on two women. Not interested in playing the get-to-know-you-game yet, I hand him his drink and return to the bar to chill. He seems to be doing well for this early in the evening. Usually it takes a few drinks and several hours mixed with a hint of desperation for a girl to give my most obnoxious buddy this much attention.

Bored with watching Justin, I've been staring into my drink now for a while. I look out and survey the crowd that's changed in the last hour. The clubbers, the nighttime partiers have arrived.

A red dress catches my eye, and I notice, along with half the men in the bar, the pretty owner wearing it—dark hair, dark eyes, and a bright smile. She's quite stunning. I've encountered her type too many times to recall. I've dubbed them the "Unapproachable Approachable." She's wearing red to get the attention, but she's looking, too. If a man she's not interested in comes up to her, it's a quick rejection. But if a man she's eyeing comes over to talk, she welcomes him. She's looking for a husband, but it will end up more a match made in one-night-stand heaven.

Yeah, she's stunning all right, but not my type.

The girl with her, the one in black, not only catches my attention, but holds it. She's pretty and cute at the same time—familiar. A memory flashes as I watch her talking with her friend. It can't be. *Can it?* Sitting up a little straighter, I'm shocked. This is quite the coincidence. I think she's the hot little redhead from the subway this afternoon. She's very attractive, even more so than I thought on the train. I wonder if she lives in the area, if this is her hangout. She exited the subway not too far from here, so it could be.

Justin comes over for a bit; the girl he'd been chatting up is now gone. "You learning from the master by watching me all night, or you gonna get out there and mingle?" He slaps his hand down on the bar and signals for two more drinks.

"The master? Yeah, you're the master all right," I reply, my sarcasm taking over. "I'm good. Just enjoying the scenery from the bar." I glance back over my shoulder and see my redhead has left.

I spin back on the barstool and down the last two gulps of my drink just as a fresh one arrives.

I must be boring Justin, because he's now talking to a girl a few stools down. I overhear her say that she loves classic rock like Smash Mouth and Madonna. Some of my brain cells die an instant and agonizing death from her comments. "Classic rock," I scoff purposely loud.

I'm still laughing at my sardonic thought when Justin says, "So, Tiff and I are gonna take off. You cool hanging here by yourself?"

"Yeah, sure." I lean back, scanning the bar one more time. I see the girl in the black dress again with her friend and two guys. I smile, because she didn't leave. From her expression, I can tell how disinterested she is in the man hovering too close to her. Her body language says everything she's not, but he keeps talking, missing her obvious disinterest.

Looking back at my friend, I say, "No problem. Go on. I'm cool."

Justin and his new potential leave, and I'm left to watch these players hit on my redhead. Would it make a difference if those jerks weren't just trying to get laid? *Stop analyzing weird crap!* Looking back at my drink, I watch the ice melt, wondering why I'm even here. It's not my scene at all. Though, these days, I'm not sure what my scene is. I think I'm ready for someone more permanent in my life, not this ongoing dating business. I've outgrown this scene enough to not make an effort, and I'll stay just to finish my drink.

I'm not an aggressive guy and know full well I won't intrude on another man's game. My redhead will be interested in that schmuck or she won't. I'll watch and see how it plays out.

A few minutes later, without a drink in my hand, I'm debating whether I should stay or go. I decide to go, but I'll check on the girl before I do. I negotiate with myself. If the guy is still there, I'll leave. If he's not, I'll go talk to her.

Just as I turn around, I'm chest to chest with brown eyes, long brown hair, and a sinful red dress.

Smiling, her hand lands on my chest. "Hi there, handsome. I hope you're not leaving."

I sit back down, because when a woman like her wants you to stay, you do. The only problem is I'm more interested in her friend. Looking over her shoulder, I scan the bar to see if she left, but that's what I assumed before, so this time I want to verify.

"I'm Charlie." She giggles for some reason when I introduce myself. I don't get the joke, so I move on and ask, "Are you here alone tonight?" Straightforward, but I need to know to clear my thoughts of the pretty girl.

She glances over her shoulder then looks me in the eyes. "Yes, it appears that way. I'm Rachel." She's flirting. "Are you here by yourself tonight?"

I'm a believer in destiny, so I don't like things forced—if I am meant to meet her, I will. Guess it's not in the stars tonight. "I am now. The friend I came with took off."

We talk, and I discover she's funny. She speaks fast, almost too fast. I hope it's nerves and not that late-night desperation.

She asks, "Do you live in the area?"

"Sort of, about six blocks away. How about you?"

"Down the street. I love the access to the park."

I offer her my barstool, but the one next to me becomes available and she settles there.

"There's a dog park around the corner from my apartment. I don't have a dog, but I find it fascinating to sit and watch the animals interact. Dogs are interesting, that's for sure." I don't even know what I'm talking about. I blame the alcohol for the gibberish.

An odd thought strikes me as she talks about some couple out in the Hamptons selling their estate. What if the redhead was brought into my life so I can meet her friend? "Can I buy you a drink?"

"Yes, I'd love a . . ." She stops speaking for a moment, and I follow her gaze, my eyes meeting bright blue ones and a black dress—my redhead. "Oh! Here's my friend. Charlie, this is *Charlie*. How funny is that?"

I can't stop the smile. It's there, natural, just for her.

She smiles at me before responding, "Very." She's speaking to Rachel, but looking at me.

"You made it off the subway?" I ask, wondering if she remembers me.

It's later in the night, the music has been turned up, making it harder to hear and hold a conversation. We do just fine, though. She blushes when we talk about the coincidence of our names. The act of blushing is completely endearing and quite adorable on her. Most of the women in this city lost the ability to blush years ago.

Being around her makes me sit up straighter, listen more intently. Remembering the strict etiquette courses I endured as a child, I adjust my shoulders back, fixing my posture as I stand, offering her my chair.

She declines and the brightness in her eyes and smile remain as we tease each other about jinxes and sodas. The playful banter is refreshing, considering we're in a bar. Our conversation is easy and comfortable, extraordinary. That is until we're both reminded that Rachel is here when she interjects some bizarre comment about me liking dogs that makes no sense. Charlie's expression indicates she thinks it's odd, too.

Not wanting to be rude, I focus on Rachel, including her in the conversation. I don't want to make her feel awkward and can tell she's feeling competitive with her friend. My eyes flicker to Charlie again when she uses a word she made up. I tell her she's cute when Rachel teases her. I wonder if she doesn't like the compliment, because she's suddenly trying to dash out the door. She probably would've preferred if I told her she was pretty or clever—which she is also.

Silent exchanges flow between them, and Charlie says good-bye before I have a chance to change her mind. I grab her hand, pretending it's a casual handshake. It's not. I feel a little desperate myself now.

She backs up, trying to leave, and I hold on, not wanting to let her go, not ready for her to walk away. I pull her toward me, watching the light in her eyes sparkle as she giggles. But her hand slips free, and she turns to leave. I should respect their decision, but this feels wrong, all wrong. The wrong girl is leaving.

"Now, about that drink," Rachel says, leaning forward, her arm draping across my shoulder.

We settle into light conversation. She has an enthusiasm when she talks that makes her appear animated. She's fun to chat with—or maybe I should say listen to. That might be more apropos.

Just after midnight, I find I'm starved and ask her if she'd like to grab a bite to eat together. She readily agrees, and we walk a block down to an all-night diner I used to frequent. Over our food, I discover she's from New Jersey and works at an auction house. Sounds depressing, selling dead people's stuff, but she says there's more to it than that.

She starts to ask questions about me, which kind of surprises me. I guess because she hadn't all night. "So, are you native to New York?"

I smile, and my mind shoots between all corners of my brain, searching for which answer I'm comfortable giving. "I'm from Kansas."

It's not a lie. I've spent a lot of time, summers and holiday breaks, down there visiting my great-aunt. Her house was more like a home than Manhattan ever was with my parents. My parents were too caught up in being a part of high society to worry about me and my upbringing.

My dad did take the time to teach me the importance of two things, or at least the most important to him: making money and meeting girls. That was the life advice I was given.

In Manhattan, you're a pawn in the game of society, a willing participant to their rules. The women here tend to attach themselves as soon as they find out I'm a local. That sounds the alarm which means I must come from money. Kansas throws them off, and it's only a partial lie, at worst, since I did spend a lot of time there.

"Kansas, wow! I wouldn't have guessed that. A small town boy, huh?" She smiles and takes another bite, hoping I'll lead into a story, but I just eat my food.

She asks a few more questions, expected ones, nothing of interest. Not saying she's shallow, but she's running through her list, checking off her requirements one by one. It's fine. I can admit we're in the age group that is seeking a life partner, so it doesn't bother me. These questions are a great way to get to know the girl, too, to find out what's important to her, what she values.

I answer her inquiries as honestly as I can and throw them back to learn more about her. After we finish our meal, we walk outside, and although I should walk her or cab it with her home, I decide to end the night. "Can I get a taxi for you?"

Her smile is friendly. "Oh, that's right. You live close by. I'll just grab a cab myself."

I step forward, spotting a taxi in the distance heading this way with its light on. I raise my arm, and it pulls up to the curb. "It was a pleasure meeting you, Rachel." And it was. There weren't fireworks, just a few minor sparks.

"I enjoyed this very much." She smiles. "I was wondering if you'd like to go out for dinner this week. Maybe Tuesday?"

Fate chose Rachel, I remind myself. "I'd like that, but I can't Tuesday." My agent texted and made me promise to focus on my goals. I don't like lying and told him I would start this week. Monday, I can let slide, but Tuesday will make me feel guilty. "I'm free on Monday."

"Oh. Um, well, I'll make Monday work. If I can't, I'll call you."

"All right." We exchange numbers.

She shakes my hand and leans in, giving me a kiss on the cheek. "I'll call you. Thank you for dinner. I had a great time." She gets in the cab, and it screeches as it takes off down the dark street, with no regard for the late hour.

I shove my hands in my jacket and walk home, thinking about my aunt's passing. My chest tightens at the loss, so I switch my thoughts to tonight, the guys at the pool hall and Rachel from the club. I don't dwell and hurry home. By the time I get to my apartment, it's almost 2:00 a.m. I climb into bed, and although I know I have to deal with my agent tomorrow, I let my mind settle on my redhead. *Charlie*. Her name makes me smile in the dark of my room. *She* makes me smile.

Chapter 3

♀

My alarm sounds at six, like it does every morning. In my sleepy state last night, I must have reset the clock instead of turning it off. Saturday morning is no time for overthinking my past mistakes, or should I say, my now-typical blunders. I turn the alarm off and go back to sleep.

By 7:00 a.m., the inevitable has happened—I can't sleep any longer. I mosey into the kitchen, starting my coffeepot that holds my Ethiopian dark bean brew. It's this month's selection from the travel-the-world-coffee-of-the-month club my dad gave me last Christmas.

I wander into my cozy living room past the bar separating the two rooms and see the funeral announcement still untouched. I sit on the couch waiting for the coffee to brew before dealing with reality. When it's done, I fill my mug and add the perfect amount of cream and sugar to cut the acidic aftertaste. I don't like this coffee, but I hate being wasteful even more, so I sip the hot liquid on the way out of the kitchen.

Grabbing the white envelope, I settle into my chair by the window—my special book nook—and pull the cardstock out to read:

You are respectfully invited to attend the funeral of
James E. Bennett Jr.
Saint Thomas Church

New York, New York
April 23rd
3:30 p.m.

The wording is plainer than I would have expected for Cherry Bennett. It's very direct and to the point, not like Jim's mother at all. She's passive-aggressive and quite the show-woman. I think the announcement is tasteful, basic, and appropriate. She didn't go overboard as she usually would. I think Jim would have approved, too. I run my finger slowly over his name, and my sweetest memory overcomes me. I try to stop the images, but they flood like a migraine, taking over.

Jim is down on one knee, the ring in hand. He's all smiles and happy tears. But all of my good memories of him are tainted now, absorbed into the pain he caused just months later. *Tears of anguish cover his face as I glance over my shoulder. He doesn't chase me. He can't.*

I return my mind to the present. Coffee, letter, morning. Yes, the here and now. After looking at the date on the announcement, I glance across the room to the calendar that hangs in the kitchen. Wednesday. The funeral is this coming Wednesday.

I recall off the top of my head what I have going on with work this week. There is a large auction featuring the East Hampton estate of two prominent Manhattan lawyers on the verge of bankruptcy on that same afternoon. Although I don't want to miss it, the funeral is more important. I know I can get out of the auction. I did assist our department head on landing the property, but Rachel could cover my tasks. She's familiar with the client.

I start my usual weekend routine of reading in the park, buying groceries for the upcoming week, and scrolling through the list of new movies for download later in the evening. Maybe uneventful to some, but it keeps me well within the comfort zone I've created. Today is a little different, though. Sitting in the park and feeling the warmth this afternoon has started to crack the hard shell, revealing a small piece of my old self. I can feel change coming, sense it. I feel it in my soul, and I welcome it.

Monday is a time for catch-up. The weekend has brought many voice mails, e-mails, and letters to trudge through before I start contacting my call list of potential clients.

Rachel pops her head up a few minutes after my arrival. "Good morning," she singsongs.

"Well, well, well, do tell," I say. Since I'm in the middle of typing an e-mail, I haven't seen her, but the silence between us causes me to turn and look upward. She's impatiently waiting for my full attention. I fold my hands over each other and relax back into my chair, giving her the audience she needs to tell her story. "Go ahead. I know you're dying to."

A delirious, happy smile crosses her face, and she starts her tale. "You remember Charlie from the other night? Well, of course you do, since his name is Charlie, like you."

I don't think I want to hear this. A small ache forms in my chest at the mere mention of him.

She shakes her hands in the air and closes her eyes as if she just remembered I was there. "Anyway, we stayed there for another drink and then went for an early breakfast, or is it a late-night meal? I don't know, but it was around one in the morning." She tends to drag stories out that could be summarized into one or two sentences, but I don't want to burst her bubble. I'm fascinated by how her mind works, and she's always fun to listen to, even if it's about guys I wish I could have gotten to know better. "We just had the best time. He's cute, funny, and so sweet. *Wasn't he cute?*" I nod, and she continues talking without even noticing me. "He paid for the drinks and the meal. I love a gentleman."

"And?" I insert my appropriately interested question to move it along. I do have a lot of work to do today, especially with the pending funeral on Wednesday.

"And what?"

I don't want to ask, but I'm a glutton for punishment, so I do. "Did you . . ." I leave it at that, hoping she gets it. She doesn't seem to be following my line of questioning, which is a first for her when it comes to gossip or sex talk.

The lightbulb finally goes off. "*Oh!* Oh, no. They have to wait until the third date."

"The third? I thought it was the second?"

"Oh my, no! That was so one month ago. I tried the fourth date after that, but I lost their interest and they would all move on. So, I deducted through my research that the third date is the magic number. Four's too long, and two dates is too soon to be a serious contender for marriage."

I smile at her logic and can appreciate the effort involved to get to this point. "Great! That sounds like a good plan."

I like her persistence, even though her assumption that all men think the same is a little off base. She hasn't factored that into her calculations. I'm also relieved they didn't sleep together Friday night, though I feel guilty for thinking it.

"Yeah, I think so, too. So, as I was saying, I had a great night. Thanks for going."

"Do you think you'll see him again?"

"Think? I know! I secured the second date for tonight." She leans forward on the top of the dividing wall.

"Wow. That's fast. He must not be from the city."

"He's not. He's from Kansas." She laughs as she sits back down on her side of the cubicle, absent from my view.

"Seriously? Kansas? I wouldn't have guessed that at all."

"I know. Don't you just love it?" I can tell she's smiling.

I glance back at my monitor as an instant message pops up. I laugh, because it's from Rachel: *I think I'm in love!*

I type back: *SLOW DOWN! I think you're in lust. Please remember to take one date at a time.*

Rachel: *Don't worry, Mom, I'm keeping that in mind.*

Her sarcasm is not appreciated. Me: *Topic change. Will you sub for me on Weds? I have a funeral to attend.*

Rachel: *Is it his?*

Me: *Yes.*

Rachel: *You want me to assist at the O'Malley/ Hurst auction?*

Me: *Yes.*

Rachel: *Of course, I'll do it.*

Me: *Thank you. I owe you one.*

Rachel: *In that case, can you cover for me tonight so I can go out with Charlie? It's a small auction downstairs, handling a few phone bids.*

I sigh, knowing how boring that auction will be, but I'll do it for her.

Me: *Yes, no problem.*

Rachel: *Thank you, thank you, thank you! Charlie, you're the best!*

Me: *You too, Rach.*

I spend the rest of the day familiarizing myself with the important items going on the block. I return five calls and twenty-eight e-mails then finish the paperwork requested by our department head.

Coffee fills my stomach instead of food for dinner, and the caffeine keeps my energy level higher than usual. This auction is straightforward from the beginning, and it ends as expected.

Afterward, I spend my evening rebelling against the winter routine I'd fallen into and walk home. It's dark out, but the day feels too nice to let it slip into mindless, forgotten oblivion. The blooming flowers and leafing trees deserve the utmost respect as nature takes its springtime course. And I, too, deserve the same opportunity to start over, leaving winter's bleakness behind. Spring has always been my favorite season. What's not to love? New life is emerging all around, while the sun warms our days.

In summer, life is in full swing, but it gets too hot to always enjoy. In fall, everything is starting to die. Winter is the worst of all, though. Everything is dead. The irony is that Jim died in April, just as life is reborn all around us.

I keep walking, but pick up my pace. I thought I was over this. *I'm not over this! This* is new! I was starting to come out of the darkness after the breakup. I was starting to move on, and I was making a good go of it. Just as my chest was starting to feel whole, his death ripped my heart apart again—this time cutting deeper. Why did he have to die? The pain is magnified more than should be allowed. He's not a saint because he's dead. He hurt me. A pathetic whimper from deep within my chest slips from between my lips. *Hold it together. You're almost home.*

I slam the door behind me, leaning against it for safety, for security. My hands press against the solid wood until it hurts. Blinking away the weak tears that have formed in the corners of my eyes, I take a deep breath. Memories can hurt, but I'm determined that *those* memories are not going to hurt me anymore. I can't let them. It's not worth it. I can't change what happened. I can't change the past. I need to focus forward, not behind.

A hot bath is in order. I fill the tub and slip into the burning water, knowing it will alleviate my thoughts of the burden of this moment as it warms me from the outside in. I sip a glass of wine and use my toes to play with the faucet. My brow and mind relax as I watch my skin turn pink where the water engulfs me. Within minutes, I find this was a much earned reward. I start to sweat about the time I see my fingers pruning. I don't like to linger and see my skin like that. I always get out at this point, not wanting the reminder of growing old.

It's easy to go about my night. I've developed a knack for shutting off unwanted thoughts. When the alarm buzzes in the morning, I'm surprised at how the time flew. I feel positive. Today is a good day. Tomorrow is Jim's funeral, but today is a good day. Today, I will sign a new client. I can't be stopped, *not today.*

I arrive at the office earlier than usual, skipping my daily coffee-shop stop. Rachel arrives, singing her usual chipper greeting, then gets to work. I want to ask about her date. I really do, but something stops me. I think it's the realization that I don't think I can handle her talking about a happily ever after with a guy I felt a connection with.

She tends to go overboard with the guys she dates, a common reaction from a woman who puts all of her eggs in one basket. Beyond wanting her dates to work out, to turn into something more meaningful, she *needs* them to. At twenty-seven, soon to be twenty-eight, Rachel Russo's desperation is starting to show in her once-cheerful expression. Her biggest problem is herself. She has a teenager's mentality regarding men and chooses the wrong guy for the wrong reasons. She doesn't give them the credit they deserve. It's still a game to her, even though she doesn't want to play it any longer. I feel for her, although she's quite inspiring in her quest to find her future husband.

These thoughts make me feel like such a bad friend that I remain quiet, losing myself in the appraisal in front of me.

A few hours after my poor psychoanalysis of the modern woman, Rachel jumps up and makes an announcement. "I just got a potential new client."

"Congratulations!" I smile and stand to stretch my body, which feels stiff from melding into the grey office chair all morning. "What is it?"

"The Bennett estate here in Manhattan."

I gulp as the pain of the knife in my back is turned and jabbed just a little deeper. "Bennett? As in James Bennett Jr.?" My throat is dry, and I struggle to form words, much less say them.

"Yes, but don't tell me you've been working with them. I just received an e-mail, but if you've been working—"

I'm quick to correct her to take away any guilt she might be developing. "No, no. That's not what I meant. I haven't been working with them on the estate. What's in the appraisal? Is there room in the spring schedule for the auction?"

"I don't know yet, but I'm thinking it will more likely be midsummer." She sits back down, confused by my strange reaction. "We're meeting with the executor at the end of the week for the initial inventory and appraisal. The deceased died recently." Her voice lowers to a whisper. "He had a skiing accident, and he was young. That's so horrible. I'm sure it's a difficult time for the family right now."

I grab my temples, closing my eyes. As the tears well up, the pain gains strength and my heart feels as if it might shatter all over again.

"Are you okay?" Rachel asks. My eyes bolt open, and I make instant eye contact with her. "You're shaking. What's going on?"

My body stops rocking in the chair before I realize I'm even doing it. My eyes soften, and I can breathe again as my irregular heartbeats realign to their natural rhythm. "I'll be fine." To end her speculation, I lie. "I have the worst headache. I think it's a migraine."

She's suspicious, but doesn't push. "I have migraine pills if you want one."

"I'm going to wait it out a bit longer. Thank you. I'll let you know."

She sits back down, and I hear her typing resume at her regular hunt-and-peck pace.

I take another deep breath in through my nose, holding it before releasing it out my mouth. Calm. I'm calm now.

I try to rationalize that Smith & Allen doesn't allow us to handle friends and family members' estate auctions. That makes sense, but a part of me wants to see what is being consigned by his estate.

I don't care about the money or his family heirlooms. I care about the book that we waited six hours in the cold two winters ago so he could have his favorite author sign it. And the shirt I had monogrammed with his initials for his internship interview our senior year. Did he still own that obnoxious alarm clock that played that annoying rap song from the nineties or the picture frame that once held our engagement photo? Those things probably won't be listed, but I'm still curious. They are the things that made up the Jim I knew, and he wasn't the Rolex-wearing James Bennett Jr. who worked on Wall Street, or the one who cared more about which restaurant to be seen at than he did about his friends.

I'm curious, but I'd probably be disappointed to discover what his life became after we broke up—what his life was becoming toward the end of us. I sweep these thoughts away, remembering that this is about business, not about him or us, and not about expectations I once held.

Rachel leaves on time, and I let her. I've been disappearing into my own mind most of the day. She lets me be when I'm like this.

I can't bear to spend another evening at home with all my depressed thoughts again, so I resign myself to the auction room and gallery on the first floor. I double-check that every piece in the next auction has the proper lot number to the catalogue and that the estimate is listed correctly. It's not my job, but I need the busywork to keep my mind occupied. The specialists have already done a thorough job, but I find the room comforting, quiet, and anything is a welcome escape from thinking about the past right now. I don't think about dinner or even remember that I miss the meal. I stay until I'm about to collapse. That's good for me, since I fall asleep without the aid of the television or the soft crashing of ocean waves from my sound machine. My mind is too tired to dream, and I sleep well.

The anxiety I avoided last night due to the auction hits me hard this morning. My first thought is that today is Jim's funeral. While I ready myself, my mind escapes into the memories of Jim in our better times, our happier times. He was always considered a catch, even before I met him at Brown University five years ago. We were in the same history class and sat alphabetically next to each other. He was different then, dynamic when he spoke and charming to a fault. His charisma made him popular with students on campus, and he was genuine in his interactions.

I didn't allow myself to fall for him right away. I was caught up in self-doubt, wondering why he would want to date me. Like most girls at nineteen, I was uncomfortable with all of the changes in my body. I was becoming a woman and still trying to identify with this new me. He was a sweet boy, who gave me endless attention and compliments—maybe he sensed I needed it. What I didn't expect was how much I would come to rely on him for his thoughtful words.

Just before graduation, he asked me to marry him. That's when everything in my world should have been blissful; instead, that's when the dreams we once shared started to shatter.

These days, I find it ironic that, no matter how much I try, I can't even remember the actual turning point that led to the end. I clearly remember the big stuff, but not the little signs that everyone says are there all along. I sigh and return to my work.

Hours into my workday, I look down and realize I'm dressed in black. I don't remember making a conscious decision to wear black, but with no recollection of choosing it, I assume it chose me. Maybe beige would've been better. I debate in my head, but don't have time to change my clothes even if I want to.

Lunch consists of a sandwich and chips from the deli downstairs. I brush my teeth afterward because I have to face his family and friends, most of whom I haven't seen since we broke up six months ago.

I let the time after lunch escape me, because I don't want to think about the funeral. So, as was typical with my old self—Jim's girl—I lose track of time completely until my phone alarm sounds, signaling it's time to leave. Taking a final deep breath, I close my eyes and remember the good times— the *I love yous*, the gentle kisses, and the hand-holding he did simply because I loved to hold hands.

When I stand, Rachel appears behind me. "You going?"

"Mmhm."

"You want me to go with you?" She leans against the wall, concern on her face.

I slip on my jacket and think about her offer. "Nah, I'll be fine." I don't know if I will, but I don't want to drag her into the mess with his family. "Anyway, you have his estate now, so that might be crossing some line or something."

She looks puzzled. "What do you mean?"

"Rachel, it's the Bennett property. *James*, Jim. That's him."

She's mortified. "Oh, Charlie. I didn't put two and two toge—"

"You didn't know. You met him one time, so I understand. Don't feel bad."

I hear her gulp, the awkwardness heavy around us. "I'm so sorry. I don't care about the estate. I'll hand it off to someone else if you want me to go with you. I will."

I hug her because she needs it as much as I do. "Thank you, but that's not necessary." When I lean back, I reassure her. "I'll be fine."

She analyzes me, searching for the truth in my eyes. "Okay, but call me if you want to talk."

"Thank you, I will."

Riding the elevator down to the lobby, I realize it's all been a ruse, a careful charade I've put on since the breakup. I do want someone with me. I want someone there who is on my side, who has my back, but I refuse to put my friends in the middle of this chaotic nonsense with Jim's family.

I stop one more time on the sidewalk, gathering my strength, and then walk with determination to the funeral.

Chapter 4

♂

Though my agent, Alec Stants, appears to be a sloth in a suit, he's surprisingly agile and fit. "I have to stop. I need air." I huff, coming to a stop and bending over to rest my hands on my knees.

"Come on! How weak can you be?" He stops, turning back to look at me. Shaking his head in mock disappointment, he adds, "This is just a disgrace that you would let an old man like me embarrass you like this." He keeps jogging in place while he annihilates every bit of my pride into humiliation.

"Who knew? Right?" That's all I manage to squeak out as I remind myself that he's only forty-two. I stand back up, pacing back and forth, attempting to regain my breath. "How much farther anyway?"

"Sad. Just plain sad. I thought for sure you'd make it halfway. We've got just three small miles left if we turn back now. That's not so bad, is it?"

I tug at my jogging pants and start in a forward motion, thinking *I can do this*! But I hate every remaining minute of it and finish out of spite and pride.

He pats me on the back while laughing. As we exit the park, he says, "See? Not so bad after all. You should make exercise a priority. It clears your head, keeps your body and mind in working order. You're pushing thirty, man. You need to stay active."

"First of all, I have a couple of years until I'm thirty. Don't age me too fast. Second, you'd prefer me out running around the park all day over writing and providing you with a paycheck?"

"Good point." He chuckles as we shake hands. He teases me as he starts to walk away. "You did better than I thought. Keep it up, and hey, send over those last two articles. I need to submit them on Monday."

I nod, acknowledging his request, and collapse on the closest park bench I can find. My mind is jammed with thoughts vying for my attention. *Thought exercise was supposed to clear your head?* I guess it did while I was doing it. I scramble to my feet and take the lazy, short way home—the subway.

A recurring thought crosses my mind—my redhead. Charlie. She's off-limits because she's Rachel's friend, but being on the subway reminds me of yesterday and how she handled herself so quietly. She has a story, and the more I think about her, the more I want to know it. *Rachel's friend*, I remind. *Don't go there.* I push the thought and the subway doors aside, and walk the remaining block home.

Sunday offers me a new perspective on the life of a New Yorker. On this one particular day, they seem to become elusive or in hiding, relatively speaking. Saturdays the streets and shops are packed with people and Monday rolls along tripling the crowds again, but Sunday, no one. There's always a seat on the subway, an available park bench, and no lines at the coffee shop. Where do New Yorkers go on Sunday?

I determine a walk around a surrounding neighborhood is in order to prove my point. Since I recovered quicker than expected from the torture—I mean, run—yesterday, I put my sneakers on again. Leaving my jacket at home, I race down the stairs and out onto the street.

The nearest neighborhood bordering mine has classic architecture and young families. Several small children play while their parents sit on the stoop keeping a watchful eye on them. Kids are interesting little creatures. How does so much life fit into such a small package?

As I turn the corner, I come across the dog park. Even though Rachel seemed to garner a different idea from my story Friday night, it doesn't hinder me from leaning against the fence and watching the dogs run free in the enclosed area.

I return home two hours later, encountering only a few people during my walk, thus proving my point. I spend the rest of the day at my computer, typing and surfing online with moments of staring out the window mixed in. I go to bed before my usual time and pay the price when I wake at three in the morning. Flicking through the late-night selection on television, I find a program I know will put me to sleep again, and it does.

Monday rolls around just as I was starting to enjoy my lazy weekend. I remember dreading these days when I was younger, but my career has given me lots of freedom that make Monday just as good as Friday. With plenty of much-needed sleep, I leave the house bright and early. I stop by The Bagelry before taking the train over to my agent's office.

Walking into his offices, I'm always surprised by his importance. He's just Alec to me—more of a friend who makes demands of my time every now and again. But here, he's *the* boss. With ten employees already bustling around the large space, it's easy to see where my commission goes. It gives me a sense of pride to play a small part in his success. He's doing better than me, that much is obvious, which makes me chuckle. No one said I'd get rich following my passion, but I've done quite well.

The receptionist calls him as I gaze out the windows of his eighteenth-floor suite. "He'll see you now, Mr. Adams." Her tone makes me think she doubted he would as she signals me around the decorative wall behind her.

I walk into his office and make the couch my own. Alec looks up and smiles. "You could've just e-mailed the articles and saved yourself the trip."

"What's the fun in that? Anyway, I haven't been here in a while and had the time." I stand up, handing him the disk. "There are five on there. Do we have takers for all of them?"

"And more. Two were due today, and I have some interested parties in your work. They're looking for something different. You have a unique voice in your writing. I'm sure they'll want them." He stands, leaning his body against the windowsill. I can tell he's about to get serious. Folding his arms over his chest is always his giveaway. "What's the big picture, Charlie? What do you want to do?"

Oh, we're having *this* conversation again. "I'm doing it."

"I think you're wasting some of your talents. I love your writing, and it sells well, but you can do more . . . bigger things. What about a book? Have you given serious consideration to writing a book?" He half smiles to ease the tension I must be revealing through my own expression. "I'm asking because I've received a few calls from interested agents and publishers."

"I . . . well, maybe it's crossed my mind, but not to any great length."

"Will you consider it now?"

"Are we talking a collection of my articles on New York or something different?"

"We can package your current stuff together and get it out there, but I think you have a great novelist inside you. What do you think about fiction?"

"I love fiction. Anything that allows the psyche to escape for a little period of time is a good thing." I look down at the floor with a better understanding of what he wants from me. "Are we talking about the next great novel—Hemingway, Salinger, King-type stuff?" I feel the pressure being applied. This is usually the point when I tend to cave into my inner feelings of doubt.

"Look." He shakes his hand at me, not scolding, but more matter-of-fact. "I know you like your free-living lifestyle. That doesn't have to change. I'm just saying if you let yourself attempt something of importance, you might succeed."

"You seem to know me better than I do, but what you forget is it's me who lives with me every day. I have accomplished a lot on my own, considering the circumstances surrounding those accomplishments—"

"You're not understanding what I mean. And being from a wealthy family doesn't constitute child abuse. Your talents are bigger than you give yourself credit for." He walks closer, lending me his hand. Pulling me to my feet, he looks me in the eye. "Charlie! You can do this and you *should* do this. Think about it and give me a call later this week with your answer."

I remain speechless and leave the room, already feeling the weight of the burden placed on my shoulders. I shove my hands in my pockets as I walk back outside, finding comfort in the small action.

The rest of the afternoon is spent staring at a blank page on my computer, willing myself to write something, but I can't. I'm not feeling it. Thankfully, I have a distraction. Tonight's my date with Rachel.

The dinner is good enough, and as much as Rachel seems to be a nice person, I'm not sure if a love connection has been made. We end the night sitting at the bar and having a cocktail. Every once in a while, she says my name or pats my knee to bring my attention back to her. But instead of my name, I think of it as *her* name—the other Charlie, Rachel's friend, Charlie. I jiggle my head a few times to shake it off, but even in my overanalytical state, I know where my interest lies, and it's not here.

I'm relieved when she says, "Listen, I like you, Charlie, but I think we might be better as friends."

I see the sincerity in her eyes and smile. "I agree. I like you—"

"We don't have to go into all that. Let's just leave it at we'll stay friends."

I chuckle. "Yes, I'd like that."

The evening ends at the same restaurant where it began three hours earlier. When we walk out, she leans forward and kisses me, a kiss that stays chaste and on the cheek. Easier to cut ties that way.

"I'm so glad we did this. It was fun, Charlie. But damn if your name doesn't throw me off every time. I keep thinking of my friend, and that just makes it weird."

I chuckle, knowing exactly what she means. "I had a great time getting to know you, but you're right."

She laughs. "Friends." Taking my hand, she squeezes gently. "Best of luck."

"You, too. Thanks again."

Right before she ducks into the waiting taxi, she says, "Call me if you want to hang out. All right?"

"Okay. Take care."

I spend Tuesday running every pro and con through my mind, on paper, on my laptop, and out loud to strangers, searching for an answer regarding this novel idea. The only conclusion I come up with is that I should write this book. And although I explained the whole deal to Tony at the bagel shop, he's more interested in the redhead I mentioned in passing. He said I should have asked Rachel for her friends' number, but that's just crass in my opinion. He's of no help with this major career decision. By the end of the day, I reason with myself. *What if I write just for me? What's the worst that could happen?*

On Wednesday afternoon, to honor my great-aunt Grace, I decide to walk. She used to say our walks were her own saving grace, before she was too sick to take them any longer. But what I forgot to tell her was our walks were my saving grace, too. I enjoyed the peace they gave me, maybe even more than she did.

Chapter 5

♀

While rushing along a side street that runs perpendicular to Park Avenue, I look down at my watch—it's almost three. These things don't start on time. There's always leeway at weddings. I hope funerals follow the same standard protocol.

I look straight ahead and notice a man in a well-tailored suit walking toward me. As he gets a few steps closer, I realize I know him. That's Charlie. He smiles, recognizing me at the same time.

"Are you following me, or am I lucky enough to run into you three times in . . . five days?" I realize how peculiar this must sound coming from a perfect stranger, but it also feels like the exact thing I should say to him, to Charlie. His name is becoming more comfortable than it should for how well we *don't* know each other.

His smile widens, lighting up his entire face. Stopping in front of me, our eyes connect for a few silent seconds, and we laugh. It's awkward and yet somehow makes me feel giddy, happy. "I think I'm the lucky one. Are you heading to work or playing hooky today?"

I look down, liking how he treats me like an old friend instead of someone he just met briefly. "I'm, well . . . this may sound strange, but I'm going to a funeral." *Very uplifting—not!*

When I look up again, his eyes brighten, and he chuckles. "Oh, I'm sorry to hear that, and yeah, strange but coincidental. I'm heading to a funeral myself."

I smile at the coincidence, but show him the appropriate sympathy. "I'm sorry for your loss. Were you close?"

"Regrettably, not recently, but yeah, in my heart. How about you?"

I look at my watch as we shift around each other, not knowing quite what to do, but I don't want to leave yet. He looks at his watch then glances at a car nearby. He needs to leave, but doesn't want to, or he would've by now. Instead, he turns and starts walking with me in the opposite direction of his intended destination.

"Not in a few months. We weren't on speaking terms, but we used to be very close. You know, I should get going." I look forward and say, "He said I was always late to everything—it drove him nuts." I smile, and a hesitant laugh escapes. We stop and stand together. I'm surprised by the ease of this interaction. "He joked that I'd be late to his funeral if given the chance."

I see opportunity flash across his face, and a smirk slowly appears. "Do you want that chance?" I stand there speechless as the heaviness of the day weighs me down, making me want to skip the funeral altogether. His face softens with sincerity and he asks, "You want to hit my funeral first, and then we'll make an appearance at yours?"

Words fumble from my mouth before I have time to think them through. "This is the weirdest date I have ever been asked out on. I just might have to take you up on your offer." I laugh, feeling awkward by my assumption. I start walking, hoping to leave the embarrassment of my words behind.

"Hey, Charlie?"

I stop with my back to him, looking over my shoulder. "Yes?"

"I'd really like your company. I could use some today."

Thinking of every reason not to, I follow my instincts and turn around, walking the few feet back to where he waits. He looks away, ridding himself of the tears that have formed in his eyes.

I wasn't going to make a big deal about it. Obviously, he was closer to the person who passed than he let on, and sometimes a stranger can offer more comfort than someone who knows your burdens, your baggage.

With a light touch, I press my fingertips against his hand. "I could use some, too—a little company that is." Sliding my hand up the sleeve of his jacket, I intertwine my arm with his, and we walk together.

Something about Charlie makes me trust him. I think it's his eyes and the truths that are so evident in them.

We don't talk as we walk, no words feeling necessary, until we reach Park Avenue, leaving the peacefulness of the street we were on. A jolt of city life hits as we join the crowds. I stop on the sidewalk and look at him, releasing his arm.

"What?" he asks, concern etching his features.

"We're not . . . I mean, this isn't a real date? I just used the wrong term earlier, that's all. I mean, you went out with Rachel just two nights ago. She's my friend."

He looks at me, baffled by my crazy mutterings. "No, Charlie, I didn't think you meant an *actual* date." He chuckles and starts moving, tugging me by the coat sleeve, playful and cute, a little one-sided grin slipping out. "What kind of date would this be? A depressing one, that's for sure."

I double step to catch up with him. "I appreciate the company. I just didn't mean to imply you were hitting on me or anything like that. We just ran into each oth—"

"We just ran into each other. That's all. Pure coincidence. It's not fate or anything like that. No worries. It's not a big deal." He stops, so I do, too. "Would you rather not do this?" No lopsided grins, no playful eyes. I see confusion and doubt instead.

"No, no. I want to. I want to do this." I wave between us. Knowing I'm giving all the wrong signals or too many different signals, I close my eyes and take a sharp breath before reopening them. With a loud exhale, instant relief washes over me. "I'm nervous about the funeral I'm going to. That's all."

"No need to be." He takes my hand, pulling me closer, and hooks it back around his arm. When we start walking again, he looks over and smiles. "Why be nervous? You have a perfect stranger here to comfort you." His words warm me over, making me smile again, too.

"This will be nothing if not interesting," I say as we approach the church.

When we walk into St. Bartholomew's Cathedral, I'm surprised at the beauty of the setting. For a funeral, this is the way to go. The church is full of people, and there seems to be an even amount of tears to joy. I think it's the glass-half-full mentality winning, though. Charlie leans down and whispers, "This is my great-aunt Grace's funeral. She was ninety-four."

"Ninety-four? Wow! She lived a long life."

"She did, but I'm glad she's moved on. The last few years have been difficult on her in that home." He straightens, standing to his full height, his body tensing under my hand. I don't say anything, even though I'm filled with questions. Gripping his arm a little harder, I try to comfort him.

A rigid-looking woman approaches us with a smile that's neither comforting nor cold—detached. She leans in and kisses him on the cheek. He doesn't reciprocate, but touches her arm for a brief moment.

"Pleased to see you here, Charles. I didn't know if you'd come."

"I loved Grace. You know we were close," he says, justifying his attendance.

She doesn't acknowledge me, not even with a glance, until it goes quiet between them. She looks me over, her eyes judging, calculating. I remember receiving this type of glare from Jim's family and friends.

She returns her full attention to Charlie. "Would you like to introduce me, or should I do it myself?"

Her tone is sharp, but he obliges her. "Mother, this is Charlie. Charlie, this is Emeline Adams, my mother."

I'm taken by surprise by the close relation, because they don't seem close at all. They don't even seem to like each other and are bordering on incivility. I put my hand forward in greeting. "It's nice to meet you."

"Likewise," she responds. Her dislike for me is as obvious as her distaste for my name. "Charlie is an interesting name for a woman."

"It's Charlotte, actually. You may call me that if you prefer." I feel like a small child in her presence, begging for her acceptance. She has an air about her that feels familiar in the worst of ways. I won't be good enough. I already know this, but the people-pleaser in me demands I try.

"If you prefer Charlie, then Charlie it is." She turns and smiles, though it holds no warmth, as she scans the room. "The Nelsons just arrived. I should greet them." She focuses back on him. "I hope you'll be civil today, Charles," she says with obvious intention to control her son then walks away before he can react.

His discomfort with the situation is apparent—his body was rigid the entire interaction. He sighs, and I can feel the tension trail behind her.

I lean over and whisper, "Your mother's great."

He bursts out laughing, and the surrounding people look at us. "You think?" The sarcasm isn't lost on him, and I like that he can find humor in the moment. "Do you want to sit back here? I think the service is going to start."

"I can stay back here, but you can sit with your family up front if you like. I'll be fine."

"No. I'd rather sit with you. Aunt Grace will understand. If she were alive, she'd be back here, too. We were sort of the black sheep of the family."

"Your strength in the situation would make her proud."

He rubs my hand that is still holding his elbow like it's meant to be there. I leave it, though, knowing he needs it, that he needs me. He needs someone on his side right now.

We stay in the back, sitting through poignant recollections and speeches describing Grace's vibrancy. Charlie stands and says, "Excuse me. I'm going to say a few words." I nod and scoot back to let him pass.

As he starts talking into the microphone, the large audience doesn't seem to faze him—he's a natural speaker. He talks about the special relationship they had and what he'll miss the most. He speaks of her as more of a mother figure than a great-aunt. His words are touching and bring my emotions to the surface, making me realize that today is going to be harder than I originally thought.

I glance to his mother several times. Her face doesn't show any emotion, but I can't tell if it's because of the plastic surgery or the lack of love she seems to bear for her son.

After Charlie finishes, he walks back to me, reaching for my hand. As I take his, he pulls me to my feet and escorts me out. He never looks back, but I do. His mother watches him, disapproving, but turns back to face the minister with her head held high.

When we reach the steps outside the beautiful, ornate wooden doors, I break the silence. "Are you sure you're ready to leave?"

"I'm ready. I said my good-bye to Grace a long time ago. We had a get-together, just the two of us, and she said her good-bye to me, as well. She was ready and didn't want her loved ones worrying over her. She wouldn't let me see her, embarrassed by her deteriorating condition." We reach the corner, and he stops. "I made peace with her loss already. Today was for everyone else." A sudden smile appears, breaking the somber moment, when he asks, "Should we catch a cab?"

I nod and watch as he hails one down. We'll be late, Jim's premonition coming true. We climb in, and I ask the driver to take us to Saint Thomas Church. The ride is spent in silence, my hand missing his elbow already. I roll my eyes at my silliness.

The cab pulls up to the curb, and we both look at each other. "So, we're here," I say, remaining tucked in the back of the cab. He waits for me to take the lead on this one, willing to do whatever I need, be what I need in the moment. While staring out at the gathered crowd hovering in the doorway of the church, I slide my hand across the seat, palm up, and wait.

Chapter 6

♂

A waiting hand—an invitation I can't resist. That's what she's offering me. I don't care if it's just as friends. I won't miss out on this opportunity. I press my hand on top of hers, palm against palm, and my fingers entwine with hers. Intimate, but what she needs. She needs comfort. She needs a friend. She needs me and I'll be her support, just as she was for me.

I watch as she sits there, stalling, so I take the lead. "Do you want to go in?"

I pay the driver to make it easier. Charlie looks at me, and I see fear overriding the liveliness of her eyes. I scoot closer, leaning over her to open the door. She slides against the vinyl seat and steps out, but her motions are stale, unnatural for how I've seen her so far.

As I exit the cab behind her, I say, "We don't have to go in if you don't want. I know a good Italian restaurant close to here—"

"No." With unsteady words, she's quick to interrupt. "I should do this."

There's only one thing I can think of doing to help. I reach into my pocket and pull out the rabbit's foot keychain. "Charlie," I say, not knowing how she'll take this. I'm hoping how it's intended. "Here, I think you could use this right now."

She reaches for the luck idol, unsure of what it is at first, but I see the moment she realizes. A small laugh leaves her mouth, and she takes it from my hand. Holding it by the chain, she asks, "Is this a real rabbit's foot? Like the lucky ones from when we were little?"

"Yep, it's real. Well, I once read that it's not a real rabbit's foot, because that'd just be gross, but a manmade one with real rabbit's fur."

"It's orange. Bunnies don't come in bright orange in nature?" She's smiling. The charm has worked.

"They also don't come with a hole and chain."

"Fascinating." She holds it in front of her face and giggles. "I don't think I've seen one of these since I was eight or so."

"That's what I said." She tilts her head in curiosity, so I explain, "My friend gave it to me last week. He thought I needed a little luck in my life."

"Luck with what?"

Damn. I should have thought this through before mentioning it. "Um, it's kind of embarrassing, but he thinks I need luck in the lady department."

Wrapping her fingers around the keychain, she holds it to her side. "I can't imagine you have problems meeting women."

I chuckle. This conversation will not make me look good no matter how I explain it. I go with the truth and hope she doesn't leave me right here on the street. "Meeting them, no." I shake my head. "But having real chemistry with them? I've struggled some."

Charlie's smile fades as she listens. Her eyes tell me she believes me, show me she trusts me. I like that I'm able to read her clearly so soon. She hides a lot of secrets in her deep blues, and I intend to find out what they are.

As if to shake off the moment we were sharing, she looks down. "Do you mind if I hold onto it during the funeral? I'll give it right back afterward."

I take her hand that's holding the charm and wrap my own hand around hers. "You hold onto it as long as you need to. Okay?"

She turns toward the church and takes a deep breath. "It's really creepy, you know?"

I hear the teasing tone in her voice, so I ask, "The rabbit's foot or the funeral?"

She smiles then nods her head in the direction of the church. "I guess both."

I follow her through the crowd at the entrance and start to hear the grumblings of gossip and shock mingling among the guests.

"Is that . . ."

"Did Cherry invite her?"

I now understand the deep breath and hesitation when we arrived. Charlie turns back to look for me. Her eyes brighten as she takes my coat by the sleeve, pulling me a little closer to her.

I watch her with new eyes now. She's graceful in her movements, but purposeful. Her chin is raised a tiny bit higher than it was before, but not in a snobbish way, more so in a self-preservation way.

She instantly drops the fabric of my jacket when a girl comes bounding toward her and smiles with tears in her eyes.

"Charlie!" They embrace each other tightly. The girl looks a few years younger, maybe college age. She tucks her face into Charlie's hair and says, "I'm so glad you're here."

"So am I, Kelsey." Charlie's voice breaks, and she drops her head onto the girl's shoulder for comfort.

The girl pops her head up, waving her hand like a fan in front of her eyes, and exclaims, "I don't want to do this anymore! I'm so tired of crying! I can't wait to hear what's going on with you." She stops, turns, and listens to a woman calling her from the front row.

Kelsey looks at Charlie, pleading with her eyes. "Will you sit with me?"

Charlie glances at me, and I nod, but she turns back to Kelsey, calm and confident. "I don't think that would be a good idea. We'll talk soon. I promise."

The girl looks disappointed, but hurries back to her saved seat with the family. Charlie turns to me, her expression eased. "Let's sit back here."

I'm not sure what to think. I haven't quite figured out the relationship of the deceased and Charlie's scandalous part in this funeral that has everyone buzzing. And I don't want to ask such sensitive questions right now.

"Are you all right?" I ask in a whisper, hoping she knows I'm on her side, even if no one else is.

"I am. Are you?"

She's interesting in her thinking. It's obvious she's in more pain than she lets on, but she still feels the need to check on me. Caring. I sit back in the pew and listen as guests are invited to speak about the deceased. I hear a few James stories, some frat Jimmy recollections, and one Jim memory. I wonder in my mind what she called him.

"Do you want to say any words?" I ask her.

"No. I don't have anything to say about Jim, not here in front of these people anyway."

The way she says his name strikes me to my core. It isn't warm, but the sadness, the hurt over his loss, is showing in her eyes. It makes me wonder if we're mourning his death or something more.

I know he was young and start to fill in the pieces of the puzzle surrounding their relationship. As my mind slips into deeper curiosity, Charlie gently leans on my shoulder and cries. I hold her head, my fingers weaving into her hair to comfort her. She doesn't seem offended or surprised, which is nice, so I slide my hand down her arm, landing on top of her hand and give a gentle squeeze. Her hand is rolled beneath mine and our fingers curl together. It's a gesture that feels different than it would in any other setting, because it feels natural. No hidden messages behind it, not sexual, just comfort.

As the minister opens the church for the viewing, the crowd falls into place, forming a line out the door. We remain seated among the continued whispers of scandal until Charlie abruptly stands. Our hands are still locked together as she starts to move toward the opposite side of the pew. When she stops to look back, our eyes meet. "Let's go."

We walk out side by side, hand in hand. She's determined to leave, and I'm determined to protect her from the gossip.

I'm familiar with these people. I grew up among the same types of people who judge so freely and give outsiders the cold shoulder. Charlie's put on a brave face, but it will stay intact for only so long before they get to her. I want to get her out of here as much as she wants to leave.

Just as we walk down the stairs, a lady calls out from behind us. "Charlotte! Oh, Charlotte!"

We stop, and Charlie looks over her shoulder, recognition then dread covering her expression. My hand is dropped before she leans forward and gives the woman an impersonal hug. They're not friends. That much is obvious.

The lady backs up—her mask and false smile in place for the rest of the world "You were late, but I know Jim would be glad you squeezed this in. He would want you here."

Charlie looks at her, waiting for her to continue, immune to her jabs.

"So, you brought a friend," she signals to me, "a friend so important in your life that you would bring him to my son's funeral?" There's no sincerity in her words, and her eyes are narrowed. She's challenging Charlie, trying to prove a point of some sort.

The tension mounts as Charlie glances to me then back to the shrewd, older woman.

I've already learned a few things about Charlie that make me want to know her better, and the list grows as she holds herself together, ignoring the woman's sharp comments.

"This is Charlie . . ." She stops, searching in her head for answers that aren't there before turning to me in horror. "Charlie . . ."

I step forward, not letting it linger any longer and not disappointing her. "Hi, I'm Charlie Adams. I'm so sorry for your loss."

"Oh!" She clears her throat. "It's nice to meet you. *Adams?* I know a few

Adams. Is your family from the city?" she asks. I can tell she's trying to categorize me.

I want to lie, but realize she might know my family. "Yes," I reply. I don't want to get into all of this right now.

Charlie's eyes find me, but I can tell my answer doesn't throw her. She has other stuff on her mind and looks like she is ready to escape this situation.

"What is your mother's name? Maybe I know her."

"Emeline Adams—"

"Oh yes!" She's pleased. "Emeline is such a doll. We sit on several committees together. Please send my love to her." Her being friendly with my mother tells me all I need to know about her. I chose to leave the confines of this super wealthy Manhattan circle, but being in the midst of it again makes me wonder how Charlie is involved with them.

It's as if it just occurs to this woman that I'm with Charlie. She's obviously questioning our relationship in her expression—what we are to each other—as she looks between us. The contempt she holds in her eyes reminds me way too much of my mother. A real emotion takes over, and tears fill her eyes. "I must get back. Very nice to meet you, Mr. Adams." She turns, and reenters the church without a second thought of the pretty girl standing quietly next to me.

Charlie seems so small, so fragile in this moment, not like the woman I've spent the last few hours with at all. These aren't friends of hers. That much is clear. She's the black sheep among them, a lot like me. I wrap my arm around her shoulders, giving her the physical support she needs to make it around the corner and away from the prying eyes of the other mourners and gossipmongers.

"I think we need a coffee. What do you say?" I want to see her smile again. I want to see that moxie return to her eyes.

She doesn't look up, staying securely tucked into my side. We're two strangers finding comfort in each other in a time of need. "I would like something stronger." Just a whisper, but I hear her.

"Okay, espresso it is, then," I say with enthusiasm, hoping that lifts her mood.

We stop, and she finds the strength to release me, standing strong once again on her own two feet. "No coffee. I need a drink. One with alcohol."

Oh, something stronger. I get it now. "Sure, there's this bar called the Subway Inn just a few blocks from here. It's dark and offers a lot of privacy."

"Sounds perfect."

I take her hand for several reasons. First, because I'm selfish and want to hold her hand, knowing full well I'm taking advantage of the situation. Second, because I also think she needs that touch, that connection with someone outside the people we left at the church.

It's been an exhausting day mentally and physically, so I hail a cab.
"Charlie?" she asks.
"Yeah?" I look down at her, her bright blue eyes shining again.
"Thank you."
I squeeze her shoulders playfully. "Eh, that's what friends are for."
Seeing her smile makes me smile, one that comes from the heart.

Chapter 7

♀

The bar is a real locals' type place. There's no jukebox or sound system so it can turn into a club in the late hours. There isn't a dance floor or modern furnishings. It's dark with old, wobbly, wooden tables and chairs and a long, worn-looking bar that runs the length of the right side of the room.

He offers to let me go first, but I pause and let him lead me.

"Come on, let's sit back here," he says, tugging the fabric at my wrist.

Following Charlie into the small, dark bar, I notice he walks with authority. I like his confidence and slight swagger. He's comfortable with who he is. I wish I were more like that. I live in the middle these days, caught between my old life and a new one I'm trying to forge.

He walks to a small table in the corner like it's reserved for him. He seems relaxed, more in his element here. Pulling the chair out for me, I sit, but he remains standing, and asks, "What would you like?"

"Whatever you're having will work." I honestly don't care what I'm drinking. I just know that I need a drink . . . or *five*.

I'm not on a mission to get drunk, but by the time we both finish our second Old Fashioned, it's starting to feel inevitable. The whiskey and bitters don't taste as strong as they did at first. That's always a sign I'm starting to be affected, and yet, I don't care. The creeping numbness is a nice change from the intense emotions of the day.

Every second spent together isn't filled with meaningless words, but I enjoy the lightness of the words we do share.

"I'm ready for another." I'm relaxed, too relaxed, maybe tipsy, definitely buzzed.

"How about we switch to beer?" He leans forward, resting his arms on the table.

"I'm not drunk," I reply, feeling defensive.

He smiles, laughing under his breath. "I didn't say you were. I just think we should slow down a bit."

"Fine." I know I'll feel bad in the morning if I don't pace myself better. "Beer it is, then. A lager, please."

"Why do I find it so attractive that you know about beer?"

"Are you saying you find me or my knowledge of beer attractive?" I rest my chin on my hand, with my elbow planted on the table and a flirty smirk in place.

"Ha! I think I'll add two waters to that order."

Even with a fuzzy mind, I know he's insinuating that I'm drunk. He calls over his shoulder to the bartender as I continue looking at him, really looking at him.

He's more than just attractive—he's gorgeous. Is it the way his long lashes fan upward toward his eyebrows as he twists his body to make eye contact with the barman? No, not just that. Maybe it's the way his jaw cuts under his chin, sharpening at the edge, displaying its strength for all to see.

Maybe.

But when he turns, looking straight back at me, I figure it out. It's his smile and the way his eyes match his every emotion. Jim had gotten good at hiding the lies in his eyes. But this is Charlie. So, despite that I can tell he's from money from the funeral we attended and his snooty mother, his eyes make me want to trust him.

"What's your story with the upper crust back at St. Bart's?" I ask, wanting to find out all I can about this handsome man, but maybe that was a bit abrasive. "Sorry about that. I kind of lose my filter when I drink."

I must amuse him, because he laughs, lightly, but it's there like he'll answer simply to entertain me. "That's all right. I like that you're straightforward."

"Good." I smile, feeling mischievous. "So I gather you're a fancy pants from the Upper East Side?"

That makes him laugh. "I was."

"Not anymore?"

"No, not anymore."

"Sounds like a story to me. You want to tell it?" I ask, all humor gone as I lean back in my chair and take the last sip of my drink.

He sips his Old Fashioned, but I can see the debate happening in his head, the momentary avoidance going on. I guess he decides he trusts me, because he says, "As I mentioned, I'm the black sheep of the family. I was cut off from my parents' money years ago. They cut off some of their love for me in the process. We haven't yet recovered from the upheaval. But that's a story for another time." He taps his glass against mine. "I hope to have another time to share it with you, but for now, let's talk about you. You don't have to, but if you want to talk about Jim, I'm here. I'll listen."

No! my mind shouts. That's my normal reaction to thinking about him, much less talking about him. I'm not comfortable in the attention focused on my past and me. I grab my water to help stave off the dryness that has overwhelmed my throat. When I set the glass down, the shock subsides. Jim's name being said in this bar, this sanctuary that we escaped to, is disconcerting.

I don't blame him for being curious, though. Charlie witnessed Cherry first hand today, and something—okay, everything about him makes me want to share more than I should. I'm not surprised he's questioning the event, so I start near the beginning, the beginning of the end, despite the turmoil I feel inside. "Jim and I were engaged—"

Embarrassment colors his face, and his hand covers mine where it rests on the table. "I'm sorry. If you don't want to talk about this, we don't have to. I knew you were close, but I guessed a boyfriend, not more."

I continue, needing to let him off the hook and not worry about missteps in assumptions. "We weren't when he passed." *Passed*, I think, twisting the word around my tongue. It doesn't sit well with me. Passed sounds temporary. I search for a word that makes it the most real to me. "Died. We broke up about six months ago."

I laugh at the irony of a fated realization. "We were supposed to be married this month. I hadn't thought of that until now." He watches me, intrigued. "I didn't break us up—"

He gives my hand a gentle squeeze. "If you're not ready to talk about this —"

"No, it's all right. I haven't talked about the breakup in a long time, and his death feels new, foreign to me. He's dead." I repeat it more for me than Charlie. His hand is warm, and though my body is frazzled from the reality of the day, I'm calmed by his simple gesture. It feels good to have someone touch me in this way. It's the kindest touch I've had in a while.

His hand slides away too soon, leaving mine abandoned and cold once again. His expression reveals he feels he overstepped a boundary. Doesn't he understand we're a team now? As of today, we're friends.

The last drink hits me harder than expected. Several reasons come to mind. I haven't been drinking that much in the last couple of months. My emotions are a tangled mess because of Jim's death, and the funeral brought everything bad about Jim and our breakup to the surface.

Charlie doesn't interrupt the long pause in my story, letting me think and talk on my own timeline. "I haven't talked about this . . . stuff in a while, and today was more difficult than I care to burden you with. Do you want to get some dinner? I think I should eat."

"Dinner would be nice."

As soon as we stand, he dashes forward, racing me to the bar to pay our tab. From behind, I say, "My treat. You got the cab."

He backs away, hands in the air, surrendering, and lets me buy the drinks.

We've sprung forward with the time change, but it's still darker than I expected. As we walk down the street, I peek at my watch.

"Am I boring you?" he asks with a smile.

"Quite the contrary. You interest me very much." I automatically wink. Oh my God! I actually just winked at him. I really need to keep myself from flirting. He's just being nice to me. I don't want to ruin this.

He laughs. "You interest me very much, too, Charlie." Then he squints. "I'm not going to wink, though, because I won't look half as good as you did when you winked."

I hit him on the arm. "You're not supposed to call a girl out on her idiocies."

"You're not an idiot, but you are entertaining."

"Changing the topic to anything other than this one. Hey look, it's dark outside. I didn't expect that." It's seven-thirty, and I'm kind of shocked how the time flew. "I knew I was hungry, and now I see why."

He smiles, and we see an old-school Italian restaurant coming up on our left. He says, "Hey, I've eaten here before. It's fantastic. Do you mind Italian?"

"I could eat Italian every night." His enthusiasm is contagious, but that he let that embarrassing conversation and wink go is full-on attractive. He's quite the gentleman.

Our table is quaint and very traditional in its appearance. We order our food and both stick to water. He still holds my complete interest as I sit across from him. His eyes reveal what he tries to hide from most.

"He cheated on me," I say, picking up where I feel comfortable. His lips separate in surprise of my admission. "He cheated and then broke up with me." I look at the checkered tablecloth and run my finger down a red line, then back up a white line. "I wish I had been the one to do it . . . but—" I shake my head, letting him know that I'm done talking about it tonight.

She fascinates me. The way she speaks, the words she chooses, she's different. Charlie shakes her head. She can't go on with her story, and I'm not going to push. I offer her a breadstick, and she happily accepts, eating it in place of talking.

Time passes, but I don't rush it. The silence doesn't bother me. It gives me time to think—to sort out what I'm doing with this woman, what I'm feeling for her. By the way my heart is clenching, I can tell I'm not going to figure this out in one day. She's much too complicated for that and intriguing, and damn beautiful.

She's stronger than she gives herself credit for. She's vulnerable and soft. Yes, she's been hurt, broken, but I don't need to fix her. There's a lot of determination in her small frame, and I have no doubt she'll mend her own heart, without relying on others to perform the task. After spending five hours with her, I just hope I can be there for the journey.

She asks about my work, and though she asks all the right questions, she seems distant. I'm not surprised. It's been a rough day for both of us. As we eat, I see lights of a happier life spark from within her. She's had a good life with a few bumps.

When our plates are cleared, panic rises. I don't want this to end. How can I justifiably keep her near me longer, though? I'm ready for this day to end, but I'm definitely not ready to let her go.

She breaks my train of thought. "Today has been one of the longest of my life. I'm so ready for it to be over."

"I was just thinking the exact opposite."

"Really?" she asks as she rubs her hand over her stomach.

I shrug. "Yeah, there's been some, um, sad parts, but you've made it a lot better."

Her eyes are a bit glassy from the alcohol, but she's held her liquor well. "Why are you so nice to me?"

"Do people treat you poorly?"

"You tend to answer questions with a question. Did you know you do that?"

"It's a distraction technique. It's also a bad habit I fall back on when I find someone so fascinating that I need to know more."

She smiles with a giggle. "Now that's a someone I'd like to hear more about."

"Maybe one day."

"All right. One day then."

I buy dinner without any fight for the tab this time. She's wearing down, tired. Lifting her coat from the back of her chair, I stand to assist.

Out on the sidewalk, she seems more serious, even a little sad. "Thank you for today. I couldn't have done it without you." She pauses to choose her words carefully. "It was bearable, better, with you there. Thank you." Leaning up, she wraps her arms around my neck in a full embrace, an embrace shared between people who are more than mere acquaintances. But I don't argue, because it feels real. I'm hoping we are, too.

Feeling her soft hair against my cheek, I slide my arms around her. In this moment, the death of my aunt hits my heart, making it ache, and I feel my body shake from the loss. Grace was the last person I hugged—the last person who hugged me before Charlie.

She now holds me with the knowledge that this isn't just for her. I feel the warmth of her inner sunshine against me, soothing me from the outside.

"I guess it's been a longer day than I thought," I say.

She sighs, mirroring my own emotions, then peeks over my shoulder and down the street. I turn my head just enough to see the taxi she's eyeing. Stepping back from her, I wave my arm to signal it over. As it pulls to the curb, I look to her, expecting the typical awkwardness present between two people in a new relationship or getting to know each other, but it's not there.

"Thank you for going with me." I stumble over my words, feeling the end coming too fast. "I'd like to hang out again sometime."

She jokes, "When's your next funeral?" A small smile flickers across her mouth, but it doesn't hold.

I laugh. She's clever. "Maybe we could hit a wedding next time."

It's her turn to laugh now. "Yeah, maybe something lighter would be a nice change." She asks the next question like she's wanted to all day. "Are you going to see Rachel again?" Her face reveals her doubts, but she doesn't show signs of regret for asking.

I like that.

I chuckle to myself. "You're asking *me* instead of your friend?"

"We're friends, right?"

"Yes, I guess we are." I angle my head, trying to figure her out. It's a wasted effort. I imagine I could spend a year straight with her and still not understand everything going on in her head. "We decided *we* were better as friends. She didn't tell you?"

"I didn't ask." Embarrassment colors her cheeks, or maybe it's the alcohol. "I didn't ask her on purpose."

Interesting. "Why not?"

She lifts her eyes up to meet mine, and I can feel her hesitation to say too much, though she doesn't seem to hold back. "I wasn't sure if I wanted to know the answer. She's usually so open with how her dates go, but with you, she didn't say anything."

Her words don't relieve me. They stress me. She's seeking the truth from me, but I don't know if she'll believe it when she hears it.

"It was mutual. The 'It' factor wasn't there. She's a great girl—"

"For someone else?"

"Honestly, yes, for someone else." I hold eye contact with her, hoping she sees the sincerity, the truth there. Then I reach, grabbing at anything that will give me more time with this beautiful woman. "Would she disapprove of us being friends?"

She moves toward the cab as I open the door for her, wishing she would stay longer. She doesn't look at me, but stops momentarily in thought before she slides into the waiting car. Her pause makes me nervous and hopeful that she's considering her options.

"I don't know, Charlie." She looks up at me. "I'd like to be friends with you, but I don't want to hurt my friend in the process. I don't have many these days."

I don't know what to say to that, because she's doing the right thing, her loyalty admirable. I know this deep down, and it says a lot about the person she is. I've already argued my best points, so I have to trust this is meant to be.

"I'll talk to Rachel," she says.

"Please do. I have a good feeling about us." I question my sanity for being so amiable.

"So do I." She smiles and says, "Thanks again. Maybe we'll run into each other sometime soon." After a quick wave of her hand, the door closes. I see her mouth good-bye through the smudged glass of the window as the car starts to pull away.

Her last name. *Shit!* I don't know her last name. I feel panic building inside and run after the cab.

"Wait! What's your last name?" But it's too late. The taxi is too far, and I stop, muttering a pathetic, "Good-bye, Charlie."

I catch a cab and call it a night. I'm too drained to make any appearances on the social scene tonight.

By morning, the previous day feels ancient and out of place in my mind. The low of my great-aunt's funeral mixed with the high of being with Charlie makes it hard for me to tuck the day neatly away in my mind. I pace my apartment, worrying and thinking about Rachel's reaction and that I might not see Charlie again. Rachel seems to hold all the cards concerning my future, and I don't like my fate resting in another's hands.

I should've gone with my instincts that first night at the bar, but opportunity and reality seem to collide regularly in my world. I went with reality, and hey, I like Rachel, just not romantically. Like Charlie said, she's a great girl . . . for someone else.

When I look at the fact, I might have wrecked that relationship on purpose, but why? I didn't know if I was ever going to see Charlie again. By the way she darted from the club that first night, I didn't think she wanted to see me again. *Ugh!* I've got to get out of this place. My nerves feel like they're crawling under my skin, itching in anxiety.

I grab my jacket out of habit from the preceding cold months of winter and jog down the several flights to the street. I feel better avoiding the confined space of my apartment—for now anyway. I walk with no particular purpose. The fresh air clears my head, allowing me the space to think about my redhead.

I'm happier than I remember being in a long time. Life is just better when you have some sunshine in your life.

Chapter 8

♀

I didn't want to get in that cab, and I didn't look back in fear that I might make the driver stop and that would lead to bad things. Things like looking into Charlie's eyes, then grabbing him by his sexy jaw, which was covered with light scruff, and kissing him. I roll my eyes at my ridiculousness, then close them, relaxing into the vinyl and indulging in the fantasy a moment longer.

As our lips get acquainted, I would hold onto his shoulders, his muscular shoulders that are straight and strong. I'd let his hands wander my sides. My breathing deepens at the thought. It's almost as if I can feel his hands on me, up and down, over my ribs and down the curve of my waist to my hips where his fingers grip me even tighter.

My head drops back as my mouth falls open. His lips leave a wet trail across my face leading to my neck, his breath on my skin awakening every nerve from its hibernation. I feel his thumb caress the side of my breast, tentative, testing. My own breathing is harsher and unsteady under the pleasure.

"Miss? Miss!"

My eyes flash open. I drop my hands from my neck and sit straight up, horrified—or would that be hornified?

"We're here," the driver says.

I shake off the silly thought and look out the window as if I need verification of what he's told me. My building. Yes, we're here. "Oh, sorry. How much is it?"

"Fifteen seventy-five."

I grab a twenty out of my wallet and hand it to him. "Keep the change." I'm so embarrassed I was caught fantasizing that all I want is to get out of this car as fast as possible, which I do.

Once inside my place, I lean against the door. My body is still warm with little tingles sprinkling across my skin in places I haven't felt in a while, places that have been ignored for too long. I release a deep breath and try to shake myself out of this crazy daydream. The liquor in my system makes me dizzy, so I pause as it rushes back to my head then I start to walk.

Yeah, it's just the alcohol making me think craziness like this. Charlie's from Jim's world. I'm sure there are more similarities than differences, and I don't think I can put my heart at risk to prove my head wrong.

I hang my coat in the closet and kick my heels off when I enter my room, working my way to the bathroom and tossing my dress onto my bed.

After brushing my teeth, I slip off my bra before pulling a tank top over my head. When I climb into bed, I realize it's not that late, but I'm exhausted. Switching on the television, I relax into the mattress with a cooking show playing in the background. Recounting the day is interesting, as Charlie's face fills every moment worth remembering. He was a bright spot in an otherwise dark day.

Thinking back to Jim's funeral, it could have been awful, even more awful than the fact that I was actually attending his funeral. The stares, the whispers—I heard it all. I saw them all gawking at me like I did something wrong, like I was the one who cheated on him. That's Cherry's doing. She's woven her web of lies and used me as her tarnished-halo-wearing son's scapegoat. She can't have the truth come out about someone in her family, much less her picture-perfect son. He wasn't all bad as a person—I did fall in love with him, after all—but he wasn't all good either.

Maybe she doesn't know what happened between us. Maybe he lied and blamed me. I don't know if I'll ever find out, but I do know I can't dwell on it. It's not healthy for me to live in the dark any longer, especially not when the light feels so good.

I'm nervous the next day while walking into work. I shouldn't be, but I am. My stomach has been twisted into mini-knots all morning. I'm blaming those for the extra drink I have in my hand right now, passion fruit and mango iced tea from the deli downstairs—Rachel's favorite.

Am I sucking up or trying to butter her up? I shouldn't have to. Charlie made the reason they aren't going on another date sound mutual. I just hope that's the truth. I really want that to be the truth, but I still need to talk to Rachel. That's the right thing to do. I raise my chin up a degree and walk with more purpose and confidence toward her desk. Yes, this is the right thing to do. My only hesitation is that she might say she doesn't want me to see Charlie again, even as friends.

"Good morning," I say, setting her drink down next to her. She is focused on her computer screen, but glances over and smiles.

Spinning around, she grabs the drink, and sips. "Thank you, and good morning to you." Her eyes flash to the drink again, then back to me. "This is a nice surprise."

As I lean against her desk, I attempt to play it off. "Yeah, I was going there anyway, so I thought I'd grab you one."

"That's very thoughtful." Her expression turns serious, and I just know she sees right through me. The guilt must be written across my face. Rachel hesitates before asking, "How are you? How was the funeral?"

I do a mental brow wipe in relief before answering. "That's actually what I wanted to talk to you about."

She turns in her chair to face me, sipping her drink. I smile and try to sound casual. "You never told me how your date with Charlie went?"

"There wasn't much to tell."

"It's not like you not to share."

She shrugs. "I just didn't because I was a little disappointed. He's a great guy, but he isn't 'the one.' "

"But you also haven't seemed like yourself." I prod, hoping she opens up, needing more and hating to see her sad.

"Paolo called to tell me he's not coming back, and the whole dating scene here is out of vogue. I'm tired of being optimistic and everything fizzling before it gets started."

Dropping my purse to the floor, I set my drink down and move closer. "Oh, sweetie, I'm sorry. Maybe it's not about always looking, but letting things happen naturally."

"I want to be married, Charlie. I want to start a family. My sister is pregnant with her third, and she's only two years older than I am. My parents are pressuring me to move home and settle down in Jersey." She turns away briefly, her finger running through the condensation on the plastic cup. "I told everyone that I was bigger than Jersey when I left, but my life here is stagnant. I've been working here for over a year, and I'm still doing the same thing. It's starting to get embarrassing when I go home for visits."

Though I'm not desperate to be settled right now, I remember how good it felt to be in a relationship, knowing that part of my life was determined and I had found my partner. That was a foolish dream, not reality.

I rub her shoulder, hoping to comfort her. "You're twenty-seven, Rach. It's not like you don't have time. You're young and beautiful, a great friend, and a lot of fun to be around."

She wipes at her eyes. "I shouldn't drag you down." Taking a deep breath, she waves her hand in front of her face. "Enough with my pity party. Back to you. Tell me all about yesterday."

I look down, now more uncertain than ever if I should talk about Charlie or not. I don't want to make her feel worse. I start with the funeral. "It was harder than I thought it would be. I expected Jim's mother to either ignore me or say something snotty. She didn't disappoint. In just a few sentences, she managed to remind me exactly how she feels about me."

"That bad, huh?"

"Yes." I close my eyes, gathering my strength because I need to confide in her. I open them and confess. "I ran into Charlie."

Her expression goes blank then several emotions flit across her face before settling into confusion. "*Charlie?* As in my Charlie? Charlie Adams?" Her arms rest defensively across her chest.

No, this isn't going to be easy.

She looks away, but I can see the hurt tinged with a bit of anger in her face. "He was at Jim's funeral?" she asks.

How am I going to explain this without hurting her more? The truth. The truth is better than lying. "I ran into him when I was walking to the funeral. We started to talk after we recognized each other."

"Then you just asked him to go with you, or he was going already?"

"No, it wasn't like that." Now that I think about it, it does seem strange, but my mind was muddled, and it felt right at the time. "He was going to a funeral, a different one. His great-aunt's." Her eyebrows are raised as she listens to me ramble on. "And it wasn't awkward, so we decided to go to each other's funerals. It was kind of spur of the moment."

"So, you took a date to Jim's funeral?"

"No," I say, feeling defensive. "Not a date. Charlie. A friend."

"Since when are you and Charlie friends? You just met him. You know I went on a date with him the other night, and though we aren't seeing each other romantically, he did ask me out first."

I grab my purse from the floor and stand upright. I'm not liking the direction this conversation is heading, and her tone is turning insulting. "It wasn't a date, Rachel."

"Well, I hope not, because that would be awkward." She turns back to her computer. "I have to get this to Mr. Allen before ten so . . ." She leaves her words hanging between us, but I get the message.

"Okay." Frustrated, I leave her alone and walk around to my cubicle. I drop my purse into the bottom drawer like I do every day, but I kick it closed harder than usual.

That didn't go how I wanted at all. I open my e-mails and start reading through them, hoping to distract myself from the guilt that's building in my stomach. The guilt morphs into irritation fast, and I start to stew.

"Charlie?"

I lift my head up and see Rachel peeking over the wall.

"Yeah?"

"I'm sorry."

"For what?"

"For being weird. I didn't mean to get defensive. I just . . . it's just Paolo and . . ." She looks down. "Are you going to see him again?"

"It wasn't like that. We're just friends."

"But you want to see him again, right?"

I gulp, not comfortable with the confrontation. "I don't know. We didn't exchange numbers or anything like that."

"Well, that's not a good sign." She shrugs and then drops below the divider wall.

No. It's not going down like this. I push back from the desk and walk around the wall. "What does that mean?"

"It means that you may have spent some time together, but it's obvious it's not a love connection since you didn't exchange numbers."

I refuse to hold back any longer. "I already told you that it wasn't like that. He was a great support at the funeral yesterday, and I think I was for him, too. We went and got drinks at a bar afterward, then ate dinner before calling it a day. It was the best non-date date I've had in a long time."

Her mouth is hanging ajar as my words sink in. "You haven't been on a date in forever, Char, so that's progress." She seems reflective as she pauses. "I'm sorry again. Ugh! I'm just in a funk. I'm actually happy you had someone there for you."

"Wait! You are?"

"I know yesterday was hard for you, and Charlie is a great guy. I bet it was good to have him there. Do you think he's cute? I think he's super cute." And like that, the old Rachel returns.

My head is spinning a bit from her abrupt mood change. "I don't know. He's nice, and it was fun to talk with hi—"

"What do you mean you don't know? Just look at him, Charlie. The man is gorgeous."

I shrug. Something deep inside of me doesn't want to admit I'm attracted to him. The problem is that my inner voice reminds me of that very fact more often than I like. That constant little voice of destiny is whispering in my ear, *"Open your mind. He's handsome and charming."*

I look down at the plain grey mouse pad on her desk, running my finger along the fraying edges before I speak again. "Yesterday was a roller coaster of emotions. I'm glad I had someone on my side." I look up at her and add, "I'm glad he was there. It's what I needed. He was there to support me no matter what those gossipers had to say."

A sympathetic smile crosses her face. "I'm sorry. I should have been there for you. I trusted that you'd tell me if you thought you needed someone."

"I didn't think I did. I thought I could face them alone, and had every intention to, but I'm not going to lie and say I didn't like having him there. I did. He was a great comfort to me. So, I don't know what happened between you two, and I don't know if I want to, but I do value our friendship and would never want to betray you, which is why I'm telling you."

Her smile turns real, happy, a glint in her eyes. "You do, you like him. I can tell." She points at me and her eyes widen as if she discovered that I'm keeping a secret from her. "You, my friend, like Mr. Charlie more than you're letting on."

I playfully roll my eyes, then pretend I hear my cell phone buzzing to distract both her and myself from this topic. She laughs, and it's boisterous and wonderful to hear. My face heats from embarrassment, and I start to laugh, too.

"I can't do a relationship right now, Rach. I won't lie, he's pretty damn dreamy, but it wasn't about that. I liked how we were yesterday. It's different between us. He's different. He seemed to understand me and not judge. He's a great listener, but he participates and talks, too." Dropping my head into my hands, I say, "Friends. We agreed to be friends. Friends only."

I feel her rub my back gently. "Keep telling yourself that, and maybe one day you'll believe it."

I return to my desk and she stays at hers, leaving me to sort through all these strange emotions. My desk phone rings, and when I answer, I hear Rachel say, "Tomorrow night we're going out. There's a place in Tribeca I want to check out. I'm not taking no for an answer, so I'll assume your silence is a yes."

I just laugh, and she knows I'm in.

Chapter 9

♂

Justin tosses me a bottle of beer as he flops onto the large chair next to the couch. I lean back after punching the couch cushion into a more comfortable shape.

"So," he says, "you want to hit it tonight? It is Friday, after all."

We're watching the sports recap from the week on television and just polished off an extra-large pizza. "After that carb overload, sleep sounds good." I moan for extra emphasis while rubbing my stomach.

"Forget that! We're going out. There are women in this city who haven't had the pleasure of my company yet." He stands and opens the door. "You've got one hour to recover. I'll text you where to meet."

I throw a pillow, but it hits the back of the door, because he's already gone.

Rolling onto my side, I stare at the television. Do I want to go out? Not really. That just reminds me of my massive failing this week. If I'd gotten Charlie's number, I would've asked her out for tonight. Short notice, but I hate those dating rules. If I like a girl, I call her right away because I want to see her. Why play games?

I need a distraction, because the wallowing will ruin the day, so I get up.

An hour and a half later, I'm at the bar of some pale blue fluorescent-lit, sleek and modern ultra-lounge in SoHo waiting on Justin to show. Two women have already approached me, but I'm not in the mood for that tonight.

Justin saunters in, and I down the last of my Jack and Coke as he orders his drink. He turns to me and asks, "New suit?"

"Newish."

"How's the scene?" He leans his elbows on the bar and scopes out the place.

"Boring."

"No hot chicks?"

"Plenty of hot women."

"So what's the problem?"

I sigh, setting my drink back down on the bar, and lie. "No problem."

My phone buzzes in my pocket. I check the text, and my eyebrows rise in surprise. I hit Justin in the chest. "Cancel the drink. We're leaving."

"What? No! I just made eye contact with the sweetie in the corner."

"The one in corner with the bachelorette party?"

"Yep."

"No. Just no. They're too young."

"They're at least twenty-one." I grab him by the tie and head for the door. "Fine," he whines, and I drop my hand. "Where are we going anyway?"

"Tribeca"

I knew what was waiting for me when I walked into the club, but I didn't expect to feel this way. My heart races, and I feel breathless. There she is— purple dress, sexy shoes, her hair is down with soft curls, eyes closed— swaying to the music. Charlie is beautiful, and I walk straight for her. Justin trails behind.

"Damn! You see that girl?" he asks, walking past me.

"I see her."

Rachel is next to Charlie, and at least three guys are vying for their attention. Justin stops right in front of Charlie, but as I approach, I shift him over.

She opens her eyes and they connect with mine. Her mouth drops open as she steals a quick breath. "Charlie!" she exclaims, throwing her arms around my neck.

Wrapping my arms tightly around her waist, I feel very possessive of her. I shoot the three stand-bys one glare each that says all they need to know: *she's with me.*

After they leave, I whisper into her ear, "Hi." No great line or clever quip, just a simple greeting.

By the time she releases me, it's just us. Rachel and Justin are heading to the bar.

Charlie looks up at me and smiles. "Hi. I didn't know if I'd see you again."

"I'm here."

Dragging her hands down the front of my suit, her fingers grasp my lapels. "Yes, you are. You look nice."

"Thanks. You look . . ." I want to say "stunning" or "breathtaking." Instead, I settle for, "Beautiful."

She's shy and tilts her face away. "Thank you."

When she looks back, she drops her hands as if she realizes she shouldn't be touching me in such a familiar manner. She doesn't know how much I like her hands on me, at least she doesn't know yet. I have hopes to clarify a few feelings tonight.

Justin hands Charlie an orange-colored martini, and Rachel gives me a JD and Coke. "Thank you."

Rachel leans forward and kisses me on the cheek. Charlie watches, studying the interaction. "Nice to see you again," I say. I look down at my drink, not wanting to give any mixed signals of why I'm here.

"You look great," Rachel replies, running her hand down my arm.

I glance at Charlie who is looking more uncomfortable by the second. Reaching over, I rub her waist in reassurance. The action isn't lost on Rachel. "Thanks." I remain staring into Charlie's eyes, enjoying the view. "You're looking lovely tonight, also."

Rachel starts to flirt with both Justin and me, but I've come to realize that's how she is with men. Justin is so entranced by her that he's hanging on her every word, which is a good distraction for her.

But for Charlie, it's too late. She's irritated, and spats out, "I'm going to the restroom."

She turns so abruptly that some of her drink splashes out of the glass. I follow behind.

"Charlie, wait up!" It's loud and I don't know if she can hear me. Guys are ogling her as she passes, a few saying hello, but she ignores them all. I call out once more. "Charlie, stop!"

She does with a huff, looking over her shoulder. Her expression's no longer playful like before. I can see her feelings are hurt. "I've got to use the bathroom."

"Then I'll wait for you."

"No, I'm a big girl. I think I can manage my way back."

"Don't do this." My hand finds her shoulder, trying to calm her.

She backs up, not wanting me to touch her. "Don't do what? I'm going to the bathroom." She's saying one thing, but her defensiveness is obvious.

"No, you're escaping from a situation that you have all wrong."

Her hand flies to her hip, and her shoulders go back. "I have it all wrong? Listen, you don't owe me anything. I don't owe you anything. The other day," she says, her hand waving wildly in the air, "was just two people doing each other a favor, I guess." Her eyes drop to the ground, and she sighs. "That's what I read all wrong."

"No, you didn't. It meant something to me. That back there," I signal toward Rachel and Justin, "doesn't."

"You don't have to answer to me, Charlie." Her voice is quieter as she lowers her hand in defeat.

I step closer, and this time she doesn't move, which is good. Pulling her to the side for more privacy, I back her against the wall. "I came tonight because Rachel texted me and said you'd be here. I'm here for you, not her."

"She did?"

I nod, and a small smile grows as she processes that information, her features softening under my gaze. "I'm sorry. I overreacted. Tough week . . . for both of us."

"Yeah, tough week." I'll blame the heaviness of the week if that makes it easier for her to accept the jealousy she just felt. "I'll hold your drink and wait here if you still need to use the restroom."

"Okay. Thank you."

I watch as she pushes the door open, her body less rigid. She glances back over her shoulder, and our eyes meet before the door closes.

I get a few looks, but no one bothers me since it's apparent I'm waiting for someone because of the two drinks in my hands.

When she returns, she's smiling. "I don't like this drink. Can I try yours?"
"Sure."

I watch as her lips press against the glass and she sips, oh so slow. "That's much better." And with that, all the bad from minutes earlier seems to be forgotten.

"Let's remedy that and get you one."

We walk through the crowd, past Rachel and Justin who don't even notice us, to the bar. I've kept my hand on her lower back, not able to stop myself from touching her.

After I buy her another drink, she asks, "Do you dance?"
"Not if I don't have to."

That makes her laugh, and hearing her laugh makes me laugh, too. "I love to dance, but I don't like the bump and grind kind of dancing unless I'm dating the guy. I don't like strangers groping me."

I look over at the dance floor. "That's all they're doing out there." I lean in closer and whisper, "And I wouldn't like strangers groping you either." Her eyes seek mine, sparkling from the spotlights over the bar. I lean back, resting my elbows on the bar so I'm eye level with her. "What do you like to do for fun, Charlie?"

Smiling as if embarrassed, she laughs under her breath. Her shy side is back. "I like to bake. I know, I know." She rolls her eyes. "My friends used to call me lame for it, but I find it relaxing. It's a science to me, an experiment."

How can I not like that? "What do you like to bake?"

"Cakes and cupcakes. Cupcakes are all the rage right now with all these cupcake bakeries popping up everywhere, but I still prefer to make my own."

"I have a terrible sweet tooth. You might have met your match." I'm not talking about baking.

"I should make you some. My coworkers have forbidden me from bringing anymore in since they all gained weight." She laughs again. "What's your favorite flavor? No, wait! Don't answer that. I'll guess."

"How about instead of guessing, you make some and we'll go from there."

"A challenge? I like a good challenge." She looks me over, analyzing everything about me physically as if that will lead her to my favorite flavor. The next thing she says takes me by surprise. "How about Wednesday?"

She's setting a date. I like that. "I'm good on Wednesday."

"You can come over after work—"

"I can bring dinner."

"And I can bake." She looks excited, probably because of the baking part, but I like to think it's about us spending time together again.

I turn back to my drink, deciding I need to finish it and stop staring at the girl. I don't want to creep her out. I order another, and we chat, getting to know each other in a different way. Although, I feel like I know her—the real Charlie—already.

When we talk about our work, she seems impressed. "Following your dreams. I love that," she says, wistful.

After another round of cocktails, we look for our friends. A bit unsteady on our feet, we can't find either of them and joke that they might be hooking up as we speak.

I can tell Charlie is heading toward drunk, so I offer to help her home.

"What time is it?" she asks as we walk out of the club, the brisk spring air hitting us.

"Late," I reply. "It's after one."

"It doesn't feel late, and I'm not tired."

I grab her elbow to steady her as she begins to sway. "It is, though. Let's take a cab." We get in the short cab line and wait.

"I can take a taxi by myself. You don't have to worry about me." She wraps her arm around my mine, holding me close, keeping her warm.

There's no way I'm sending her in a cab this late by herself. I'm going with her. "No, it's fine."

"Well, if we're sharing a cab," she says, approaching the curb. We're next. "Let's go to yours. I want to read some of your writing."

I grin to myself and tease her. "I don't know if you're in any condition to read right now."

"I'm not ready to go home, Charlie. I can call Rachel if you're too tired."

This girl is complete trouble. "Okay, fine." I give into her. "We'll go to mine."

"You made a rhyme."

"I think you're drunk."

"I'm not drunk," protests the drunk girl next to me. She ducks her body into the taxi, and we take off after I give directions. "You live in a fancy schmancy part of town," she says. Her body is snuggled against mine.

"You'll be disappointed then."

"I doubt I could be disappointed with anything when it comes to you."

I look at her, shocked by her comment, but she smiles all smug before resting her head on my shoulder. She's trouble, and I debate whether I should be taking her to my place. I have nothing to hide from her, but the way she's acting, I'm equally nervous and excited of where this might lead. I won't take advantage of her, but her cuteness is wearing my willpower down.

I rub my hands over my face, knowing I drank too much as well. I'll pay for this tomorrow, but I'm going to be happy in the now.

"I like it," she says when we arrive. Dropping her purse on the entry table, she does a slow spin, taking it all in. "It suits you."

"I hope that's a good thing." I toss my jacket on the couch.

"Yes, it's a compliment."

"A drink? Water, beer—"

"Please. Whatever you're having."

I grab two beers out of the fridge and twist the caps off, tossing them into the bowl on the bar. I've had a weird obsession with collecting beer caps for a few years now. I watch her from the kitchen as she looks at my bookcase, running her finger along my desk. She moves to the window and looks out.

"You have a balcony," she states. "Can we go out?"

"Mmhm." I hand her the bottle and open the door for her.

We drink in silence for a few minutes, enjoying the calm compared to the loud thumping of the club. It's breezy and a little chilly, but not cold tonight. She sets her beer down on the small bistro table and leans on the rail, stepping out of her shoes.

"You're short."

That makes her giggle. "Did I kill the illusion?"

"Ha! Not for me."

"Wait until you see me without makeup then. It's all a mask to hide the hideousness."

Setting my drink down. I think I'm also done drinking for the night. Playfully nudging her with my elbow, I shrug. "Whatever. I bet you look even prettier without makeup."

She bellows in laughter, her head dropping back. "Now that's a challenge I won't accept." She turns more serious as she faces me. "Charlie?"

"Yeah?"

Shifting her weight onto one ankle, she nervously asks, "Can I kiss you?"

"What?" Not what I meant to say at all. Her face falls. Damn it! She threw me off—

"Never mind. It was silly. I just haven't been kissed in so long, and I miss —"

I step forward, closing the gap. Cupping her face in my hands, I kiss her, cutting off her words and ending her doubts.

Chapter 10

♀

My body leans against him, relaxing into a kiss that makes me forget who I am. He kisses me like I'm the most desirable woman in the world. And at this moment in time, I believe him.

The whiskey from earlier clouds my head as I press my body against Charlie's hard chest. His strong arms hold me to him as if he's afraid I'll disappear. I won't. I can't. I'm lost in him as my body sparks to life, erupting in a passion different from anything I've ever felt before.

I let go and give into my desires. I give into him because I want to, because he's so damn sexy, but most of all, because this gorgeous man, who was supportive and by my side just a few days ago, turns me on and wants me. It's nice to feel desired, to feel pretty and sexy. By the way he's kissing me I can tell the feeling of want is mutual. I just hope I can make him feel how much I want him, too.

His hips press forward, trapping me between him and the railing as his hands secure me, drawing my body closer. It's hard to breathe and hard to move, but there is nothing I'd rather be doing than this.

As his tongue caresses mine, I shiver in delight, causing him to still.

"You're cold. Let's go inside." He takes me by the hand and grabs the two bottles with the other.

Walking inside behind him, I feel the warmth of the apartment. I tremble, but if I'm being honest, I'm trembling from his touch, his kisses, and the building urges inside, not the temperature outside.

Releasing my hand, Charlie sets the bottles on the coffee table and turns off the kitchen light. I don't want an awkwardness to consume me, which can happen if I start overthinking this, so I step forward as he turns on the lamp by the couch.

"Charlie, kiss me."

He hurries to me. "My pleasure," he whispers then kisses me. His lips are soft but firm, and his hands grasp me, kneading me with purpose. I'm unsure if his purpose is the same one I feel. Doubt creeps in without warning. *How far am I going with him? How much do I want? Am I ready? Am I ready for this? For him?*

I kiss him harder and hope the moan he releases into my mouth will shroud my doubts. Our lips part and our breaths blanket each other as we pant for more. I hold him behind the neck as he rests his forehead against mine. I keep my eyes closed, not wanting reality to ruin the moment.

Too much time to think will be the downfall of our activities—activities I'm enjoying far too much to end. So I open my eyes, pleasantly surprised to meet his blue ones. They're darker than usual, dilated, serious, and wanting.

"I can tell you're overanalyzing this, thinking too hard," he says. His voice stays low and suggestive.

"I don't want to think. I just want to feel again." I speak the honest truth.

"Just feel." His words float breathlessly between us, but hold so much weight in their meaning.

Just feel.

Just feel.

Just feel. The words repeat in my head and become my new mantra, giving me the moxie to lead him down the short hall to his bedroom. I stop upon entering, looking around. It feels so intimate in here, not bachelor pad-ish at all. It's warm and inviting. He releases my hand as I step toward the bed and sit down. There's a chocolate-brown loveseat under the window with some pillows that appear to be used a lot. Maybe he reads there. I would. It looks so cozy and comfortable.

The furniture in the room isn't matchy-matchy, but works well together. Every piece feels as if it always belonged together. His comforter is a grey-blue, reminding me of his eyes.

Charlie's voice brings me back to him before I have a chance to analyze the framed photographs on the wall. "We don't have to do anything you don't want," he says, sitting down next to me. He entwines his fingers with mine and places our hands on his thigh.

"No, I want to do this—"

"Do what?" He looks at me, his eyes gleaming with curiosity.

"Be here. Do this . . . you know . . . oh, I don't know. Just kiss me, damn it!"

A sly smile makes its way across his face as his hand lands gently on my cheek. Caressing my skin with his thumb, he chuckles under his breath, then kisses me exactly how I need to be kissed. It's mind-blowing.

I relax, feeling the gentle pressure of him while letting his clean and masculine scent infiltrate my body. I sigh into his mouth, and he kisses me harder until I'm lying on my back. I use my heels to dig into the mattress, pushing myself farther up. He slides up the bed with me, our lips never separating. His hand slinks up my leg and over my dress, settling on my ribs.

I like the gentle weight of his chest on mine and the way my tummy tingles as he balances above me. His knees are between mine, nudging them apart to make more room. I should feel weird or awkward because it's been so long, years in fact, since I've been with anyone other than Jim—but I don't with Charlie—I don't feel either of those. Instead, his touch comforts me as his mouth cherishes me.

I feel his right thumb run lightly over the side of my breast. Losing more of myself in the moment with each second that passes, I push my body into his hand, wanting the same thing he wants.

A deep groan rumbles through his chest, and his kisses become more intense. He leaves my lips and trails wet kisses over my jaw down to my throat. He works his way to my ear, his breath heavy and hot. "You're so beautiful." His words are but a sweet sigh.

His hips press forward, and I can feel how large he is. He thrusts his pelvis into mine, and I arch my back, relishing the sensation.

It's been too long. I missed this—the butterflies, the excitement and anticipation, the intimacy of being this vulnerable and yet comfortable, with someone. I didn't feel confident in the beginning of my relationship with Jim, and it makes me note how much I do with Charlie.

He stops after he kisses my shoulder. Maneuvering the strap of my dress to the side, he nibbles at my collarbone.

"Mmmm," I hum, not meaning to do that aloud, but not caring that I did.

Charlie's left hand moves under my bottom and squeezes. A giggle escapes when I smile.

"God, I love your laugh."

He looks up at me, his lashes framing his baby blues, and he smirks. Yep, smirks. I'm weak to a smirk, always have been, but his is especially devilish. My knees fly together, gripping him between them, and I don't bother letting go.

His hand slides down my thigh before touching the back of my knee. His fingertips draw figure eights before he swerves over my calf muscle to my ankle, pausing on my foot. My shoe is removed and dropped to the floor, the other one following with a thud.

We're clothed, but I feel so much closer to him already. My heart is open and bare to him, welcoming him. With that realization, my mind is made up. I'm going to enjoy my night and stop worrying about the past.

Chapter 11

♂

Her hands flatten across my chest then she fists my shirt, pulling me to her, wanting more just like I do. I can't stop my hips from seeking a connection of their own. I have a beautiful woman lying beneath me who is everything I've been missing in my life and more, and I don't want to screw this up. My heart skips a beat every time I look into her pretty blue eyes, so I avoid them, trying to control my emotions.

I groan when our bodies press together. I love the feel of her, but hold myself above her, not wanting my full weight on her slender frame . . . yet. I'm not sure how far she wants to go or how far we should, but something tells me tonight isn't the night for us to make love. She's more than tipsy, though not drunk, but even so, I would never want to take advantage of her that way. I saw how she calculated the aftermath of her decision a few moments earlier and how her eyes brightened when she made up her mind. She wants to be here and that makes my heart soar in ways I haven't felt in a long time.

I kiss her, loving the feel of her lips, the taste of her mixed with hints of beer. I love the way she kisses with passion, as if this is the last kiss she'll ever give. Little does she know, if she'll let me, I might want to kiss her forever.

She suddenly pushes me up, sliding her body into a sitting position then swings her legs off the bed. "I'm gonna take my dress off, and since your being dressed like that gets me all hot and bothered, I can only imagine you're even better without clothes. I want you shirtless and pantsless. That's only fair, right?"

She's bold, and damn, that's attractive.

"Yep," I say, "that'd be the only fair thing to do."

I want to rip her clothes off and then my own, but the virtue of patience holds great rewards. So I calm myself despite everything I'm feeling inside. Behind my back, I shake my hands one at a time. I'm not used to these kinds of nerves. Women never make me nervous, and yet this one . . . she entices me into her world without even trying.

I look her over, my eyes lingering on the curve of her cheek. I worry that if I rush, all of this will happen too fast, and I won't get to appreciate our time together. One deep breath follows another. "Come here."

She moves closer. No obvious doubts cloud her eyes. I'm rewarded with a smile when I run my hand up her arm and over her shoulder, caressing the back of her neck before taking the top of the zipper pull and dragging it lower.

"You look incredible in this dress, but I can't lie and say I'm not looking forward to you out of it."

Running her hand over my chest, her fingers begin to unbutton my shirt and yank it down my shoulders. She undoes one of my cuffs then the other, and my shirt falls just as her dress does. I take a deep breath when I see her in front of me, all creamy skin dotted lightly with freckles and goose bumps. Her waist curves in, and her stomach is flat but soft.

Her strapless black bra and panties pop against her pale skin. There's nothing fake about her—just wonderfulness in its natural form. Watching her as I undo my belt, I slip my shoes off and socks, then pull my undershirt up and over my head. I step out of my pants and leave them on the floor. She smiles and giggles as if she's remembering an inside joke. She's irresistibly adorable. I grab her, taking her by surprise, and laugh as she squeals.

"Men don't usually like woman laughing at them when in such a precarious state." I take her hand in mine and rub her palm up and down my precariousness. That wipes the smile right off her face.

Releasing her hand, I seize the opportunity to watch her as she continues to touch me. I want to drop my head back and close my eyes, letting her work her magic, but my desire for her is stronger. I weave my fingers into her hair and pull her closer, less gently than before, letting need determine our pace. Kissing her abruptly, she melts against me, so I wrap my arms around her waist until she's steady again. A quick flick of the fingers and her bra clasp is undone.

"Impressive," she mutters.

With my eyes closed, I breathe her in. She's all the air I need. "You did this to me. You made me want you." I'm not just talking sexually, but I can't tell her that, not yet.

I press my pelvis harder against her hand and hope I can impress her even more. Her breath staggers as she grasps me tighter, making me moan in return. "That feels so good."

I can't lie. It's been a while and even longer since I liked a girl this much.

Her smile turns mischievous, her fingers grip me with intention then she stops. "I was calling *this* impressive. As for your other skills, I hope you're bringing your A-game tonight." She winks then squeezes for emphasis before stepping back and letting her bra fall to the floor.

I hold her eye contact, though, I desperately want to see her in all her naked glory. My confidence builds, with a little arrogance mixed in, and is in full effect. "Oh baby, let me tell you, I'm gonna be the best you ever had."

She cocks an eyebrow, playfully challenging me, her own confidence skyrocketing. "Don't tell me. Show me."

I look at her, taking in her entire body. I've never seen anyone as sexy as she is in this moment. "I intend to do just that."

I lunge at the woman, moving her to the bed. Charlie's not shy, but she shivers now that she's exposed to me. Lying down together, I rest my elbows on either side of her head and push her hair away from her face. I look into her eyes, now that I can see them, feeling our connection deep inside.

Pushing up on my hands, I see all of her displayed for me—her bare shoulders, her breasts, her stomach and belly button. Her eyes close as my own follow her lines, admiring her body. I like how feminine she is, shapely.

This woman was already driving me crazy with lust, but now her perfection is here to tempt me into sin. I feel myself hardening from the fact that she's beneath me and knowing she wants to be here.

I jerk against her, an erratic, involuntary thrust that elicits a squirm and panting breaths from her open mouth. I watch her reaction as I touch one of her breasts, her eyes opening as I appreciate the feel of her in my hands. "Sexy. You're so sexy, Charlie."

She lifts her hips, arching her chest further into my hands. With a gentle squeeze, and then one a little harder, I learn what she likes, what turns her on. Leaning down, I lick around her nipple, taking my time. It tightens and perks, teasing me until I kiss the pink tip like I'd kiss her mouth. She's starting to move around a lot, the intensity getting to her as much as it is me.

"That feels so good . . . been so long," she mumbles. She turns her head to the side. "More." She rubs her pelvis against me. "More."

Lowering my body again, I press hard against the apex of her thighs, giving her the pressure she needs, giving me what I want. I start a slow rhythm that builds as I suck on one breast while squeezing the other, then switch. Her hands are on my head, encouraging, encouraging, encouraging.

That's when I start to move quicker, our underwear keeping a safe barrier between us. Her fingers grab hold of my hair, and she pulls hard as she tremors beneath me, calling my name. Her warmth and demand overcome my focus, which is hanging by the last thread of strength I have, and I follow her into ecstasy. My mind is fuzzy as my body resonates with pleasure.

I drop my head into the nook of her neck as my body falls on top of her. I give us time until our breathing has synchronized then look into her sparkling eyes.

"Hi," she says. Even in the dim light, I can see her cheeks blush with color.

"You're blushing—"

"Yeah." She looks away from me, and I don't like that. "I do that. It's annoy—"

"It's pretty on you." I kiss her, hoping to wipe away the embarrassment that's seeping in. "Hey, don't do that."

"Do what?"

"It's good. *This* is good."

She wiggles out from under me, sits up, and closes her eyes. "Good, yeah."

But I see through her. She's going to blame the alcohol. I can tell because I see regret taking over. As soon as I sit up, I wrap my arms around her and pull her onto my lap. She leans her head on my shoulder, and I kiss her neck.

I whisper, "It was good. It was fantastic, in fact, just like you are. Don't overthink this or twist it into something bad."

She sighs. "Can I use your bathroom?"

"Only if you stay tonight."

That makes her smile again. "Well, if you're going to blackmail me then I guess I have no choice, I suppose." She's coming back around to her usual self, rolling her tired eyes as her smile widens.

A playful hit to my chest tells me she's happy, so I flip her down, onto her back again. I kiss her once, twice, three times nice and quick before she can escape. "Stay with me because you want to, not because you feel you have to."

She plants a kiss on my chin. "I want to stay. Now get off me, you big oaf. You got me all . . . sticky and sweaty. I doubt you want sticky and sweaty in your fabulously soft sheets. What thread count are these anyway?"

I laugh, once again amused by how her mind works. "They're eight hundred—the perfect mix between stiff and too silky."

"I think I should worry that your sheets have been so thoroughly thought out."

"Oh, you should definitely be worried, but not about my sheets."

She rolls out from under me and stands, her hands cupping her breasts. She's covering herself, but she doesn't understand how hot she looks— swimsuit model hot. Turning around and sauntering toward the bathroom, she wiggles her ass and winks. "Worried, huh?"

I throw a pillow at her, making her giggle. "Yes, worried, very worried if you keep that up, you tease."

She peeks out from the bathroom. "I'm not a tease, and if I remember correctly, you're a lot sticky and sweaty yourself."

I jump to my feet. "We should shower together then."

That makes her laugh. "Um . . . yeah, no. Too soon for that business."

On that note, she shuts the door, and I fall backward on the bed as if I've been shot. I realize, I have been shot—right through the heart by Cupid. Damn that little cherub. When I least expected it, my life has been completely derailed, and yet, I'm excited to move in the new direction.

I rush to the kitchen and grab two bottles of water from the fridge, setting one on each nightstand.

When she returns, I pass her, stopping to steal one more kiss. She happily obliges me. Her breath is minty, which makes me curious if she used my toothbrush.

"Help yourself to something to eat. I brought you a bottle of water over there."

She slaps my ass and says, "Thanks."

As I shut the bathroom door, I can see her crawling under the covers with a smile on her face. I hurry, wanting to climb in bed and hold her until she falls asleep.

When I come out, I slip under the blanket and sheet and scoot next to her until we're touching. She rolls onto her side, her back against my chest. I take her hand and drape my arm over her, holding our hands against her chest.

Chapter 12

♀

I open my eyes slowly. It burns, so I clamp them shut again. The silence is deafening, unsettling, and the weight over my ribs, although warm, is concerning. I startle, realizing there is a person snuggled against my back.

My body stiffens, tense with unease as a million memories race through my head. *Charlie.* Happy eyes, wet kisses, tickles, sparks, tingling, release.

The thoughts engulf me until I realize I drank too much. I shouldn't have come back to his place. I knew this would happen. I felt the sexual tension building at the club. All the laughs, little touches, flirting, warm breath laced with Jack Daniels heated my face and sent sensations straight to my core.

My body betrayed me when my mind was vulnerable and he whispered sweet words to me last night. I know they were lies to comfort me, but I became weak to the gorgeous man who has become my friend . . . *was* . . . is . . . oh God, I hope we can still be friends.

He might not want to be once he wakes up and realizes that after six months of abstinence, I'm a complete wanton whore. Maybe he already thinks that.

Oh no! My hands dart to my vagina, and relief washes over me as I discover my panties are still on. I mean, I think I would remember having sex after all this time of, well, not having sex, but I needed the confirmation just to make sure.

I slink out from under his arm, and although he stirs, he doesn't wake. It's 5:39 a.m., and I'm wide awake with worry. I should leave and give him his space to wake up in peace. Hopefully, he'll forget about this romp, and maybe, just maybe, we can get back on track with our friendship. I've enjoyed the time we've spent together too much to throw it away on drunken escapades.

Though last night . . . yeah, that was quite enjoyable, too. I feel my face heat with embarrassment as memories of me shouting his name come to mind. God, he must think I'm such a narcissist considering that's my name, too. He's going to think I'm a total freak who gets off on Charlies or, even worse, someone after his money. I knew he was from money, but I'm reminded of it again as I look around his apartment in the dim light of the early hour.

I trip over my bra, but I catch myself while stumbling. I put it on then feel around in the dark room for my dress. I find his pants, his shoes, and his shirt before I find my clothes.

I slip the dress on over my head and let it fall into place before twisting my arm to zip it up. *Shoes.* I need to find my shoes. I locate them several feet apart, and they remind me of his strong hand caressing my legs and then taking my shoes off before we got even more worked up. I had already been worked up last night before we came here, but I think I held it together enough to cover my nerves.

His face is so handsome and sweet while he sleeps. But once dressed, I don't look back at him, though that's all I want to do right now because I don't want to just look back, I want to crawl into bed and cuddle with him. That might make him feel awkward in his own home, though, and how mortifying would that be, if he asked me to leave? Last night was near perfection, and I'm not willing to let the light of day mess with my memories. So, I'll protect them and leave before being asked.

I tiptoe into the hall and find my purse in the living room, on the table by the door. I look around once more before sneaking out. I like his apartment, and I'm envious of his balcony. Apartments with those are hard to come by unless you pay a fortune, which by the looks of this place, he might have.

I leave the building without further debate. This is the right thing to do. It shouldn't be, but it is. He was a willing participant last night, but I started it by asking him to kiss me, and the alcohol led to more. I just hope he forgets my forward behavior and, even more so, forgives it.

Chapter 13

♂

The rustling at the end of the bed draws my attention, and the emptiness of my arm wakes me. I look toward the sound and see her standing there. Her dress slides fluidly over her head and down her body. The sun has yet to break the horizon outside the large window, but there's enough light to see once my eyes adjust to it.

I glance at the clock, 5:45 a.m., and it's the weekend. We could have slept in. I wanted that. I had blissful dreams with her in my arms.

Continuing to debate whether I should say something, she bends down and puts her shoes on. I should let her go. She's embarrassed or regretful . . . the words make my chest ache. Or maybe she thinks I'm the one who's regretful. I don't regret last night. I never will. I would hand over my Man Card to be able to cuddle with her a few more minutes.

I remain silent as she ghosts around the room gathering her belongings then disappears into the hallway. Did she not want last night? Is it going to be chalked up to a drunken mistake? It won't for me. I remember every kiss, the feel of her skin under my fingers, her breath as it covered me, and the sound of her voice as she came apart. Anxiety fills my lungs and my heart, but I let her leave anyway.

I grab her pillow and smack it down over my face, inhaling her scent and hoping we can recover from this.

Damn! I forgot to get her phone number . . . again. It might have been the distracting nightclub or the alcohol or the kissing that made me forget my mission, but I'm irritated that I forgot all the same. Although I do know where Charlie works, it's Saturday and she won't be there. I contemplate calling Rachel, but there are no guarantees she'll give it to me. Besides, I don't want to go through her friends. I want her to give it to me, for her to *want* to give it to me.

I never go back to sleep. I can't. Images of being above her and feeling her orgasm under me have left my mind reeling. Remembering her sneaking out is starting to override the good that was last night. I'm left wondering what went wrong and, more importantly, where we go from here.

She didn't stay, so that makes me think she regrets last night. I hope not, but reality is descending into my chest, making my heart hurt that we may not be meant to be together. The start of this relationship is full of complications, and I don't know if either of us is strong enough to work through those.

I pull on a pair of athletic shorts, T-shirt, socks and sneakers. I have pent-up energy, ideas of settling down, and stress that needs to be burned off. Once I hit the pavement outside, I'm off. I feel sluggish until I reach the park, falling in line with the other joggers who are up early to take advantage of the peacefulness and cooler temperatures. It makes me wonder if they have a mind full of thoughts to sort through like I do.

I push myself hard as I round the turn that leads back to my building. My goal is five miles, and I have two more to go to reach it. Somehow, it seems easier when I set my own pace—fast when I'm irritated and slow when thoughts of Charlie arise.

I can't stop my mind from lingering on all that I've learned of her. She's complex and understated. Her personality sneaks up on you and wins you over. She doesn't have to be the center of attention, but you can't ignore her beauty—inside or out.

She's taken over too much of my headspace, so I try to harness it, pushing all thoughts of her to the back of my mind until I'm ready to deal with them. Today's not that day.

After showering, I pull on some sleep pants and sit down at my desk. I haven't written anything this week, not being in the right frame of mind. Aunt Grace's passing has been weighing heavily on my heart.

The impending family dinner I have to attend for the reading of the will agitates me, even though it's more than two months away. I shouldn't go. I don't think Grace would care. It's going to be more hassle than it's worth, but something inside of me, something way down deep, tells me I should be there. I should be the one to talk about my great-aunt, to represent her the way I remembered, to show who she really was. No one else understood her like I did. She didn't hide her true self from me. She didn't put on the charade in front of me. No one else will serve her memory as well as I will. I have to be there *for her*.

I open my bottom drawer and pull out a thin flat box tucked under extra file folders and desk supplies. I haven't looked in here in months, but I feel the need to now.

The top photo is a black and white one taken of Aunt Grace last spring. She was lively that day, and in a mischievous mood. She'd just had her will changed and shared that with me. I wasn't comfortable speaking with her on such matters, and I'm not greedy and don't want for much, so I told her to give everything to charity if she wished. I would love to see my family's faces when they are told she changed the will and gave it all away to strangers. But Aunt Grace never revealed what changes she made. She had a sly sense of humor, and we'll find out soon enough if she had her last laugh.

I smile before placing the picture on the coffee table and return to face a blank document on my laptop. The cursor taunts me, daring me to start a novel, daring me to step outside my comfort zone.

I stare.

Time passes.

Nothing.

My intimidation level peaks, and I close my laptop before walking away from it in frustration. I stand in my kitchen, leaning against the counter. Looking back at the computer, irritation stings, but I know this is not about the writing or lack thereof. This is about Charlie and her sneaking out this morning. I haven't been able to shake that away, to let her go.

I don't fixate on women like this. I date, sure. But it's been a while since I was in a committed relationship. *Committed* makes me scoff. My last girlfriend should have been committed. The irony in the word.

I make up my mind on the spot. I'm going to find her. I'm going after Charlie.

After throwing on a pair of old jeans and a T-shirt, I slip on my sneakers and jacket. I grab my wallet, phone, and keys before rushing out the door. The funny thing is I don't know where I'm rushing to. I know I want to see her. Correct that—I know I *need* to see Charlie, but I don't know anything about where she lives. In a city of eight million, it's not easy to track people down without knowing a last name or phone number.

I stop on the corner and dial Rachel. I'm not in the mood to be polite. I'm desperate to fix this mess or settle it once and for all. The phone rings four times before I hear a familiar voice.

"Yo, bro, what's up?"

I pull the phone from my ear and look down at the screen, positive I just dialed Rachel. I stare at it in confusion for a second before I remember last night. "Justin?"

"Yeah, why you calling my woman before ten in the morning?"

"Your woman?"

I hear him laugh. "Dude, you were holding out on me before. Why'd you never mention Rachel?" He lowers his voice to a whisper. "She's a bombshell, a total hottie."

"Bombshell? Is it 1952 and I forgot?" I shake my head needing to end this ridiculous conversation. "Hey, I need to speak with her. Is she awake?"

"She's awake all right, but she's indisposed right now."

"Okay, seriously, I don't want to hear about your sexual exploits. Ask her if I can get Charlie's number. It's important."

"*Oooohhhh.* I see. Charlie boy has fallen for girl Charlie. A girl who shares his name— it's kind of narcissistic, don't you think?"

"The difference between you and me, my friend, is I don't like her for her name, but because of who she is. You would go after a girl Justin in a heartbeat, but it'd be attached to a very butch girl and wouldn't be that appealing."

"True dat."

I roll my eyes. "I'm too busy to get sucked into some rapper's lingo with you right now. Get me Charlie's number. Her address would be even better."

"So what you're saying is you will speak the rapper's delight another time if I get you her address?"

Now, I laugh. "Yeah. Sure, homeboy."

He turns away from the receiver and calls, "Hey sexy! Charlie, your friend . . . what's her address?" I hear voices in the background but can't understand. "Yep, for Charlie." I hear her say something before he comes back on the line. "She knew it was just a matter of time and wishes you luck."

"Great," I reply sarcastically. He gives me the address, and I hop in a cab.

Charlie doesn't live that far from me, which makes me happier than it should. I pay the driver and stand in front of her building. It's small, five stories, but quaint and old. I like it because it has history and personality in its architecture.

Justin got the door code from Rachel before we hung up. Rachel is very trusting or else very supportive me. Either way, I appreciate it, because

I'd rather be rejected face to face than through an impersonal intercom system. I jog up four flights, taking the stairs by two, and walk down the hall to apartment 4A. With my hand in the air ready to knock, I take a quick breath then tap the wood door with firm knuckles.

Waiting.

Waiting is torture. I hear light footsteps and see the other side of the peephole go black before one, two, three, four locks, and a chain are opened.

I know I've fallen hard for the woman when everything slows as if in a movie. The door swings open, blowing her red hair delicately from her shoulders as her face shows her surprise.

Chapter 14

♀

"What's your last name?" he asks, standing just outside my door. He's out of breath and intense, as if everything in the world depends on my answer.

His handsome face makes me breathless as his eyes penetrate my soul.

"Barrow," I say before I have a chance to stop myself. I don't mind telling him my name. It's not a big secret or anything. It's more that I still don't understand why he's here, much less how he knows where I live and how he got into the building.

"Barrow? As in wheel?"

It's a typical reaction. "Yes, Barrow is my last name. It's Scottish."

Charlie is still staring at me, but I don't know what I'm supposed to be doing, what he's expecting from me.

I shift to the side and make an offer. "Would you like to come in?"

This was my second mistake today, and it's only 10:15 a.m. My first mistake was that I should have stayed to see how this played out, but I don't deal with rejection well. Jim hurt me enough. I'm not ready for more pain.

"Yes, I'd like that very much."

I close the door behind him, relocking one of the deadbolts, and stand there feeling awkward.

He looks around my small apartment then turns back toward me. "I don't have your number either."

"You apparently have my address."

"About that—"

"I have a feeling that Rachel is behind this." I walk away, waving my hand in the air carelessly.

"She wished me luck."

"That doesn't surprise me."

He watches as I walk into the kitchenette area. I can see him standing there staring, so I ask, "Coffee or orange juice?"

"Orange juice would be great. Thank you."

I fill the glass and hand it to him. He drinks over half before setting the glass down on the granite countertop, swiping his thumb over the corner of his mouth. My mouth might have dropped open watching that little bit of juice-tainment. My own glass remains untouched, since I'm still stuck on the fact that Charlie is here in my apartment and looking as hot as he does. I only saw him once before in casual clothes and that was on the subway. I wasn't paying that much attention then. I am now and he wears them well.

"Why are you here, Charlie?" I ask because I need to say something instead of just gawk.

"Why did you leave this morning?"

"You came here to confront me?" I can't stop my defensive tone. "I had to do the walk of shame in an evening dress and heels, and now you're here to make me feel worse?"

He steps closer, but I turn around to focus on cleaning the mug and bowl in the sink. To focus on anything that allows me to think clearly, because I'm not so sure I do when he's around. I can't look him in the eyes right now. He must think I'm horrible or, even worse, slutty for my drunken antics last night. I practically ravaged the boy with my mouth.

"No, that's just it," he says, not sounding as sure of himself today. "I didn't want—"

"I'm sorry about last night. I know it was wrong, just a stupid drunk mistake. I hope we can get past this and still be friends." I hear nothing behind me, silence holding court, so I continue, hating the tension that separates us. "The other day meant a lot—"

"Why are you so nervous?"

"Huh?" I ask, glancing at him to see his eyes are still on me.

"You're nervous. I don't mean to make you nervous or upset you. I can go if you want."

"No!" I shout, startling him. I laugh, anxiety laced with shaky giggles. He smiles at me, and a calmness engulfs me. I take a deep breath before explaining. "No, you don't need to go. I'm glad you're here. I should apologize." I take a step toward him and smile. "I'm sorry about this morning and I'm sorry about last night."

His smile falters before he regains his composure, and as much as I want to ask what just went through his mind, I don't want to push my luck either.

"You're sorry about last night?" he asks, studying my eyes.

"Well, yeah. We had such a great time until the alcohol went to my head and I attacked you." I feel my face heat, remembering how I begged him to kiss me. "I'll understand if I've ruined everything, but I want you to know how much I've enjoyed our time together, as much as one can at a funeral." I'm rambling and can't seem to stop myself. "I was referring to talking with you at the Subway Inn afterward and then—"

"Stop, Charlie. Just stop."

My mouth clamps shut, and my heart hurts because I can hear the words coming from his mouth before he even says them. I grip the edge of the counter and close my eyes in preparation.

"You didn't beg me, and you didn't ruin anything. I want to be friends with you."

Those aren't the words I expected at all. "So, you're not mad at me?"

He shakes his head, and a small smile reappears. "No, I'm not mad." He rubs behind his ear and says, "I was hoping we could be mo—"

My oven timer sounds, drawing both of our attention.

"My cupcakes are ready."

I can feel his eyes on me as I take the cupcake pan out of the oven and set it on top of the stove. Looking back at him, I ask, "You were saying?"

"You do bake." He sounds surprised.

I nod. "Baking relaxes me."

"Eating relaxes me," he says, joking, then looks down at his feet like he said too much.

That makes me smile. *He* makes me smile, and the tension that was there a few minutes ago has evaporated. I don't feel the need to fill any voids with ramblings or explanations or any more apologies. I can be me, Charlie's himself, and this is right.

Even though we haven't talked everything through, we're on the right track. We're friends again, just how we were meant to be.

Chapter 15

♀

He frosts. He does dishes. He's funny and smart. *Is this guy for real?* I watch as he looks over the frosted cupcakes and carefully chooses one. It doesn't slip past me that he chooses the one I was going to pick. It's the largest in the batch. That amuses me.

He appears to be on the verge of drooling, but looks up and smiles, presenting the cupcake to me. "The chef should get the biggest one."

No, he's definitely *not* for real. Men like this don't exist among us mere mortal women.

"Thank you," I say, taking the cupcake from his hand. Our fingers touch by accident, and like last night, my stomach twists in giddiness to be near him. "Grab one and come on." I nod for him to follow me.

He picks his cupcake after a second careful perusal, and follows me to the couch. I feel like this should be awkward right now. That *us* like *this* would be uncomfortable for some reason, especially after last night, but like all the times I've spent with Charlie, it's not. It's easy, which brings up an earlier thought I had. *Is it too easy with him? Is it even possible to be too easy?* I'm going to drive myself insane with all of this overanalyzing.

"How are you doing?" he asks, peeling his wrapper down on one side.

"I'm good. It's been a weird week, but I'm holding up. How are you?"

He's about to take a big bite, but stops and says, "I've been thinking about my great-aunt a lot."

"I'd love to hear about her if you want to share."

He sighs, and I can't tell if that's good or bad. "If you don't mind, I'd rather not today."

He looks at his cupcake and a small smile returns. "These look great." His mouth opens wide, and he closes his eyes as he takes a big bite of the small cake, frosting spotting his cheek. Opening his eyes, he catches me staring. Looking embarrassed, he asks, "What?"

I laugh. I shouldn't, but I do. "You've got . . ." I start saying as I point to the left of his mouth, then swirl my finger wide in the air in front of him, ". . . a little frosting there."

His tongue darts out and licks. "Here?" Charlie rubs his finger where I first pointed.

"No, over more."

He sticks out his tongue and searches his cheek again. "Still there?"

"No, a little more to the right."

He wipes aimlessly around his mouth, missing the spot, so I reach over and wipe the chocolate off with my thumb. I linger just a second before laughing.

"Thanks," he says, all mischievous smile and happy eyes.

I'm quick to retract my hand, because that was probably inappropriate. Actually, I'm positive it was inappropriate. Looking down, I take another bite of my cupcake instead of licking my thumb like I want. Self-conscious that he sees right through me, I try to distract by saying the first thing that comes to mind.

"So, why'd you track me down? Just had to know my last name?"

"Yes, and I want your phone number." His confidence is attractive.

He finishes his cupcake, and I nibble on mine.

"What do you want my number for?" I take the empty wrappers and get up to toss them in the trash.

"Usually they're given so people can reach you, talk to you, and schedule time together—"

"Okay, okay." I smile. "So, you want to do those things with me?"

"No. I just collect numbers." His sarcasm drips.

"Fifty-five," I say, deadpan.

"Fifty-five?"

"Yeah, you can add that to your collection."

He laughs, sinking back into the couch cushions to get more comfortable. "You're funny, real funny." He chuckles as he folds his arms across his chest.

I return, leaning against the arm of the couch. "Make yourself at home."

He gets my humor. "You have plans today?" He may be asking, but his body position tells me he has no intention of getting off this couch anytime soon.

"Oh yes, I have very fancy plans today. I was going to clean the mess I made in the kitchen, order a pizza, eat about a half dozen cupcakes, and watch movies. You want to stay? I mean, I'm sure your day can't be as exciting as mine, but you're invited to the grand event." I roll my eyes because my day sounds so lame, even if I do play it up in a joking manner.

"Sounds like a good plan, and I'll buy the pizza."

He'll stay? Charlie wants to stay and spend the day here . . . with me? "Really?"

His face contorts. "Did you not want me to?"

"No, of course I did. I just didn't think you'd want to."

He sits up straight, questions filling his eyes. "So, you invited me on the pretense that you didn't think I'd accept? Does that mean," he stands and takes a few steps toward the door, "you don't want me to stay? I can go. I'm sorry for bothering you."

"No, no, no. That's not what I meant. I invited you because I want you to stay. I just didn't think you'd *want* to."

He stops in front of the door, looking at me, reading me in that way I'm starting to become accustomed to, a way that makes me feel like he cares. He's looking beyond the surface, seeing the real me underneath my words. "I'd like to hang out with you."

"I'd like that, too. I'm not letting you buy the pizza, but you can pick the first flick."

His body relaxes, and I can tell he'll stay.

"Deal." He runs and jumps on the couch, kicks his shoes off, and props his feet up on my well-worn coffee table. Pointing at his bare feet, he asks, "Is this okay?"

I nod, giggling. "No socks?"

His eyes dart to his feet, and then he looks embarrassed. Dropping them to the floor, he hurries to explain. "Wow! That was rude of me. I forgot I wasn't wearing socks. I was in kind of a rush to get out the door."

"It's okay. I keep it casual around here. You can kick your feet up. Soda?"

He lifts his feet back onto the table, crossing his legs at the ankle and leaning his head back on his linked hands. "Yes, please. Let's get these grand plans started."

"Go ahead and find a movie. My movie collection is in the large drawer in the TV console, or you can choose one from pay-per-view."

I walk back into the kitchen and stack the dirty dishes in the sink to deal with later. I fill two glasses with ice and pour soda in both then wait for the bubbles to fizzle down. Sneaking a peek over my shoulder, I spy him kneeling in front of the television, flipping through the cases. His shirt has risen, and I get an eyeful of those sexy back dimples above his jeans.

Dirty thoughts of him are swirling around my head when he asks, "How about *A Fool's Future*?"

My eyes meet his, and I immediately turn back to the sodas, pretending to be busy and hoping he didn't see me checking him out. Sounding flippant, I say, "Sure, if you're up for something chick-flicky."

"I've never seen it. But if you own it, it must be good."

I walk to the couch, setting the drinks down on the table before curling up on the side opposite where Charlie's taking up space. The DVD starts as he takes a few sips of his drink.

"Thank you—"

"No worries," I reply.

"Thank you for letting me stay."

I stretch my legs out next to me and nudge him with my foot. "Thanks for staying. Now hush. I love this movie."

He chuckles, and a happy peace fills the room.

We polish off a medium extra-cheese and pepperoni pizza, two more cupcakes each, and sit through a rom-com and a gangster movie before we fall asleep.

I wake up around 4:30 p.m. Our legs are tangled between us on the couch, and my foot is between his thighs. *Oh my.* Just two small inches north of my toes and . . . I wiggle my foot out super slow so my mind doesn't linger in the gutter.

He also fell asleep, but stirs, his eyelids barely rising. His eyes are more grey than blue under the haze of sleep.

"Hi," I say. My voice is raspy from the nap. "Guess we were both tired."

He may look drowsy, but light reflects off his eyes, making them shine. "Yeah, we were up kind of late last night."

I don't know if it's his soft, comforting expression or his words, but I feel warmer. I'd like to say I'm blushing, but the heat is not just in my cheeks. It's all over. I sit up, grabbing my drink and taking several large sips to try and cool down.

Charlie sits forward, swinging his feet to the floor and scrubbing his face roughly with his hands.

"You want to go for a walk? I could use some fresh air." I offer because I could use some, too, though maybe more for the cool breeze than the freshness of the air.

"I'd like that."

We put our shoes on and I grab a jacket before we make our way down to street level.

"I like this part of the city. Lived here long?" he asks.

"Not that long, but I always liked this neighborhood. Jim wanted to live uptown. He considered Murray Hill once as a compromise to me, but that was still more uptown than I wanted. His parents disapproved of my suggestions, because they wanted him close to them." I laugh at the memory. "A five-minute cab ride was too far for their liking."

"You lived together when you were still dating?"

"What can I say? He was very convincing."

"He convinced you? You didn't want to?"

"I did, but I didn't. I'd never lived with a guy, so it was big step. We were engaged at the time, but I think I was scared something would happen and then . . ." We stop at a corner a few blocks away from my apartment. Charlie doesn't move. He faces me and waits for me to finish. "And then all that stuff *did* happen, and I'm here now."

"It suits you."

"What does? Being single?"

He laughs, a real gut chuckle. "No, your apartment and this neighborhood. It suits you."

I look up at him and smile. He makes me feel good about myself, about my choices, and about what my instincts told me a long time ago. Instincts I didn't trust and was talked out of back then. "Thanks, Charlie."

We cross the street and buy a coffee from a bakery. We get it to go so we can continue walking and enjoying the late April day.

I notice he watches me in a protective way. He steps closer when people pass us on the sidewalk as if to guard me. He held his hand in front of me when I was about to step into the crosswalk and a car ran a red.

"Do you mind if I ask you something personal?" he asks.

He makes me feel safe. So when he wants to know something, I feel secure in sharing myself with him. "Not at all."

"What's up with Jim's family? From what you've told me and from the funeral, I gather you didn't get along?"

I stop to admire the necklaces and earrings in the window of a shop. Even though I don't like the topic, I'll answer anyway, because I'm not the downfall of that relationship. I say this to myself a lot to counteract all the passive-aggressive comments Cherry used to utter under her breath. One day I hope the negativity from back then won't reside in my head any longer.

"It wasn't that we didn't get along," I say. "It was more that I wasn't the one they wanted their son to marry. I'm not from their world, and I didn't fit in, like ever, even when I tried. And trust me, I tried."

"If you have to try that hard, then it's not worth it. They're not worth the effort."

"I was in love." I shrug as we walk on, tossing my cup in a nearby trashcan.

"Love makes us do stupid things. The old saying is true. Love is blind."

"You too, huh?" I nudge him in the ribs.

"A story like that requires heavy alcohol, not coffee."

I'm enjoying our time together too much to upset the vibe. I smile in sympathy. Understanding not wanting to revisit old heartache, I don't push. "You're not like most guys I've met here. Why are you so nice, Charlie?"

"What, you don't know any nice guys in Manhattan?"

I can tell he's teasing, but he truly doesn't understand how rare a man he is. "I know one." I want to touch him again, even if just in a teasing way, but I shove my hands in my pockets to restrain myself.

"You probably say that to all the guys."

My smile grows, and I feel happy. "Ha! Yep, my charm works every time."

"I bet it does. I just bet it does. So, it's Saturday night. No hot date?"

"He's hot, but more of the platonic kind," I say, kind of wishing we hadn't decided to stay just friends.

"Come over here. I want to show you how platonic I can be."

"Who says I was talking about you?"

He doesn't shrug or slump. He's all cocky, confident again. "I think I'm the hottest platonic friend you know, excluding last night, of course."

Yep, there was nothing platonic about last night. "Is that so?"

"It most certainly is," he says, holding his hand out. "Now c'mere."

"You sure do hold yourself in high regard." I walk toward him, taking hold of his hand. "Can I confess something?"

"Confess away."

"Is it sad that last night," I say, peeking over at him, "was the most action I've seen in a long time, and that was with a friend?"

Squeezing my hand before wrapping his arm around my shoulders, he laughs. "Yes. Actually, that is one of the saddest things I've heard in a while."

I attempt to elbow him in the ribs. "Ha ha. Where's your hot date, then, show-off?"

He blocks the hit, holding me even tighter against him to keep me from escaping. "She's right here."

Smiling, I lean my head on his shoulder. While I love the feeling of being in his arms again, I'm uncomfortable with the swirling emotions he evokes, so I change the subject. "I'm still hungry, are you?"

"You devoured half a pizza and I don't know how many cupcakes earlier. That wasn't enough?" He's back to teasing, letting me know we're good. Looking up at him, his eyes are blue and happy, and that makes me giggle again. "You want to order something at your place?"

"No, let's stay out."

"Come on. I'll let you take me out for some grub."

"You'll let me?" He winks, laughing. "Fine," he says, rolling his eyes with a sly grin on his face. "I'll buy. By the way, this act of yours is so transparent, Ms. Barrow."

"What act would that be?" I ask, raising my eyebrow at him.

"You just want to go out so you can show off your hot platonic date."

Now that makes me really laugh. "You always see right through me, Charlie." That's truer than I'd like to admit.

The weather is perfect, and we are friends again. I don't think this night can get any better, until it does with one simple gesture. He pulls me closer, until I'm as close as I can get to him. I wrap my arm around his middle, and I don't fight this feeling of security he gives me. I revel in it.

Chapter 16

♂

Ha! Yep, my charm works every time, she said in response to my flirting. Flirting? Is that what I was doing yesterday? Yes, that's exactly what I was doing.

She's clever and intelligent, funny, and, yes, charming. And yet, she doesn't seem to realize it at all. I hate speaking ill of the dead, but Jim was an asshole. It sounds like he put everyone before her and then cheated on her, too. *Prick!* If he were alive, I'd be having a serious chat with him. No one deserves to be treated like she was, but *she* especially didn't deserve it.

When I looked at her yesterday and she was smiling, her expression all glorious and happy, any earlier aggravation over her leaving dissipated, and I felt happy, too.

That was the first day we spent together as real friends, friends who knew where they stood in each other's lives, friends without preconceived notions and no heavy judgments. I didn't expect for us to end up in that place when I showed up on her doorstep that morning, wanting her last name and phone number, but I also realize that sometimes the best things take time. For her and for now, I'm willing to be here as her friend.

I can't get something else she said off my mind, so the next day, I bring it up again.

"I've been thinking about what you said about living with someone and how you worried that something would happen," I say, gauging her reaction. I take a lick of my ice cream and wait to hear if she responds.

She glances up from her hot fudge sundae, but returns her focus to digging out the cherry that's fallen to the side of the bowl.

I continue because we're friends, and friends should be able to talk about anything. Leaning closer to her across the small table, I explain, "Something could happen, yes, but that something could be good or bad. It's a gamble, right? On the positive side, it's a risk that can pay off."

"On the negative side, I lost in the end," she replies. It's obvious she's uncomfortable.

"You could have won just as easily. You couldn't predict that Jim would cheat. It sounds like it surprised you and wasn't something he'd done before." I watch for her reaction. She gives so much away in her expression. I doubt she's even aware of it.

"I don't know if he cheated before. I like to think he didn't." Charlie stabs her spoon into the ice cream, dropping her hands to her lap, and looks me directly in the eyes. "But I won't ever know now, will I?"

"I think it's going to be a matter of trust."

She tilts her head, and the late afternoon sun lights her red hair from behind, giving her a soft halo effect. I force my eyes down to the melting ice cream in my hand to keep myself from staring.

"We should have just gone to dinner," she says, deflated. "I'm hungry and not for ice cream. You up for fish and chips?" She perks up at her suggestion.

"I'm up for anything." And I am. Everything feels like an adventure with her.

While walking down the street, she smiles looking over at me. "I'm glad you called."

"I'm glad you answered."

She laughs, her sweet grin staying in place long after her laughter stops. She looks around as we turn a corner, and her face is serene, her eyes revealing her happy thoughts. As she tucks her hands into her pockets, she says, "I like spending time with you. Yesterday was nice just lounging around. There doesn't seem to be that pressure that often exists between friends or . . ."

"Lovers?"

"Lovers!" She bursts out laughing. "No one uses that word anymore, Charlie."

"What's wrong with lovers?"

"Ew, stop saying it," she chides, poking me in the side. I love how touchy-feely she is.

"Lovers," I reply in a deep voice, then change it and do a bad British accent. "Lovahs."

"Stop it! God, could you imagine being called someone's lover?"

I scrunch my nose. She does have a point. "Sounds so seedy. By the way, I've been following you this whole time. You know where you're going?"

"Sounds debaucherous. Yes, of course, I know where I'm going."

"I don't think debaucherous is a word."

"It's a word."

I chuckle, glancing over at her. "No, I don't think it is."

"You wanna bet?"

"You're a stubborn little redhead, aren't you?"

"How about putting dinner on the line for it? And yes, comes with the territory. Stubbornness and fiery-tempered."

"I can't see you as fiery-tempered."

"I'm not. I'm just saying that's one of the stereotypes of being a natural redhead." We turn the corner, and she says, "I think it's all of the fake redheads out there that are fiery-tempered and giving us naturals a bad rap."

"You've thought about this, haven't you?" I chuckle, making fun.

She shrugs with a smile on her lips. "I overthink everything."

"I can believe that."

"Stop it," she playfully replies. "Now, back to debaucherous."

"Yes, please do get back to debaucherous." I know it's not a word, but I'll play along for her since she's so eager to prove me wrong. She's cute when she gets that tiny, determined line between her eyebrows. Another giveaway on how strong she is as a person. "Okay, the loser buys dinner."

She stops in the middle of the sidewalk and pulls her phone out, typing in the search box. Listening to her sound out the word is quite adorable. "De-ba-cher-ris." She puts a hand on her hip, and her lips purse. "Hm!"

"What'd you find?" I ask, peeking over her shoulder.

She spins out of my reach and says, "Back away, back away. I didn't search right. Let me do this again."

I snicker on the inside. I know she's not going to find it, but I like her tenacity. I step back and cross my arms in fake annoyance, but I can't stop smiling as I watch her fingers zip across the screen. "Don't forget about the *u*."

"The *u*? Where does that go?"

"Well, in debauchery, it goes after the *a*."

She types some more as a huge smirk crosses her face before it falls just as fast. Without looking at me, she tosses her phone into her handbag and says, "Come on. Guess I'm buying."

I'm obnoxious, so I fist pump. I also do a little consoling and a lot of trying to restrain myself from laughing, because she apparently is a sore loser. I wonder if that's a redhead trait, too.

Her eyes roll as she pouts. "Stop it! So it's not a word. It's close to a real word."

"If you want to use debaucherous, I won't judge."

"Why do I not believe you? See? I can already see you judging me. It's in your beady, blue eyes."

"Beady? I've been told I have enchanting eyes, soulful even, but never beady, baby."

That elicits a laugh from her, which makes me laugh, too. "And you're not conceited at all, are you?"

"Nah, not conceited, just speaking the truth."

"Ugh, and you're insufferable, too."

"Ha!" I smile.

She bumps me with her body to the right. "If you can contain your self-indulgent glee for a while, we can eat. We're here." She presents the door like a game show hostess.

"I don't know if I can contain myself. You might have to help me with that. Teasing—"

"More like taunting."

"Okay, taunting. Taunting you is so much fun. It'll be hard to stop."

"Shush it and come on," she says, grabbing me by the wrist and dragging me inside.

I've never been here. I've never even seen this place before. "Should I be worried, Charlie?"

"Nah, it's the best in the city. The guy is from England. He knows his chish and fips."

"Don't you mean fish and chips?"

"Nope. Just go with it."

I laugh. "You're killing me with the funnies today. You know that?"

"Yep, I sure do. You should stick around. I'm a real riot."

"I just bet you are." Yes, this is turning into quite the beautiful friendship.

Sitting at my desk on Monday, I catch myself staring out the window at the leaves budding on the tree outside. On Sunday, Charlie twirled a leaf between her fingers when we walked through the park. We sat by the pond near The Boathouse Restaurant, watching joggers as they passed by, kids playing tag, and couples strolling hand in hand. I lay back on the grass, staring into the clear blue sky, letting my eyes drift closed, when her head came to rest on my stomach.

I may have stopped breathing for a moment. In actuality, I know I did, but trying to play it cool, I inhaled long and slow until I was breathing normally again. I don't think she noticed. If she did, she didn't say anything. Just as I lifted my head to look at her, her arm reached into the serene air and caught a leaf as it floated down from above. Wordlessly, she smiled and admired the new green leaf of spring.

We lay there for a few minutes when she suggested we go for ice cream. It was almost a relief to get out of that position. Her closeness, the intimacy of the moment tugs at my heart, and being a typical guy, it also turned me on. I wanted to touch her, hold her, make her sticky and sweaty again, but that's not who we are now. So, ice cream it was instead.

Back to the blinking cursor on my laptop, I start typing the first words that come to mind and let my fingers tap over the keyboard unrestrained for the next two hours without a break. Somehow, I manage to write my first full chapter to a novel that I have no clue of what the story is. And yet, the words flowed like a river, steady and strong. The words "My Everything" stand out to me as I write them, and I've found my title.

After I save the document, I read the first few lines over, getting lost in them again.

My Everything ~
I want to say I fell in love at first sight. That would be the romantic version, but that's not the truth. I fell in love with the woman who would become my sun, my beacon, my compass, my everything when I sat next to her at a funeral and saw the depths of sadness and true beauty for the first time.

I miss Charlie. Just three days into . . . whatever this is, and I miss her. She's captivated me and makes me use words like 'enchanted' while writing. The word 'beguiled' has crossed my mind three times since I've known her. But damn it, men aren't supposed to use those words, much less think them. I stand and pace, rubbing my temples to alleviate my anxiety. One glance at my watch and I know I have to see her. A plan is formed and I'm out the door within twenty minutes.

"Holy sh—"

"What are you swearing about over there?" I call to Rachel without looking up from my monitor.

"Turn around, Charlie," she says. She giggles and her laugh sounds like it's directed more *at* me than humoring me.

I spin in my chair and gasp. "Charlie!"

"Charlie," he says, greeting me. His voice is smooth and charming as always.

My heart is racing, my hand is tapping against my chest, and instead of greeting him like I should, all I can think about is what I look like right now. I would have worn a different outfit, put more makeup on, and spent more time styling my hair.

While he's standing there grinning, I take a second or two to admire his great posture and his strong shoulders.

"I hope I'm not interrupting. I mean, I know I'm interrupting. Your work, for example—"

"It's all right. I'm glad to see you. How are you?" I pretend to be all business-y, but it's hard around him. I want to frolic and eat sweet treats in his presence, but I roll my eyes for using the word 'frolic,' even if just in my own head.

"Other than a problem with speaking, I'm good. Great in fact."

I'm waiting for him to tell me why he's here, but he takes a few moments to look around before his eyes land back on me. "I wanted to see if you were free for lunch?"

"Yes, she is," Rachel shouts over the cubicle wall.

"Hi, Rachel," he says. He chuckles quite loud, drawing some attention from nearby coworkers.

I stand and peek over the divider wall. "I thought we had plans?"

"Oh, I forgot I have tooooo, ummm . . . damn, I need a pedicure. I have to get that done." She can't look me in the eyes when she lies, so she stares at the monitor in front of her. "You should go to lunch with Charlie." And like that, I've been brushed off.

I turn back around to face him. I love Rachel for freeing our date, but I also hate her for being so obvious. I try to hold back my giddiness over seeing Charlie for the third day in a row by hiding my face and ridiculously big smile as I reach down and grab my purse. "It looks as if I'm suddenly available if you want me."

His mouth quirks up in a devilish smirk. "Yeah, I guess, you'll do," he teases.

We walk to the elevators in quiet confidence, but I see Mr. Smith standing by the front desk. "How are you today, Ms. Barrow?"

"I'm well. Thank you, sir." Wanting to escape, but not wanting to be rude, I introduce Charlie. "Mr. Smith, this is my friend, Charlie Adams."

"Charlie Adams." He interrupts the introduction to ponder aloud, "You look familiar."

They shake hands as Charlie replies, "We met at a benefit last year, sir. My aunt Grace was in charge of fundraising for the School District #8 art department. The public schools there lost most of their funding, so she organized the ball."

"And what was the outcome?" Mr. Smith asks.

"Over four hundred thousand was raised. It compensated for more than the deficit and eight scholarships were set up."

"That's good news. I bet your aunt was quite pleased."

"Yes, sir, she was. She recently passed away, but she left this world knowing the arts wouldn't be lost on the next generation."

"I should hope not or we'll be out of business, too," he jokes, but becomes more serious. "I'm sorry for your loss. She was a very nice woman."

"Thank you."

Charlie and I smile. I say, "We're going to lunch."

"Well, I'll let you get to that. Nice seeing you again, Mr. Adams, and I'll see you at the meeting later this afternoon, Ms. Barrow."

The elevator doors open and I feel the light touch of Charlie's hand on my back, guiding me in front of him. He drops it as soon as we enter the elevator and I can't stop the disappointment from the loss.

"Where are we going?" I ask, curious.

"How about a deli?"

"There's a great one in the lobby, but it gets crowded at lunch, so we probably won't find a table."

"I don't want to stand and eat. There's a deli a few blocks from here that I've eaten at before."

"Deli on Madison? That place is great."

Fifteen minutes later, we sit down, placing our sodas and order ticket on the table. He bought lunch, claiming it was because he showed up uninvited. I'm thinking he doesn't see how happy I am to see him again. "So what brings you to this part of town, Charlie?"

He plays with the straw's wrapper before wadding it between his fingers. When he looks up, he says, "You do." He shrugs. "I missed you."

He always makes me smile, but I laugh lightly, too, because I like that he missed me. "You missed me?"

Leaning forward after looking around us, he whispers, "Yeah, I missed you. Is that so strange?"

No. Not strange at all. I'd been thinking about him since we parted after dinner yesterday.

"What?" he asks. "Are you laughing at me because I can admit I missed you?"

"I think it's great you can admit you missed someone, and I wasn't laughing." I giggle.

"That. That right there is laughing."

"No, that's giggling."

"Aren't we too old to giggle?"

"Speak for yourself, old man," I tease.

He laughs now, but turns away when our number is called. Tapping the table once with his palm, he says, "I'll be right back."

I watch him as he walks toward the back of the small restaurant to claim our order, enjoying the view. *Damn it!* I look out the window when I'm busted staring at his ass. When I look back, he's gloating—I mean smiling —all the way back.

I try to tamp the heat I feel that wants to redden my cheeks, giving my guilt away, but I think it's too late.

"Here." He sets the food down in front of me. "Eat and maybe that will distract us enough to not talk about the fact that I just caught you ogling my ass."

"I wasn't ogling." I feign annoyance at the accusation, although I totally was ogling.

"You were sooo ogling."

"I hate you, Charlie." I laugh, joking with him.

"Yeah, I hate you, too." He teases with a smug smile set in place.

I seriously love our friendship.

Chapter 17

♀

What is it about Charlie that makes me happy and provokes daydreaming?
I think about this while doodling on a Smith & Allen pad of paper. I wish I
wasn't smiling. I must look insane, but just thinking of him makes me
smile.

A tap on the shoulder startles me right out of my thoughts. I turn around
and see Rachel standing there with a cocked, all-knowing eyebrow. "That
bad, huh?" she asks, sounding sympathetic.

I laugh lightly before answering. "Bad? No, not at all. Good. Too good, in
fact."

She smiles. "Walk with me to the kitchen."

I follow her down the corridor and around the corner where the kitchen is
located. Although there are no doors on either of the doorways, it feels
more private than our cubicles. I stand and wait. I know it's coming. I was
busted fair and square with my head in the clouds.

"Café mocha or hazelnut today?" she asks.

"Ummm, mocha. Thanks."

She operates in silence, but when she hands me the flavored coffee, she
says, "You like this guy, don't you?"

So many thoughts—maybe they're excuses—flutter around my brain. I'm not sure how to answer, so I respond as honestly as I can. "I do, but not in that way. We're friends. That's all."

"*Really?* Just friends? Because I don't remember the last time you doodled *Rachel* on a notepad with swirly bits and hearts around it. You have it so bad." There's a playful lilt to her words.

I roll my eyes and laugh. Yep, she caught me, but I'll argue to keep my goofy pride intact. It's embarrassing being caught acting like a high-school girl with a crush. "First of all, I don't have anything 'so bad' except an over-sweetened coffee in my hand. Second—"

"Why are you blushing, then?"

I sip my coffee as a distraction, and also to give myself a few seconds to clear my head and allow the pink cheeks to dissipate. "As I was saying, Ms. Interruptus, we are friends. *Only friends.* Nothing more. I'm just happy when I spend time with him, but that's where it ends."

She saunters past me, shaking her head. "Keep telling yourself that, dollface. Keep telling yourself that."

I slump against the soda machine after she leaves, wondering if the drawn hearts are more telling than I'd like to think. I like drawing the curve of them, but maybe . . . just maybe . . . *nah.* I shake myself out of this notion and toss the coffee.

I return to my desk and grab my phone. Walking down the hall toward the bathroom, I stand near a window in a spot that a small fake tree blocks from prying eyes. I shouldn't be doing this, but I can't stop myself. I press the button then duck down and put the phone to my ear.

"Hello there. I didn't expect to hear from you today." Charlie's voice is calm, and I can almost hear the smile in his tone.

My heart leaps a little just at the sound of his voice. I look around, peering through the leafy branches to spy on nosy coworkers, otherwise known as Rachel. "I was just thinking about you and—"

"Oh you were, were you? I like that."

"Hush, smuggsters."

His laughter fills my ears. "So, what can I do you for?"

"That has to be one of the perviest phrases ever."

"Perviest. The word perviest is pretty perverted sounding."

"Well, yeah, it's pervilicious."

He chuckles. "My gut can't handle your humor today. What's up?"

"Nothing much. Like I said, I was just thinking about you. Are you busy later this week?"

"Are you asking me out on a date, Ms. Barrow?"

"That warrants an epic eye-roll, and since you can't see me right now, please hold while I proceed to do just that." I hear him humming *When The*

Saints Go Marching In while he waits for me to eye-roll him. So I do.

"All right, I'm back." I giggle. "Not a date. Just two friends hanging out together. I was thinking Saturday, if you're free."

"What time?" I hear shuffling on his end.

"I don't know. I'm free all day. We could have another movie marathon."

"You want me to come over to nap with you again? Admit it, Charlie, you are a Saturday afternoon napper, and you liked the company."

I shrug, though he can't see me. "I'm not ashamed. Are you?"

"Nope, not at all. How does two work for you?"

"Perfect napping time."

"What can I bring?"

"Beer. I have none." I want to ask something, but I'm nervous of the answer I might receive. "I can make dinner if you're also free in the evening?" So the question I really wanted to know the answer to might have been wrapped up in a casual package, but it's still there.

"What kind of guy do you take me for? You think I'd nap with one woman then have dinner with another? What a low opinion you must have of me."

I love that he didn't make me ask. "Not low, quite high actually."

"Oh really? You can tell me more about that on Saturday."

"Yes, I look forward to filling your head full of compliments and ego-boosters."

That earns me a laugh. "Charlie?"

"Yes?" I lean against the wall and grin from ear to ear.

"I have to run, but just so you know, I've been thinking about you, too."

"Well, in that case, maybe you can toss a few ego-boosters my way on Saturday, too."

"Happily. I'll see you then."

"Okay. Bye."

"Bye."

I end the call and lean forward, pressing my forehead against the window. Two days. That's all. I can wait until then. The cool glass calms my warm skin, and I realize that I already want to call him back to chat again. I don't, though, because I know he's busy and I should get back to work, but for a brief moment, I think that maybe I do have it bad.

I like him too much to risk it away on a fling or frivolous relationship I don't think either of us are ready for, so I pocket these feelings away. They're troublesome and could lead to heartache. "Only friends," I remind myself. *Only friends.*

Later that evening, I'm home and it's dark outside. I want to curl up on the couch and flip through the channels for something I don't have to think about while watching, something I can zone in on and zone out on real life.

I grab my uninteresting meal out of the microwave, and carry it on my oven-mitt-clad hand over to the couch, but I don't make it there before someone knocks on my door. I detour and look through the peephole. I see him and feel the giddiness bubble up inside. Charlie knows I can see him, because he's all smiles and funny faces. I unlock the door and open it wide.

"And to what do I owe the pleasure?" I put my free hand on my hip, and sway them with sass.

"I couldn't wait until Saturday." He smirks, holding up two white bags in his hands. "I come bearing food."

"So what you're saying is that you find me irresistible?" I present my awful, tasteless meal to him. "Anyway, I've already got dinner covered."

He laughs, but says nothing as he walks past me straight into the kitchen.

"And the market on worn-out workout pants," he says, unpacking the bags on the counter, "but I won't hold those against you. By the way, that's not dinner."

I kick the door shut and lock the deadbolt, following behind him. "Don't judge my comfy leggings. There are only two holes. And if this isn't dinner, what is it?"

He looks over the little black bowl of steaming food still sitting atop my mitt-covered palm. "I don't know," he replies, scrunching his nose. "But you're not eating it." He picks it up and tosses the tray into the garbage can before I have a chance to protest. "I have food. Go sit over there in your holey pants and I'll serve."

I'm liking this idea a lot. "Who am I to argue with that?" I toss the mitt over my shoulder without care, and hurry to the couch to wait and be served.

I smile because he makes me want to smile, sometimes too much, making my cheeks hurt. Very much like right now. Flopping onto the couch, I cross my legs like a pretzel. I hear drawers opening and closing, silverware clanging together, and a wine cork pop open.

"You need any help?" I holler because I see him turning in circles looking for stuff.

"I got it," he says then flashes me a self-assured smile. "Hope you like lo mein." He hands me a plate along with a fork and napkin. "And I bought a sauvignon blanc because I have no idea what goes with Chinese food, and I like this one."

"Thank you. This looks great. I'm starved."

"Dig in."

When he joins me on the couch, that comfortable silence exists between us again, surrounding us as we eat. But tonight, I find myself wanting so much more, wanting to talk, even if just to joke. He's quick and clever and makes me laugh.

"Did you know you have a bull's-eye on your chest?" He lifts his gaze from my chest to my eyes as he takes a bite of the saucy noodles.

"Oh," I say, looking down at my T-shirt, "it's from college. My roommate has one, too. We made them as an experiment."

He chuckles. "I'm sure you proved your hypothesis true if the experiment was to draw every guy's attention straight to your breasts."

I cover my mouth with my hand so it doesn't get ugly when I burst out laughing. After catching my breath, I ask, "So it worked?"

"One hundred percent, baby. By the way, you don't need a bull's-eye to get a guy's attention."

"Are we still talking science here?"

"Maybe chemistry. What do you think?"

I set my fork down and take a drink of wine, keeping eye contact. "I'm staying neutral on that subject."

He narrows his eyes at me, but a wry smile appears. "Playing it safe will never get you anywhere."

"Sounds like you know from experience." I finish my last bite and set my plate on the coffee table. Angling my body to face him, I take my wine in hand. "Tell me about you. You've been good at keeping your life a secret."

Stabbing his fork into his noodles before spinning it around, his expression darkens, though I know he'll try to cover. That's what he does. He has secrets and a past that certain topics bring to light. Most wouldn't notice the look he gets in his eyes or the way his smile falls, even in the briefest of moments, but I do.

"I haven't kept my life a secret. You know all about me." He sets his own plate down and takes a sip of wine.

"Okay, let me rephrase. Tell me about your past, your childhood, growing up in Manhattan because I know you did, though you don't talk about it, and went so far as to tell Rachel you grew up in Kansas."

"I don't talk about it because it's uninteresting and stereotypical."

"Nothing about you is stereotypical," I add.

"I think that's my line." He shifts to face me, his long legs stretching across the couch and landing next to my hip.

I turn and straighten mine, mirroring him. "Is that what you do? You feed lines to girls?"

"Not to you. I speak only the truth."

"I'm special, then?" I prod his hips with my toes for more information, pressing for the details that make up who he is.

He takes another long sip, his eyelids dipping closed to savor the drink.

After a few seconds, he looks at me with a small smile. "I don't know how to answer that."

"That's not the part I want to know about anyway. Why don't you like to talk about your past?"

He looks uncomfortable for the first time since I've known him, other than at his aunt's funeral. "I don't like to do the whole woe-is-me thing, because I've had a good life, a spoiled one. I'll come off like I'm complaining, and I'm not."

"Then don't put on a production or say what you think you should to appease me. Just share who you are. Friend to friend."

He looks down as a soft chuckle rumbles around his chest. "Friend to friend," he repeats with an amused scoff. Swinging his legs off the couch, he stands and walks to the bookcase near the door. He peruses the titles, not looking at me. "I was a rich kid from Manhattan. I went to the best schools in the city, and I partied too hard."

"Where I'm from, that isn't stereotypical at all—"

"It is here. I'm sure Jim was no different. I might have met him, but I can't remember."

I don't like Jim being dragged into the conversation, but I understand why he was. I've never liked to think about that part of Jim's life. I know Charlie is right, and that hurts a little, but I remain quiet, encouraging him to continue. I may not want to talk about Jim's life, but I do want Charlie to talk about his.

"My dad worked too much, and my mom worked the scene for social status. They weren't bad parents overall, and I only had one nanny when I was younger, but when I decided to change my degree and go in a different direction . . . let's just say they weren't very supportive and my life plan didn't go over very well. I was also arrogant and had a chip on my shoulder. That didn't help my cause."

"What was your cause?"

"To be anything other than what I was at that time. I had good times, don't get me wrong, but I had sort of an awakening one day. I realized that the life I was living wasn't what I wanted anymore. I wasn't who I wanted to be anymore. So I made up my mind and made changes."

"And your parents didn't approve of this new you?"

He comes over and sits down beside me. "You see, my dear Charlie, I am what one in proper society would call 'a disappointment.' It's not that I have any regrets, because I don't. They cut me off when I changed my major, which meant no more school for me. I shoved my independence in their face by doing everything I could to prove the point that I didn't need their money. The problem was that I went about things the wrong way.

They reminded me of all my failings in life, and I reminded them of the shallowness of their lifestyle. We've butted heads for years over this."

"You made a choice in life, and because of that choice, you basically lost your family?" I summarize, now understanding the aloofness between them at the funeral.

He taps me on the nose three times. "Ding, ding, ding." He lies back, closing his eyes as if the weight of the conversation exhausts him. "I don't like the world they live in, and threatening me with money doesn't do any good. We're at an impasse of sorts. I find it hard to spend time with my family and most of my old friends, so I don't."

He acts strong, but I see it causes him pain deep down. Maybe I shouldn't have brought this up when he's been so sweet and brought din—

I feel his hand on mine. "Stop that."

"What?" I reply, my voice low like his.

"That," he says, smoothing his thumb over my temple. "I can almost hear the cogs turning in there. Don't overthink this. I made choices, and I'm good with them. I'm more than good. I'm happy, and I wouldn't change a thing. I had Grace—"

"But Grace is gone."

"I have you," he says, like that's the most natural response in the world.

And I couldn't agree more. That response should scare me, or at the very least worry me, that I'm filling some void in his life, but it doesn't. The void I fill is not one left vacant by his aunt. No. He carries her in his heart. I'm here for different reasons. I'm not sure what those reasons might be, but I like being in his life no matter what they are. "Yes, you do." I move my hand down to where his are resting in his lap and entwine our fingers. Curling my legs up, I snuggle into his side. "I'm tired, and you stuffed me."

"You stuffed yourself. I've never seen a girl eat so much."

"Shush it." And just like that, the heaviness is gone, and we're back to us again.

Chapter 18

♂

We've grown close, Charlie and I. She's vivacious. That's another word she's made me use for the first time ever.

Everyone underestimates her, including her boss, and even her friend Rachel. They think of her as a wallflower or a bookworm, more the quiet type. Maybe she is with them, but with me she's not. She's vivacious. And her spirit is contagious. I've found myself unpredictably addicted to her.

So, even though I spent this past Thursday evening schooling her on the ins and outs of Manhattan then beating her at two games of Scrabble, I'm back at her place on Saturday afternoon at two on the dot.

I knock, a knock I use just for her. It goes something like one knock, then two quick ones and another one. As I stand there trying to contain the goofy grin that gives away how happy I am to be here, I hear the same knock from the other side of the door. That does it. I have to smile and punctuate it with a gut-chuckle. She's clever and amusing.

She swings the door open, laughing. I'll never get enough of that sound.

"You didn't think I was paying attention, did you?" she asks, her smile giving away her happiness, too.

"Eh." I feign disinterest. "I knew you were. You're more observant than others give you credit for."

She steps aside, and I stride in, heading to the fridge and putting the beer away, starting to feel at home here in her apartment.

"Aww, is that a compliment?" she asks, following me.

"Was that a fishing question? Do I not give you enough compliments?"

She tilts her head down as if embarrassed before she responds. "You do. You're good like that." Clasping her hands, she rubs them together. "Let's get this marathon going." She walks to the coffee table and bends over. Although I should be ashamed for checking her out from behind, sadly I'm not. Then again, I'm not sad about it either.

She squats, and her eyes meet mine. One major eye-roll from her and I move to the couch . . . so I'm in front of her. Yeah, so she caught me. It's not the first time and it won't be the last.

With five movie cases stacked in front of her, amused, I say, "You mean business today."

She laughs. "A marathon means business. So, what's first? I have two girlie flicks, two testosterone movies, and a thriller."

I lean forward, spreading the movies across the table. "Do you have a preference?"

"No, you can choose."

"Hmmm . . ." I look at each cover. I've seen two of them, but I don't want to ruin this for her, so I don't say anything. She went to a lot of trouble to get a variety, and I appreciate that. "How sleepy are you?"

"Pretty tired. I had an auction that went later than expected last night, and we were short two assistants. I didn't get home until after eleven. Why?"

I hold up one of the guy movies. "This is the one."

She smiles. "Perfect."

Just as I suspected, twenty minutes in and she's fast asleep. The blinds are closed, and the room is dark, except for the television screen. The movie was noisy, but I've turned it down to let her rest. This is one of the movies I've seen before. I picked it because I knew she'd fall asleep, and she did.

We're lying lengthwise on the couch. My arm is draped over her ankles, my fingers toying with her socked feet. Over the next forty-five minutes, I watch her more than the movie. I've always thought it was strange when people say sappy things like "you look younger and more at peace when you sleep." Until now. She makes me want to move down to her end of the couch and hold her, instead of her feet.

My mind lingers on the thought before I make my mind up to do it. What's the worst that can happen? It's cuddling. I mentally kick myself for using that word. Being cautious and slow, I work my way up and switch sides, sliding between her and the couch cushions. I stop breathing and stare as she adjusts, but she doesn't wake, so I settle all of the way down and tuck my arm under hers, holding her to me.

I don't remember falling asleep, but I did. When I wake up it's a little darker in the room, and she's rolled my way, facing me, her bright, wide, happy eyes watching me. My eyes go wide, and excuses tumble from my mouth. "I . . . this isn't . . . I guess I just fell—"

Her hand touches my cheek and with a faint smile, she says, "It's all right, Charlie. I like snuggling with you."

"Is that what we were doing?"

She giggles, pushing my chest lightly. "You're a snuggler. You're a napper and a snuggler."

"I prefer cuddler," I say, just to clarify.

"Cuddler, snuggler. Same thing."

"I can tell you're rested by how fast you're talking."

"I'm not talking fast," she declares, the words rushing out.

I close my eyes, still smiling. "C'mere." With the arm that worked its way under her while we were sleeping, I roll her over so that her head is on my chest.

It's nice that she doesn't fight it. She even wraps her arm over my stomach, and I can feel her breathing level out.

"I like this," she says, but I hear the worry in her tone. "I've never had a guy friend like this, one that I felt this close to before. Do friends do this?"

I embrace her fully with both arms and place a light kiss on the top of her head. "Yes, good friends can do this and we do this."

Around five thirty, we venture out to the grocery store down the street. Watching someone in their element is always so interesting. Charlie's guard is down, and she's feeling rejuvenated after the nap. She greets a checker by the name of Bill as she reaches for a basket. I take it from her, offering to carry it, and follow her to the small produce section of the corner market.

"What are you hungry for?" she asks.

"We've eaten Italian and Chinese together. How about Mexican tonight?"

"Oooh, that sounds yummy. I make killer nachos."

"Well, I can't pass up killer nachos."

We get the goods, and I toss some ice cream into the basket before we head back to the register. As she chats with Bill while unloading the basket, I notice he keeps glancing at me. Maybe I'm a little paranoid, but it seems like he's sneering when Charlie isn't looking. I give him a closed-mouth smile in acknowledgment. I know this game. He doesn't like me encroaching on what he considers his territory.

Sorry, buddy, I think to myself. I lean in, my chest touching her right shoulder, and rub my hand up and down the middle of her back. "I've got this," I say, winking at her. My eyes lock with his.

She turns in my arms, which puts her even closer to me, more intimate to the outside world, and smiles. "Are you sure? I don't mind. You did let me hog the couch all afternoon."

I smile, enjoying the fact that she just told Bill how we slept on the couch together. "Yeah, I'm positive." I should probably downplay the pleasure I'm feeling and try not to sound so chipper. "Really. I want to buy them, and I'm the one who benefited on the couch." I think about leaving the conversation there, insinuating everything, but I don't. I don't want to make her feel uncomfortable in front of this guy. "I love a good cuddle, remember?"

She turns around as she puts the jar of jalapenos on the counter. When I meet Bill's eyes again, I smirk with a cocky shrug thrown in for good measure.

He leans forward, trying to block me out. "That'll be twenty-one dollars sixty-three, Charlie."

She giggles and nods her head toward me. "His name is Charlie also. What a weird coincidence, huh?" she asks, looking back at me.

"Yeah, weird," Bill mumbles. I can tell he's not amused like we are.

I pay the man and grab the bags. She walks out the door, waving good-bye to Bill. Dropping my shades down over my eyes, I add, "Thanks, man. I'm sure I'll being seeing you again real soon."

Only the sound of the door chime is heard, since he doesn't respond.

We make it about ten feet down the street before she looks up at me and asks, "So, are you always that obnoxious?"

"What?" *Oops, I think I'm busted.*

"What?" She scoffs. "Yeah, you're just the picture of innocence. I think you know what you did back there."

"I'd think any woman would be flattered to have two men—"

"Territorially pissing over them? Yes, that's oh so flattering, Charlie." Her tone is flat, not her normal teasing.

"Hey." I grab her wrist to stop and get her attention. Lifting my sunglasses to the top of my head, I ask, "Are you mad? Because I can't tell right now."

She looks down the street, then pushes me backward, moving with me so we're out of the main path of the sidewalk. "No, I'm not mad. I'm just not used to the attention."

"If you want my opinion, and I know how you live for that," I lean down to her eye level so she knows I'm serious, "I think you just never noticed all of the attention you actually get."

The woman can hold eye contact with a straight face very well. I must admit, it's a little intimidating. Then the side of her mouth quirks up, and her cheeks pink when she says, "Stop. You're too complimentary, and I'm not comfortable with all that . . . you know, attention stuff."

I shouldn't do this. I really shouldn't bring Jim up at a time like this, but I have to. She needs to know how special she is, even if I have to give her constant reminders to undo the damage of that relationship. I take her hand in mine and start walking again. I want her to feel safe and keep this conversation casual.

"There's this girl I know." I look down at her. "She was hurt. I mean, someone hurt her heart, broke it. Despite having this broken heart, she brought light to everyone around her without even realizing it."

I notice she squeezes my hand a little tighter before she speaks. "Charlie —"

"No, let me finish the story." She keeps walking, silent and listening as I continue talking. "Every day I spent with her, I discovered something new and amazing about her, something I didn't think even she realized about herself."

"I don't have low self-esteem anymore," she says. She's trying to stay calm, but I can tell she's getting defensive.

"This is just a story, Charlie." I glance over at her, and she seems deep in thought.

"Then tell me more."

"I found myself wanting to spend more and more time around her and her light. One time, I walked into a dark, crowded club, and she was the only one I saw. No one shined as bright as she did, and she alone was the one I wanted to talk to."

She stops walking and turns into my arm, resting her forehead against my chest. Holding her in the middle of the sidewalk, I say, "Jim didn't know what he had, or maybe he'd forgotten. Not everyone is that forgetful." I tilt her chin up to look at me. "You need to know that you're beautiful and stronger than you think you are. *And hot.* So I might get a little overprotective or . . ." I hate that I'm about to say this, but do it anyway, ". . . jealous. That's because the time we spend together is perfect to me, just like you are."

I feel her body shake as she sniffles. She drops her head down just as the tears begin to fall. A soft giggle, and then a full-on laugh, erupts as she steps back. With a playful hit to my chest, she says, "Damn, you are good with the compliments. I might have to keep you around."

My chest tightens, knowing that everything I said, everything I just professed, has been twisted in her mind, leading us back to where we started. I drop my sunglasses back down onto my nose and take her hand tightly in mine again. After releasing one long sigh, I say, "C'mon. We've got some nachos to make and movies to watch."

"I'm thinking a Scrabble rematch is in order."

I laugh out loud. "That's my feisty girl."

She smiles to herself, then leans her head on my arm. We start walking again, leaving the deeper stuff to be dealt with for another day. It's hard to get mad at her, even if she is oblivious to what this is, to what we are. She'll see the truth one day. As for me, I look down at our hands clasped together, and yeah, this isn't so bad.

Chapter 19

♂

"So, destiny brought us together?" I ask her as we walk down the street.

"I'm leaning more toward fate. Destiny has nothing to do with fate." She says this like it's a fact. It is . . . in her head.

"I always thought they were the same thing."

"No, no, no. Not at all." She looks at me like I'm crazy. Charlie's so damn cute. "Fate is a negative outcome."

"So we weren't destined to be, well, what we are?" I ask, playing the innocent just to hear more of how her mind works.

"We became friends because of the funerals. That's pretty negative, in my opinion." She sounds almost disappointed by this realization. I know I am.

"Destiny is positive then?" I egg her on, because I love having conversations like this with her.

"Destiny is the exact opposite of fate. Destiny is the belief that forces beyond your control want you together and will make that happen. And you call yourself a writer!" She smirks in amusement, because she loves to prove me wrong, and is proud in doing so at this moment.

"And I always thought you were my destiny."

"Ha! I think I'm more your fate." She jabs me in the ribs then grabs my wrist, pulling me into a kitchen store.

I follow her through the tight aisles packed with cooking utensils and pans, but I'm still curious about the fate/destiny topic.

Picking up a rubber spatula, she states, "I like the red. Maybe I need to add more red into my life."

"Red is daring. Are you ready to commit to making such a bold statement by using a red spatula in the privacy of your own home? Sounds crazy if you ask me."

She doesn't respond to my sarcasm. She's gotten good at ignoring it. "Yes, I should be more daring. Look at Rachel. She loves red and wears it all the time."

"You're not Rachel." I scrunch my nose. I like Rachel, but Charlie . . . she's so much more.

"I know I'm not Rachel, but she's daring and she's happy."

"She has low standards if Justin is the one who makes her happy. You aren't happy?" The thought of her unhappy bothers me.

"No, but I'm happy when I'm with you. There's a difference."

"You've lost me again."

"Seems to be easy to do."

"Maybe you need to give me a map of Charlie Barrow, so I can keep up with the different detours your mind takes." I chuckle at my joke.

She points a peeler at me. It's red. "Maybe you need more red in your life, too."

I spin her around by the shoulders and muss up her hair just a little before kissing her playfully on top of her head. She's laughing. She loves it. I can tell. "I think you're all the red I can handle right now."

She stops, tilting her head, her eyes wide with curiosity. "Just right now? Is this not an ongoing thing we've got going here?"

These little moments of insecurity on her part work in my favor. Without telling me directly, she's letting me know she likes being in my life, too. So I tease a bit more, keeping her on her toes. "Are we back to the fate and destiny thing again?"

She stares into my eyes for a few seconds before shaking it off and turning around. Dropping the peeler back into the canister, she rounds the corner. "You're exasperating, Charlie. You know that?"

"Yes, ma'am, I do." I peek around the corner. "But that's why you love . . ." I catch myself, ". . . hanging out with me."

With an apple-shaped kitchen timer in hand, she smiles, redirecting the conversation to a topic she's more comfortable discussing. "Timers are antiquated. Why buy a timer when your oven and microwave both have the feature? It's like timer overload." Her arms go into the air as she glances back, but then she keeps walking—the timer is just a distraction tactic. "I need cupcake liners," she says before taking off toward the back of the store.

I stand there a moment, watching her through the open racks of supplies. She's mumbling to herself. That's a nervous habit she's started doing the last couple of months. Sometimes I wonder if she only does that around me, if maybe I'm the source of her anxiousness, but I don't dare bring it up. I don't want to make her feel self-conscious.

Roaming down the aisles, I find her in front of an impressive display of cupcake liners. Her finger taps her lip as she contemplates her choices, as if cupcake liners will ever matter in the grand scheme of life. "What kind of cupcakes do you want on Saturday?"

"I'm not one to turn my nose up at a cupcake, so any kind you like," I reply, resting my shoulder against the case.

She leans forward and picks a pack of liners that are white with a lime wedge design on the side. "I'm thinking of making margarita cupcakes."

"I've never heard of cupcakes the flavor of cocktails. It's genius."

This elicits a giggle from her. She takes her liners, and I trail behind as she proceeds toward the checkout counter.

Walking out into the early June heat, we both pause at the store's door before we're hit with the sun's harsh rays. "I freckle easily," she says, looking at me.

"I know." I've watched freckles slowly start to cover her nose and cheeks as the warmer weather set in. I even made my heroine freckle. I recall a passage of my book that I wrote the other day.

My Everything ~
Though she considered them blemishes, he loved them. He loved every unique little sun spot on her, and often let his eyes drift from one to the next, making invisible patterns on her beautiful skin.

"Charlie?" she asks, breaking into my thoughts.

"Let's go get you a hat," I reply. I hope she didn't notice my momentary mental disappearance.

She walks from one awning to the next, staying in the shade as much as possible.

Ducking into a corner store, I see a shelf in the front with baseball caps. "Yes, you need a Mets hat," I say, convinced this is the right choice as I put it on her head.

"No, the Cubs." She scans the shelves for a Cubs hat. She won't find one, because this is New York City, and no store here is stupid enough to carry a Cubs hat.

"The Cubs? Are you crazy, woman? Talk like that can get us hurt in this city. I almost could have tolerated you supporting the Yankees, but the Cubs? No can do." I shake my head at the horrid thought. "Maybe we should go to a Mets game this year. The smell of peanuts and popcorn, a cold beer on a hot day, watching one of the best baseball tea—"

"A Yankees game?" she asks, putting on a Yankees hat.

"You're hilarious," I deadpan. "The Mets. Always the Mets. Their games are more entertaining." She rolls her eyes, and I decide I can't stomach seeing her face under such an abhorrent logo, so I swiftly remove the offensive hat. "You're a New Yorker now, pretty girl. It's decision time. The Mets or the Yankees?"

"Why do you like the Mets so much? Don't the Yankees have more history?"

"The Mets are the underdogs. I liken myself to them. Oh, I know what's going on here. Don't tell me Jim was a Yankees fan?"

I knew I shouldn't have said it the second the words came out. But they did, and though I know it's painful for her to think about him, I'm glad she's faced with these memories. She's been more open about her life with him, and how she felt after they broke up. The hardest part has been trying to help rid her of the guilt she feels over his death. *Why should she feel guilty?* He was the ass who cheated on her. He was the ass who ended it with her. She has no reason to feel guilty, but maybe that's what happens. Maybe the living carry the burden of the deceased.

She takes the Yankees hat from my hands, tosses it back onto the shelf, and slips the Mets hat on. "I think it's time for a change."

I nod in agreement. I can feel the tension from a moment earlier lift. "That hat looks good on you."

Putting one hand on her hip and one behind her head, she wiggles her hips for me, showing off. "Why thank you, kind sir."

"Come on. I'll buy the hat after that little show."

Back out on the street, she hooks her arm with mine as we stroll. I've been meaning to tell her something, but haven't found the right time. I just say it, because I hate not being open with her.

"So, I was asked out yesterday." I wait for her reaction.

She doesn't look my way, but busies herself with the small shopping bag in her hand. "Oh yeah?" She's trying for indifference, but I see through her. We may not know every secret about each other, but we've learned to read each other pretty well.

"What do you think about that?"

"That's kind of forward of a woman to ask you out."

I nudge her. "You know what I mean."

She points across the street. "You want a coffee?"

I point to a bistro next to the coffee shop. "You want food and a drink?"

That makes her laugh. "I can eat."

"Good, because I can drink."

We walk into the little café and ask for a table outside. It's midafternoon, and the crowd reflects that in their business attire. I met her at her work because she had a half day, and we've been walking around shopping for the last two hours.

"It feels good to sit down. These shoes are not made for walking." Her eyes meet mine and she adds, "Ironically." She takes her hat off and tucks it into her purse.

"No, but they're sexy on you so they're worth the pain, right?"

She gives me a mischievous smile, and a pale pink colors her cheeks. Someone else might think it's from the heat, but I know different. "Always with the compliments." She leans down to rub her ankle and says, "Yes, they are sexy, which was the initial appeal, but I only wear them to work, so I don't think they were one of my best purchases."

Leaning down, I lift her ankle onto my thigh and rub gently. "Then wear them for their intended purpose."

She watches as I caress and massage. Resting her elbows on the table, she asks, "And what is their intended purpose?"

"Is this where I'm supposed to give you my best line?" Her body is relaxing before me, her pretty eyes looking right back into mine.

"No, this is where—"

"Hi, can I start you off with drinks?" The waitress asks. Charlie drops her foot to the ground, the intimate moment we were sharing interrupted.

I should look at the waitress, but I'm too fascinated by the emotions playing in Charlie's eyes to look away. I order wine. "Do you have Rombauer Carneros Chardonnay?"

"I believe we do. Let me look that up," the waitress replies, turning her attention to the menu. "Yes, we carry that. Two glasses?"

"The bottle, please."

"Would you like to hear the specials tonight?"

I break my stare from Charlie and look up. "I'm feeling adventurous. Surprise me with the special. Charlie?"

"I'll have one of your specials, too. You decide."

The waitress smiles and then says, "You won't regret it. They're both delicious. I'll be right back with your wine."

I want to pick up where we left off, but something tells me that ankle massages and the topic of sexy shoes and their intended purposes are over. We sit in amiable silence until the wine is uncorked and poured.

After a sip, she says, "Tell me about this date." She's not looking at me, and it makes me wonder if me dating really does bother her.

I lean forward, wanting her eyes back on me. As soon as she looks my way, I say, "I never said I was going." I take a sip—okay, it's a gulp—and hold eye contact.

"Why wouldn't you go? You don't like the desperate type?"

That earns a solid laugh from me, and a little giggle from her. "If I went out with every woman who asked, I'd never get to spend time with you."

"Flattery will get you everywhere."

"Apparently not," I say, raising an eyebrow.

She squirms a little under my gaze, but I'm just speaking the truth. We've gotten so close over the last couple of months, yet we still aren't talking about what we are to each other or want to be.

She turns back to face the street, sipping her wine nervously, or what I like to call *jealously*. I can see it in the way her eyes study every woman who glances my way. I can see it in how she tries to pretend I didn't make that dig at our relationship, at us, and her avoidance of becoming more than friends with me.

"How's the book coming along?" she asks. Another obvious sign of how she gets annoyed at herself for feeling jealous—she changes the topic.

"Swimmingly."

"That's not a word," she says, leaning back, relaxing again. Avoiding.

"Are we going to play this game again?"

"I'll bet dinner on it."

"I've eaten here before. Dinner can be quite expensive." I wink to antagonize her. "You sure you want to take that bet?"

She straightens her spine, defensive. "I can afford it."

"I'm not judging you, Charlie, just letting you know." I hope she doesn't think I'm teasing or taunting her. I know this place is more on the higher end. I would've ordered something different if I'd known she'd be buying, something less expensive.

"You must be very confident?"

"I am. And you like my confidence."

She rolls her eyes in that cute way she does when she feels I'm being arrogant then grabs her phone from her bag and searches for 'swimmingly.' Dropping her phone into her purse with attitude, she takes another large gulp of wine. "Sometimes you really frustrate me, Charlie Adams."

I'm right on the word, but I have a feeling it's the thought of me dating that really frustrates her. "I know." I lean in close and whisper, "And it's so fun to push those buttons of yours."

"Speaking of buttons, how many dates have you been on in the last six months, anyway?"

I'm so right. She attempts to wrap her jealousy into a casual question. Our food arrives, but it feels intrusive to the moment we're having.

When we're alone again, I reply, "Not many. I've got pork." Her eyes flash to mine. "I've got pork *loin*. You should get your mind out of the gutter."

She laughs. "I like being in the gutter. Ooh, I got salmon. You want a taste?"

I nod and open my mouth. She slips the fork in and drags it slowly back out. "Yes, yours is delicious. Open up."

Feeding her a bite of mine, I watch her lips gently cover the tines of my fork and pull back.

"I like the pineapple chutney with it. What does 'not many' mean? Under fifty, more than three?"

I can't keep from laughing. She's so jealous. Why will she not admit this to herself? I want this relationship to become more, but only when she's onboard of her own accord. I won't push to make this happen, but I'm willing to wait and see where this goes.

Until she says, "Maybe you should date."

I stare at her in astonishment. "Really?" Lame response, but that's all that's coming to me right now. Questions start to fill my head and get me wondering. Maybe she's seeing someone. Maybe she wants to see someone and feels guilty because of me. "Are you dating?"

"No."

I watch her take a bite of her food, chewing so slow before she takes another sip of wine. "Why not?" I ask.

"Just haven't been feeling it, or maybe I haven't met the right one yet."

That's a punch to the heart. I should wait to respond when I have a rational reply, but my heart overrules my head. "I think I'll call her back right now and set it up."

"Why?" Her words are rushed. "What's the big deal? You can't wait? I thought we were eating?"

Relief washes over me. She may know how to push all of my buttons, too, but even she realizes she went too far this time. I smile at her, glad she stopped this silly game before it turned ugly. She cares more than she lets on, that's for damn sure. Now, how can I make her admit she wants to be with me when she can't seem to see it herself?

This is the challenge I face. Nothing great was ever achieved by taking the easy route, I remind myself.

"You're right. We are, and just for the record, Rachel is the only one I've been on a date with since we met." I hold up my wine glass and offer a toast. "To good food and the two of us living in the here and now."

Chapter 20

♂

The first of July brings hotter weather, it's lighter later, and I find my mind drifting off to the thought of beaches, vacations, and Charlie in a bikini. I wonder if she wears bikinis. With a body like hers, I hope she does. That's a nice image.

I'd like to spend more time picturing Charlie in a bikini, but I need to concentrate on the book because the first part of it is due to my editor soon. Turning back to my laptop, I continue writing.

My Everything ~
Her laugh didn't sound like bells chiming, or birds singing. It was better than that. Her laugh was hardy and sometimes punctuated with a snort or two at the end, and I absolutely could not get enough of it. I was willing to embarrass myself on purpose just to invoke it.

I often wondered if she was onto my games, but she never said anything. Although sometimes, just sometimes, I also wondered if the laugh was coming from somewhere other than the superficial stuff that supposedly caused it. I could see it in her eyes. That look. That look that told me it was more, that there was more between us than ridiculous jokes and cocktails. She was happy and laughing from the heart.

Her eyes gave her away. She felt more, just like I did. But now, it was time to test our relationship and tell her. Her beauty tonight made me think impossible things. Impossible things and heartfelt confessions, such as adding a future to our past and present.

I save the document, ending it there for the day. Writing this book has been draining. I know it's not what Alec expected from me. Hell, a love story isn't what I expected to be writing either, but that's exactly what's being written. That's what is flowing and needs to be told.

The hardest part of this process has been relying on Charlie to lead me in the direction of the story. She's been guiding me to the ending all along, completely unaware. Sometimes I worry that neither the story, nor we, will get the happy ending we want and deserve, but I try to believe and hold onto hope.

I'm giving her time, because I've never felt like this about anyone. I stay in this relationship, this friendship with her, because I realize that this might be it. This might be all we ever are, and being the loser I am, I'd take it. I'd settle for this if *this* is all she can give me. She's the one, but she's skittish from being burned by love, so I'll just have to show her I'm the one for her.

Time is what's needed. I'm the impatient sort, so time has become my torturer.

My phone buzzes, inching across the desk in front of me. Justin's calling. "What's up?"

"Just got a call from my girl. Rachel said you need to come up here today. Charlie might need you."

"Why, what's going on?"

"Something about an auction and Charlie crying. That's all I got from Rachel. When emotions get involved, I tune out. You know this, dude."

I shake my head. "Yeah, that's real appealing to the ladies, I bet. How *ever* does Rachel resist your charms?"

"She doesn't. The woman is insatiable."

"No, don't go there," I say, cringing. "Let's get back to Charlie. She's at work?"

"Yeah, something about some dead ex-boyfriend and an auction today."

Jim's estate is being auctioned and it's happening today? "I've gotta go. Bye."

I hang up and call Charlie's cellphone, but there's no answer. I grab my wallet and keys and take off.

Grabbing a cab because it's faster, I hurry into her building on Madison and up to her floor. I approach the reception desk. "I'm here to see—"

"Charlie Barrow."

S.L. Scott

"Yes," I reply. I'm surprised the receptionist knows.

"I remember you from the last time you were here."

"Good memory. Can I go back?"

She leans forward on her elbows, and her smile grows wide. "She won't be at her desk. There's an auction in less than an hour. She'll be gone for a while. Do you want to wait here with me?"

She's flirting. I know all the telltale signs. Her eyes are wide and focused on me with a little glint in them. She readjusts until the V of her top is highlighting her cleavage. She leans forward, even at the expense of it appearing odd and uncomfortable.

"Thank you, but I need to find her. It's important."

She sits back, not wasting another minute of her time on me now that I've shown no interest. With a dismissive wave of her hand, she says, "In that case, she's down on the first floor in the gallery or the auction room."

I hurry back to the elevators and down to the first floor, rounding the corner to find the entrance. When I enter the auction room, it's empty. I call her name out a couple of times anyway. "Charlie?"

A man pushes through wide double doors off to the back and props them open. I see people milling about back there. Walking into the large gallery, I look for her, but still nothing.

"Charlie!" I hear Rachel call me, and I turn. Her heels echo in the large room as she hurries over. "I'm glad you came. She acted like it didn't matter all day, but now . . ." She sighs and looks around. Leaning in, she whispers, "This is the first time I'm clerking an auction on my own. I want to be there, but—"

"Don't worry. You go do your job. Where is she?"

"She's by the jewelry display case." She points to the back left of the gallery.

As I walk over there, I notice all of the stuff going on the block today. A leather couch. A painting that looks like the ones sold at the corner of Washington Square, but the expensive version, and a crystal vase. Everything is very traditional, formal, the painting an exception. From the photo frames to the dining table and chairs, the items piece together the mystery of who Jim used to be, but I don't see much of Charlie in the belongings.

I round a large china cabinet and see her standing in front of a jewelry case, not touching it, but staring at the backlit glass box. When I touch her back, she startles. "Hey there." I'm hoping I can calm her, support her, be whatever she needs me to be for her.

Being discreet, she wipes underneath her eyes with the back of her hand, and the action alone shows me how vulnerable she is to what's happening.

"I thought I was over all of this, but seeing it here . . ." Her eyes drift to mine. "Why do these things affect me this way?"

She wants answers I can't give her, but I search for the right thing to say in her time of need. "These objects are a reminder. That's all. It's not him. It's just stuff."

She turns and hugs me, squeezing me hard while pressing her cheek to me. I wrap my arms around her, appreciating every moment like this that I'm given, and try to steady my heart.

She looks up and says, "Your heart is racing."

"I hurried here to see you." It's not a complete lie, but me rushing over here has nothing to do with why my heart is beating so fast right now.

That makes her smile, but she sees through the lie. "So, Rachel called you?"

"No, Justin."

"Rachel called Justin to call you?" She laughs lightly as she wipes at one of her eyes again.

"Something like that. You want to blow off this place and go somewhere else?"

She looks around. "I want to stay for a while longer. Will you stay with me?"

"Of course." I follow her as she walks over to a desk hidden behind a screen and reaches into her purse, pulling a flask out. That makes me smile. "You drinking on the job, Ms. Barrow?"

"Rachel gave this to me. Maybe I should ask her why she has it at work." She laughs again, but this time it's hollow. "Guess she figured I needed it more than she did today." She takes a quick swig, scrunches her nose at the taste, and hands it to me.

I look around first. The auction is about to start, so the potential bidders have left, but the screen is hiding us from the public anyway, so I take a quick sip. The whiskey burns as it coats my throat. "I didn't know Rachel was a whiskey drinker. Maybe I should have given her another chance." I take a risk and joke.

That wins me a dirty look and a punch to the arm. "Ow!" I grab my arm and play along. It never hurts, but it makes her feel good that maybe she's strong enough to do a little damage.

She takes another gulp and tugs on my shirt. "Come on. I want to show you something over here." She leads me back to the display case and points at a ring in the middle on the top shelf. It's sparkling and simple in design —platinum with diamonds scattered around. "That's my engagement ring."

I lean in closer. "Really?"

"It's Tiffany's, but it wasn't that expensive." She smirks, glancing at me.

"Cherry hated it. I loved it. Simple, beautiful, not showy. He gave it to me because he said he thought the ring was pretty and reminded him of me. He bought it with me in mind."

"It's very pretty. You gave it back when you broke up?"

"No. When we moved here after college it was quickly replaced with what was deemed a 'proper' ring. Four perfect carats. Princess cut. Platinum band. It was breathtaking. I was so surprised. I loved it until, one night at a dinner party at his parents' house, Cherry told the story of how she forced him to go shopping for a ring worthy of the Bennett name, and that she picked out the new one." She stands up straight, turning her back to the case and sips from the flask.

The auction has started, and two employees remain back here, waiting to move furniture when the auction is finished. They're burly guys who don't look like they will tell on her for drinking.

I take another sip after her, impressed how she's drinking the straight liquor without complaint.

She goes to Jim's couch and sits down heavily, dropping her head back. "God, I loved this couch. It's ridiculous how expensive it was, but it's so comfortable."

I smile and sit down next to her, handing the flask back.

She rolls her head to the side and smiles at me when our eyes meet. "The whole ring thing was a joke to Cherry. They were laughing at the little band that Jim bought me in college. They were laughing at us, taking away from the sweet proposal. He gave me a ring that he knew I'd like, a ring that fit who I was. That night, he took it all away by laughing with her. He held my hand up to show the new, Cherry-approved ring to the other guests." She slides across the leather and says, "I gave Cherry's ring back to him the night we broke up. By accident, though, I forgot and left the other ring in my dresser drawer when I moved out. I had hidden it there for months, like I was protecting it or something."

The silence that falls is weighted with sadness, and all I want to do is erase all the bad. I speak before I have time to think through what I'm saying. "I'll buy you the ring if you want it."

She sits up, stunned, and then her expression softens. She smiles while touching my cheek, and whispers, "You would, too, wouldn't you?"

I lean into her hand. "Anything for you."

She falls gently against me and places her head on my shoulder. "You're too good to me." She takes a deep breath and exhales. "I don't want the ring. His mother sent it back to me with Jim's funeral announcement. I gave it to Rachel to add to the sale a month ago. As much as it hurts to see it here as another one of his possessions up for sale, I don't want it anymore. I have the memories, and the memories are less tainted than the jewelry."

She closes her eyes. When she opens them again, she says, "When I look around at all of this stuff, all I see is a life that never was. Empty promises in the life I shared with him." She points at a table. "That picture frame held our engagement photo. I served our first meal in our apartment on those dishes. That crystal vase held the flowers he had auto-delivered on a weekly basis to our house, not for me, but to make an impression. It was a life I never wanted and never adjusted to. It's a life that felt hopeful at one point, but it was forced. I see that now. These things were his and Cherry's, never mine. The only thing I was ever allowed to contribute is that cheap painting. It's all I could afford, but I loved it all the same. Cherry hung it in the guest bedroom. I used to read in that bedroom, just so I could look up and see it."

I knew that piece stood out. I glance over at the painting one more time, and it makes me smile. It's a painting I would be drawn to if I saw it for sale somewhere other than this auction.

She sighs, looking at me. "I'll hold onto my memories. I'm ready to let this stuff go."

I squeeze her hand. "I think you're a smart and wonderful woman. You know that?"

She sits up and laughs. "Yeah," she says, polishing her nails like she's told how awesome she is all the time. "That's why you love me so much."

"Just one of the many reasons." That statement is truer than she allows herself to realize. I chuckle to myself, and as I look into her bright eyes, I see the Charlie I've wholeheartedly fallen for return—the happy, snarky, and beautiful woman that she is.

Chapter 21

♂

Charlie looks so relaxed as she sits on Jim's couch—her former couch—and her mood has shifted compared to when I first arrived. She doesn't look sad, but seems contemplative.

"I talked to Jim's sister, Kelsey, today. She stopped by earlier."

"You were close?"

"I thought so, but things have changed. I've changed. We chatted for a few minutes, but it was strained. I think I'm the outcast now, a little stain on the image of perfection they had of him."

"Own it, Charlie. Stay true to yourself."

That makes her smile, mischievousness sneaking in. "You're right. I've always been the outcast in their eyes. I should be proud they couldn't change me." She angles her body toward me and says, "You never told me about your first love, black sheep." She pokes me in the chest for extra emphasis on her little pun.

"You're a clever one." I sit forward, reaching to ruffle her hair, but she ducks away too fast. So instead, I ask, "You want to stay here and see how this all plays out sales-wise? Or, I can buy you dinner?"

She stands. "You know the way to my heart, big boy. Let's go." She takes my hand and pulls me up with her.

After sneaking out the back, we don't go far, because there's a bar across the street she wants to go into.

"You meant a liquid dinner, right?" When she starts to laugh, I'm reminded of the part in my book I wrote this morning.

"I'm cool with whatever you want."

"Two Jack and Cokes, barkeep," she calls, as we slide onto stools at the bar.

"You trying to get me drunk?"

"Absolutely. I'm trying to get us both drunk."

"Both of us drunk turns into—"

"Debaucherous behavior?" Her eyes and sly smile give away her devilish mood.

I chuckle. "I'll give you debaucherous, though we both know I totally won the bet on that word."

The drinks are set in front of us, and I pass my credit card over.

She toasts. "I think I love the word more now that I know it's wrong. It's an outcast, like us. To outcasts and black sheep, Mr. Adams." She hits her glass against mine, making the liquid slosh.

"To outcasts and black sheep, Ms. Barrow."

After taking a long drink, I watch as she relaxes her shoulders. She looks carefree, more like the woman I know—the woman I spend time with on Saturday afternoons.

"You're not getting out of the love story, by the way," she says, taking another sip.

I look down at my drink and wish I could smile, but the memories aren't good. I spin my glass around twice, watching the ice cubes melt and hear them jangle together. Her eyes are on me. I don't have to look at her to feel them, but she remains quiet. I finish the liquor then tap the empty glass on the bar twice to signal the bartender that I need another.

When I'm ready, I look at Charlie and start to talk. "Her name was Stephanie Dardusko. Wow. I haven't said that name out loud in years. It still makes me chuckle. Sort of how you amuse me on a daily basis."

"I hope you aren't teasing me," she says, faux-pouting. "I'm vulnerable tonight."

"I thought teasing was all we did? Teasing is what we're good at."

"Well then. I'll take that as a compliment, and by the way, change the subject much?"

"Fine, fine," I say, rolling my eyes. "I met Stephanie one summer when I was in college. I came home to the city for summer break. I was partying too hard, but you've heard about that. I was drunk and horny, and Stephanie was, too." I set my drink down and turn toward Charlie. "That's real attractive, huh? Drunk and horny. Can you tell we both had high standards back then?" Remembering what an idiot I was embarrasses me even now.

"I'm not here to judge you." The way she says that makes me believe her. She's here to support me, to get to know me better, to know the man that all of these stories created. "How old were you?"

"Twenty. We hooked up, and the summer passed in a drunken haze. We partied in the Hamptons, at the newest nightclubs, the hottest restaurants, and we had sex . . . a lot of sex, everywhere. We were oblivious to the rest of the world, so we did stupid stuff. The problem is that summer ended, and I had to return to reality, to school. She came with me and lived in my apartment that year. She was just there doing nothing but drinking, continuing the party that we started in Manhattan months earlier."

I rub my eyes, realizing this is affecting me even more than I thought it would. Maybe I haven't put my own ghosts to bed.

"We were together almost ten months before we had our first fight, and when it did happen, it was bad. I was too sober and she was too drunk. She was yelling before I even walked in the door. I could hear her screaming all the way down the hall. I thought she was cheating on me with someone, but when I opened the door, it was just her. She was belligerent and throwing things. Broke all kinds of stuff. Shattered a picture of me and my buddies. Destroyed some of my textbooks. She just went crazy."

I pause to take a deep breath, the image of her freaking out running through my head.

Charlie's hand rubs my back as she asks, "Are you all right? We don't have to talk about this, if you don't want."

"I want you to know all of this, everything about me, even the bad." I turn on the stool toward her and finish my story. "I remember noticing how beautiful she was in her rage. It was the most passion I'd seen from her in months. That's when I realized how bad she'd gotten. I didn't complain because I loved her. I had fallen in love with her that year. I liked having her around, having her at my apartment. I liked coming back from class and seeing her there waiting for me. I liked all the wrong things about her. I couldn't be someone's entire world, because it sets them up for disappointment. When she flipped out, I saw the truth. I saw who she really was and how bad she'd gotten. I think I had seen it before that night, but didn't want to admit it.

I was more screwed than I knew at the time. Later that night, I found the remainder of a line of cocaine on my government textbook. Now that I think of it, that's kind of ironic. Very anti-establishment of her. It was like her way of telling the world to screw off. Next to the cocaine, I found bank receipts. I guess that was her way of screwing me over."

"She stole money from you?"

"Over the course of ten months, she took just over fifteen grand without me knowing. It was from my private account, not my parents'. In high school, I never spent much money when my friends and I went out. They all had money, so I saved mine."

She's looking down at her lap, and I can see the pain in her expression, her sympathy for me. She whispers, "You loved her. So, what happened?"

"I broke up with her and kicked her out that night. Needless to say, I knew she had the money for a hotel." I try to keep the sarcasm out of my tone, but it's there. "The next day, I saw her leaving a neighbor's apartment. They were kissing."

I look back at my drink, the humiliation creeping back, and say, "It hurt to find out she was stealing from me, because she didn't have to. I gave her money all the time. I would've given her more. But to see her making out with that guy . . ." I exhale, hoping to release the pain I'm surprised I still feel over Stephanie.

"One of my favorite qualities about you is that you trust people. You believe them good until they prove themselves otherwise. Don't change that." She leans closer and asks, "Do you blame yourself?"

"For her stealing, nah. Sometimes I do wonder if she was hooking up with that guy on the side, though. She met me in that party environment, and then a few months later, I changed. I was a serious student again. Sure, I still drank and went to parties, but only on the weekends. I guess she thought I was one way, and then when I went back to school, I was different. I conned her. Not on purpose, but in reality that's what happened. I'm sure following me to college was quite boring for her, compared to our life that previous summer."

"You're too good, Charlie. You believe you're to blame for the drugs and the fight, as if you created the person she became? You didn't, and she could have done something with her life. She should have been going to school or working, but she chose to lie around doing nothing." Charlie touches my knee, and the sensation takes over, running up and down my body. Her touch. *Her* comforting *me* now.

"She was that way when you met her at the party, remember? Drunk and horny. She used you, and yet you're blaming yourself for her actions."

I take a gulp, letting her words sink in. "That's an interesting perspective."

"It's true. You were handsome and rich, just the target she was trying to bull's-eye."

I chuckle. *"Were?"*

"Were what?"

" 'Were' good-looking? You don't think I'm good looking now?" I ask, teasing.

That makes her laugh, lightening the mood. "What if I tell you no?"

"You'd hurt my ego."

"And if I tell you yes?"

"I'd pop my collar and might even strut a little," I say with a wink.

"Oh, this I've got to see. Charlie, you're very handsome, but I also think you already know that."

I stand, pop the collar on my shirt, and strut the length of the bar. "Like what you see, baby? Is this what you want?"

A woman leans back and says, "If she doesn't, I do."

"Hands off, lady, he and his inflated ego are all mine," Charlie says, leaning back then laughing.

I whisper to the lady, "Sorry, I'm taken."

Straight-faced, she states, "The offer still stands if you two break up before you leave tonight."

I smirk. "I'm hoping she keeps me for a while." As I start to walk away, she slaps my ass. "Wow!" I rush back to my stool. "Did you see that?"

"I sure did, and I can't blame the lady. You do have a nice ass."

"I'm good-looking and now I've got a nice ass? It's time to get you home. You're obviously drunk if you're complimenting me freely."

"Am not."

"You so are." I slide off the stool and hug her head to my chest. "But I still love ya."

She giggles, wiggling her way out of my silly hold.

I sign the tab, and a few minutes later, we're out the door and I'm hailing a cab. Charlie leans her head on my shoulder again as we sit back in the taxi. The sounds of the city lull us both as our emotions from the day start to dissipate.

I hop out, helping her out of the cab in front of her building. "You gonna be okay?" I ask because, even though I'm not drunk, I've drunk enough to know that I'd try to take advantage of the situation if I escort her up to her apartment.

"Yes, I'm fine." She leans forward, grabbing the front of my shirt and pulling me closer to her. "Thank you."

"For what?"

"For coming to the auction, for the drinks, and for sharing a piece of you, an important piece."

"You're welcome. Thank you for listening. Hey, and Charlie? Next time, call me if you need support. That's what I'm here for."

"And to think I thought you were here for the entertainment."

"You've sorely underestimated me and my skills, then," I say, grinning.

Unabashed, her eyes check me out from head to toe. Backing away, closer to her door, she says, "Maybe I am drunk. Goodnight, Charlie."

That's odd. I've never caught her eyeing me so blatantly. "Goodnight."

As she swings the door open wider than necessary, I hear her mumble, "Very skillful indeed."

She's going to be the death of me if I'm not careful, but her mumbling and how exposed we were with each other tonight makes me think she's in just as deep.

Finally.

Chapter 22

♀

Admiring the neighborhood and brownstones, I smile while walking to Charlie's apartment after work. I like coming over here. We don't spend much time here, because we both prefer my large comfy couch, but today he called and said he was making me dinner.

When I open the door into his renovated building, I almost trample an older lady. "Oops, I'm sorry. Please excuse me."

"No worries, dear."

I start up the stairs, opting to skip the small elevator, but stop when she asks, "You're Charlie's girl, right?"

Huh? Interesting question. Turning around, I say, "I'm not sure. We're friends, though."

She gives me a warm smile. "Your name is the same as his, right? Charlie?"

"Yes, that's me," I reply, smiling for so many reasons, the main one being that Charlie has talked about me. "Please forgive me. I don't know your name."

"I'm Charlie's neighbor, Mrs. Lackey, but you can call me Veronica."

"Well, it's very nice to meet you, Veronica."

"You, too. I've tried to get a few juicy details regarding you out of

Charlie, but the boy doesn't kiss and tell." She scoffs, snapping her fingers like she's out of luck.

That's funny, so I laugh. "Maybe that's because we don't kiss, so there's nothing to tell."

"No kissing?" She sighs. "I miss kissing. My Johnny was a great kisser."

"Kissing is very romantic. Was Johnny your—"

"My husband of fifty-three years. He left me too soon, but I know he watches over me now."

"He sounds wonderful," I say, moving closer to the wall so I'm out of the way of the door.

"Why don't you and Charlie kiss?"

She's not shy, that's for sure. "We're friends, not dating."

Her expression is surprised, which means Charlie didn't explain all the details regarding our relationship to her. I'm curious how he explained "us" to her. I have a feeling he'll get out of delving into this matter, so I decide to invite her to join us. Plus, I like her moxie.

"You know, I'm heading upstairs to dinner with him. I'd really like if you joined us. I know Charlie would enjoy that, too."

She waves me off. "No, no. You two lovebirds need your time alone. I don't want to impose. I'm going out for my evening walk before that August heat wave hits us."

"It's no imposition at all. If you change your mind, you know where he lives."

"Thank you. Go off now and have fun, and kiss that hunk of yours. It doesn't have to be all about the sex these days. Sometimes pleasure can be found in the simplest ways. Good-bye now."

"Oh, we don't hav—" The door swings closed before I can clarify that Charlie and I are just friends, friends *without* benefits. Well, at least none of those types of benefits.

I head upstairs, knock on his door, and wait. He never keeps me waiting long, and the door swings open. I walk past him and say, "I just had the most interesting conversation with Veronica from next door."

He takes my purse from me and sets it down on the bar as I pull off my work jacket. "Who's Veronica?"

I look at him astounded. Veronica knew about our sex life. Well, kind of, so I assumed they were close enough for him to know her first name. "Veronica. Mrs. Lackey?"

"Mrs. Lackey's name is Veronica? That's all kinds of sexy."

I tilt my head, annoyed. "I'm gonna pretend you did not just say that. Anyway, how is Veronica sexier than Charlie?"

He laughs and sets a glass of iced tea in front of me. "No name is sexier than Charlie. Just saying."

Now that cracks me up. "I sort of set you up for that one."

"In more ways than one."

"What are you cooking me tonight?" I ask, being nosy and heading into the kitchen. "It smells amazing."

"I roasted a chicken."

"Really? You know how to do that?"

He looks at me funny. "I know some cooking basics. Do you cook or stick primarily to baking?"

"I don't burn toast and I know how to make scrambled eggs, but I'm a baker."

He hip bumps me out from in front of the oven. "We'd make a killer cooking team. I can cook and you can make dessert. We could eat and get fat and live—"

"Happily ever after?"

"Yeah," he says, a smile overtaking his features. "Or something like that."

I stretch across the counter for my glass of tea. When I turn back, I catch his eyes on my midsection, but he quickly looks away. *He's so busted!* Cool air hits my exposed stomach as my shirt rises up. I pull it quickly back down and drink my tea, pretending like I didn't just catch him eyeing my bare skin.

Trying to act casual, I watch as Charlie bends down, taking the roasting pan out of the oven. The muscles in his arms tense and define from the heavy weight of the dish. He bends over, and his own T-shirt slides up as his jeans hang down just enough to reveal the top of his black boxer briefs and lower back dimples.

I shouldn't, but I do. My eyes linger, following the lines of the muscles on his sides that lead to his abdomen. A couple of drops of tea land on my chest, and I startle.

"Missed your mouth."

Flustered, I look up and see him pointing to my chest. Embarrassed, I become defensive to stop the nonsensical emotion. "Yes, I guess I did. My mind is on other things tonight."

So confident and cocky . . . and sexy, he asks, "Like me?"

"You're not going to get me to blush tonight." I snap at him, my words clipped. I'm well aware that I was the one busted this time.

Charlie walks close, so close, and drops his arms forward on either side of me. He's trapped me between them, and although I shouldn't want this with a friend, I do with him. I want it more than I should. I love being this close to him, but instead of giving in, I hold my own, standing my ground —shoulders back, straight face in place. His head moves even closer to mine, but he keeps our bodies apart on purpose.

"I bet I can."

I stare into his blue eyes. My heart is pounding in my chest as his breath hits my face. I like that I can smell a trace of mint. It makes me think he freshened up just for me. I often find myself reacting to him in ways that I wouldn't to others. Maybe it's because I like these games we play, the ones that involve our heads and our hearts.

"I dare you."

His lips are on mine as soon as the words leave my mouth.

I want to kiss him back. I want to lose myself in him and this kiss and the moment, but my heart is still pounding, and the fear of losing him as my friend wins out. I tilt my head down, leaning forward and resting my forehead on his shoulder for a moment, feeling the heat between us overwhelming me, and take a deep breath. Hoping to clear my head of these thoughts of more with him, I duck under his arm and scurry into the living room.

I don't stop until I'm on the balcony in the warm air of the evening. Is a cool breeze too much to ask for? I need to douse this fire burning inside me. A cool breeze should help me wrangle these crazy ideas that are shouting inside my head to be heard. Ideas that maybe, just maybe, I should risk our friendship and date him, or at least kiss him some more. But it's August, so I'm out of luck.

Bending forward over the railing, I close my eyes and take another deep breath.

"I can't back down from a dare," he says from behind me.

"You cheated." I don't look at him. I'm teetering on that line, and seeing him, seeing his handsome face will weaken my stance. I'll ruin everything by jumping him, and that won't be good for either of us. Couch snuggles, Saturday afternoon cupcakes, beer, and movies I watch just because he wants to—all of it will be gone if I don't control myself.

"How so?" he asks, joining me, a safe distance separating us. His back is to the railing as he watches me, waiting for me to say something that will argue the fact that he made me blush.

If I were being honest with myself, he lit a blaze, not just a blush, but that's too much reality for me to admit.

"That was a cheap shot." I shift onto my right foot and try to hold steady, though I'm unnerved.

"It wasn't a shot. It was a chance I took."

"I don't like being used to prove a point."

"Who said I was using you or proving a point?" He inches closer, keeping his arms crossed over his chest. His biceps are distracting as he advertises them so flagrantly in front of me.

"You weren't?" I ask. I already know the answer. "You took advantage of the fact that I haven't been kissed in a long time. It's been forever, which is too long. I think it's been since you, if you must know. So throwing temptation like that in front of me is cheating, not to mention that you knew exactly how to get the reaction you wanted." I huff defiantly.

"I kissed you because—" The sound of a knock on the door interrupts us. "I'll be right back."

I find relief in the distance between us, but I'm disappointed I don't know what he was going to say. I'm so screwed up when it comes to him. I've had so many new feelings, maybe old feelings—the ones that I tamped down months ago. Like Charlie, I can't ignore them any longer.

He makes me feel emotions I haven't felt in a long time. I'm hoping that means I'm ready to date. I've had no interest in that since Jim and I broke up. I can tell I'm ready to touch and be touched—kiss and be kissed. I liked that kiss. I liked it a lot. I wasn't aware I was touching my fingertips to my lips until I drop my hand down.

I steel myself for the potential of more, hoping this isn't a mistake. When he comes back, I'm going to kiss him. Two can play this game, and I intend to score. I laugh at my slip. I mean win. Yes, I intend to win, not score. And if I happen to get to kiss him again in the process, then I'll take one for the home team. I'm ready for action . . . to prove a point, of course.

I see Mrs. Lackey walk into the living room and smile so sweet as she looks at the two us. "I hope you don't mind me stopping by—"

"No, not at all. Would you like something to drink?" Charlie asks her as I walk inside from the balcony.

"If you have sherry, that would be nice," she replies, and looks down for a moment, as if she's being naughty.

He chuckles. "I'm sorry, I don't have any sherry, but I do have white wine."

"Join me for a chat on the couch and we'll all have a glass of wine together, then." She's kind of bossy, but I like her.

I sit down beside her on the couch as Charlie gets the not-so-subtle hint and retreats to the kitchen. She turns toward me and states rather bluntly, "You like him a lot. Are you in love?"

My eyes go wide. "I think you've assumed the wrong thing about us."

"No, I haven't. You, dear, aren't allowing yourself to see the truth."

"What are we talking about, ladies?" Charlie hands us both a glass of wine with a smile.

Veronica looks right at him and says, "We were talking about how much Charlie likes you."

I gasp in surprise. "I . . ." I stutter, shaking my head. "No, we weren't. We were talking about—"

He's looking at me all smug, loving the fact that I've been put on the spot, and then winks just to add to the fun before turning back to her. "Mrs. Lackey, I think you're a troublemaker. I'm going to need to keep my eye on you."

She laughs, patting my leg. "I think Charlie here is more your type. Keep your eyes on her lovely face and all will end how it should." She smiles, but I see her matchmaker sneaky side slipping out, and that makes me giggle. She's full of grand ideas when she asks, "I want to dance. Will you dance with me, Charlie?"

He offers her a hand, helping her up and pulling her to him with a flourish and a spin. "It would be my pleasure." Going to his music system, he flips through a few stations until he finds what he's looking for.

Charlie melts my heart when I hear Sinatra waft from the speakers. He strolls back to Veronica, and like a gentleman, takes her by the hand. They sync their steps and sway to the romantic music.

She's beaming as she smiles up at him. I can't hear what she says, but when the second song comes on, she claims she's tired and insists I take her place.

He smiles and nods to encourage me to get up, and I do. I do because he's that persuasive when he has that look of . . . of . . . *like*? No, it's more than that. That look isn't like, it's so much more. I know because it's how I'm looking at him right now, and all of my earlier resolve to prove him wrong, to win, is gone. If losing is dancing with someone or even kissing someone who cares for you like I undoubtedly care for him then call me a loser.

I take Veronica's place and slide my hand into his as he places his other hand on my hip. I hold his shoulder with my left hand and step closer, wanting to be as close as I can without offending Veronica by being too overt.

He's warm to the touch, and being this close, dancing with him is nothing less than intoxicating. Closing my eyes, I lean my cheek against his shoulder.

My hands are released as his arms wrap me in strength, protection . . . *love?*

In this moment, this moment right now, I wonder why I've been fighting this when it feels so good to be with him. I've been resisting his charms and handsome face, beautiful smile, and happy eyes since I first laid eyes on him on the subway last March. *Why did I keep myself from the happiness he so freely gives me?*

That's when I realize everything we've been through, everything we've become to each other has led us to here and now.

He won't hurt me.

He's not Jim.

Chapter 23

♀

"When I hold her, my heart comes to life, sparking into fireworks that are bigger than the two of us. Our souls bond together, sending us straight into the stratosphere. The world holds endless possibilities, the universe is our playground. Our hearts remain captivated by the other as we take this journey together," he whispers into my ear.

My knees start to buckle from the feel of his breath along my neck. Goosebumps cover me, undermining any willpower I have while listening to his seductive words.

"I wrote that today," he says, his fingers splayed on my lower back, rubbing with gentle pressure.

"Charlie?" I run my hand over his heart.

A timer buzzes, startling us, and we stop dancing. He looks me in the eyes and says, "Hold that thought."

He walks into the kitchen, and I get my wine, taking a sip and hoping to grab hold of the moment we just had once more when he returns. My courage to tell him how I'm feeling is seeping away with each ticking second. Standing next to the couch where Veronica sits, I take a deep breath.

"It's time, dear," she says, encouraging me.

"Time?"

"Don't waste any more time. You don't know how long you've got."

"I know you're right," I reply, "but I think I may need just a little more." She purses her lips in reproach, so I start to justify myself, hating that she's disappointed in me. "I don't want to just throw all my emotions on him. He's busy with his book. I don't want to burden him right now, but I promise I'll tell him soon."

I think she sees right through me, but doesn't call me out. Patting my leg, she says, "Just don't take too long. Other women won't."

Doing a double take, I eye her as that thought settles itself in my head. Other women won't? Other women won't waste time? Other women will tell him how they feel? Other women will try to take him if I don't tell him first and take him off the market? Other women will try to take him away from me. I place my hand over hers and whisper, "I'll tell him this weekend. We always spend Saturday afternoon together. I'll tell him then."

"That's my girl." She smiles with full faith in me, and that makes me smile, too.

When he returns, he announces, "Dinner is served." Our eyes meet, and he's well aware that the moment has passed. He sighs then looks to Mrs. Lackey. "Hope you're hungry."

She stands, giving me a reaffirming smile. "I am."

Chapter 24

♂

The bell chimes above the door, and the standard friendly greeting is called out. "Welcome to The Bagelry." I make my way up to the counter. Tony looks up from loading the fresh baked goods into the display case and smiles. "Morning, Charlie. How's it going?"

"I'm good." I point to one of the bagels. "Onion today. How's business?" I look around and every table is full. "Booming, by the looks of it."

He laughs as he drops the bagel into a brown bag. "No complaints. Coffee?"

"Yeah the usual, straight up."

He turns around and pours the brew into a to-go cup. With his back to me, he asks, "Writing?"

"Some. Not as much as I should. My mind has been a bit a preoccupied."

"Tell me about her, or is this the same one you mentioned before?"

"One and the same."

He sets the cup in front of me and leans on the counter, lowering his voice. "Bring her in sometime. I'd like to meet the girl that's occupying all that headspace of yours."

I slide the money across the counter, telling him to keep the change, but add, "It's complicated—"

"If I had a dollar for every time I heard that. Listen, Charlie, life is complicated, but women, they're more than complicated." He should've been a bartender with all of this advice. It's good advice, though, so I continue to listen. "One of the most important things I've learned in life is that complicated isn't always bad. Sometimes complicated is just complex."

A short line has started to form behind me. "Seems I have some stuff to think about, then."

He smiles, returning to his jovial self. "Like I said, bring her by. I'd like to meet this complicated woman. Anyway, she sounds good for you. I have a feeling you've had it too easy with the ladies."

That makes me laugh. "Yeah, maybe. Hm. I don't know." But I know deep down he's right, pretty much about all of it. "Thanks for everything."

"See you soon."

I walk outside and stop to sip my coffee. My phone rings, and when I see the screen, I smile before answering. "Dude, you finally back?"

Conner laughs. "Yeah, I'm back for a while. I received a few threats from my parents last spring after I extended my trip by two weeks and then spent half the summer in Europe."

"They need their shipping tycoon of a son to come back and run the business full-time now."

"Basically. My dad needs to hit the links again. Ever since he retired in July, he gets irritable if he has to miss his Friday golf game."

"So you're working today?"

"That place runs itself. You want to get some lunch?"

"It's nine thirty in the morning."

"Yeah, but the diner is always open."

I look at the bagel in my hand and debate momentarily. "I'll meet you at the diner in twenty."

Conner is already seated in a booth by the window when I arrive. I toss my little bagel bag down and slide in across from him. "Were you even at the office when you called?"

"No. I was here, but I have my laptop."

"So you're running a multimillion-dollar business from a diner and a laptop?" I wave at Shirley, our regular waitress, and she starts pouring the orange juice she knows I'm going to order.

Conner shrugs nonchalantly. "I didn't ask to run my family's business."

"But you did accept the job."

"No, I was forced into the job."

"Forced? You sure don't mind living off the money the business brings in."

"Same old argument, Charlie. Get over it. You could've been running your family's biz, but you walked away. Now you sound bitter. What gives?"

"Not bitter, just simple observations I've made."

"Changing the subject because this one bores me. Fill me in on what I missed these last few months."

"Not much—"

"Jada said you missed her last three parties."

"When did you talk to her?"

"Last week in Atlantic City."

"Jada in Atlantic City? I thought she didn't gamble anywhere but Monte Carlo."

He laughs. "She made an exception for me." He points two fingers at me accusingly, and says, "You, my friend, are causing the ladies all sorts of stress."

Shirley sets my drink down along with my toast. I don't have to order here anymore. She knows my selection already. Ordering the same thing almost weekly for five years makes it pretty obvious. "Thank you."

Her face is pleasant as she stands ready, coffeepot in hand. "You're welcome, Charlie. All good?"

"Yep. All good, and you?"

"Same old, same old. Enjoy your food."

Conner is now reading e-mails. I don't know if they're personal or business, so I pick up our conversation where we left off. "I'm not stressing the ladies out. They're stressing themselves out."

"I get it, Chuck. Everyone does. You didn't want everything handed to you." His voice turns mocking. "You wanted to 'make it' on your own and prove your parents wrong. It's all very admirable and blah, blah, blah, but what gives on the social scene? What did we do to offend?"

I started staring out the window around the quoted "make it" line.

Since I remain silent, he says, "Dude, I'm not trying to hassle you here. It's just, what's going on with you?"

"Just because I don't go to a party doesn't mean I'm not living life."

"No, but it's not just Jada's party. It's also Jenn's last month and Susi's last week. You're stepping back again. Why?"

I feel defensive, although he has every right to ask. He's my one friend from the old days I talk to on a regular basis, the only one who supported my decision back then. "Same reason I wanted out in the first place. I don't like to stand around and talk about a fashion show some girl attended, and I don't care about the party the weekend before out in the Hamptons. I don't care about that stuff, and they don't care about what I'm doing. I found myself reevaluating what I consider a good time, and I figured out it's not those people."

"Then what people are living up to your standards these days?"

"It's not like that, and you know it. You make it sound like I'm the snob."

"And you're not?"

"I don't owe anybody anything, Conner."

"You're right, you don't. As your friend, I'm curious as to what's going on. I see the changes in you. I saw the change before I left—the moodiness, the unenthusiastic attempts at parties, all of that. Now that I'm back, I see even more changes. Is it Justin?"

I scoff out loud. "Justin? Justin can be entertaining, but he's doing what I did at twenty-one. I'm not looking to revisit those days again. It's fun every once in a while, but my liver appreciates not having to work that hard."

Our breakfast is served, and everything seems to calm between us as we eat.

I know he's going to give me shit about this, but I still feel the need to say something. I brace myself for the taunts I know are coming and say, "I met a girl."

"I knew it! You are so transparent, man."

"I don't want to talk about her, though."

His fork goes clattering down onto the plate. "You say something like that then follow it up with no deets. That's BS and you know it."

"We're friends. That's all."

"Since when do you have girls in your life who are just friends?"

Shaking my head, annoyed, I try to justify my position. "I'm not that bad. I never was, despite what you and the rumormongers chose to believe."

"I've known you since you were five, Charlie. I've been in awe of your skills with the ladies since I was twelve. I also know that you're no angel."

"That, my friend, is in the past. That is part of the life I chose to leave behind, because whether it was at the end of the day or the morning after, it didn't change the feeling inside me that I didn't want to live like that."

Ignoring my answer, he redirects. "Back to this girl. She's different?"

I feel my chest ache, like I'm sharing a secret I shouldn't, but can't resist doing so all the same. I nod as I take a big bite of eggs.

He leans back in the booth and sips his coffee while watching me. "You can stick with that nonverbal reply shit, but just so you know, it says more than your words ever would." He laughs and puts a fifty-dollar bill on the table. "She must be some girl."

He lets me off the hook, and we finish our breakfast in lighter conversation.

Out on the sidewalk, we stand in silence a minute before he raises his hand to hail a cab. "You want a ride?"

"No, I'm heading home."

As the cab pulls to the curb, he asks, "So, this girl . . . when do I get to meet her?"

"That seems to be the question of the day." I shove my hands in my pockets and briefly wonder if I want to introduce her to him. He's my friend and one I trust, but I kind of like keeping Charlie all to myself. "Maybe soon. I don't know." I shrug.

He laughs as he climbs into the backseat of the taxi. "All right. Well, you let me know, and in the meantime, baseball, Sunday at my place. Two o'clock. If you're not busy with your girlfriend, that is."

"I'll be there."

When he shuts the door, I turn and walk down the street in the opposite direction. He's left me with a lot to think about—my old life and my new life—how much do I want them to overlap? I worry more about them colliding than overlapping. I don't know how to prevent that from happening, but even in one of the largest cities in the world, I know it will.

First, I need to concern myself with my family's dinner this weekend. I still can't bear the thought of going, but maybe bringing Charlie, bringing someone on my side, is what I need to do.

I lean against a brick wall and dial her number.

"Hello," she says. Her voice is sweet, happy.

"Hi."

"What are you up to today? Writing?"

"I'm heading home now to start. I just had breakfast with one of my friends. So, I was wondering about something, and you have every right to say no. I know it's last minute and not the most thrilling thing to do on a Saturday night—"

"Wow, with a setup like that, how can a girl resist? I'm on the edge of my seat here, wondering what you could possibly ask me that won't be the most thrilling thing to do on a Saturday night."

I laugh, because she makes these things easy, makes me comfortable. "It's a family dinner. I mean, a dinner . . . at my family's house."

"Oh." Her voice perks up.

"Well, it's really the reading of my aunt's will."

"Oh." She sounds more somber now.

"Dinner will follow." I close my eyes and shake my head. "I know how ridiculous this is. I shouldn't have ask—"

"Of course I'll go. I want to be there for you, if you want me."

"Yeah? Yeah, I want you there, which is why I asked. I'll understand if you think this is weird."

"Truthfully, Charlie, it is kind of weird, but I think we got over weird when we went to the funerals together. So I'm in. What time?"

"I'll pick you up around six."

"Hey, before we hang up, about our Saturday ritual, or what's become of our ritual as of late."

"Yes?"

"Well, since we're doing the family-reading-of-the-will thing that evening, I guess we'll be skipping said ritual, huh?" She sounds disappointed.

I'm disappointed by that thought, too. "What would you say if I still want to come over and, you know, continue the ritual?"

"I'd say I'd like that."

"Maybe I can bring my clothes over and get ready at your place then?"

"I think that would be a great plan."

"Good. Then I'll see you on Saturday at two."

"Are you free at noon?"

"Yep." I don't hesitate when it comes to spending more time with her. "I'll bring lunch."

"I'll make cupcakes."

"You pick the movie."

"I'll make the couch up."

"Make the couch up?"

She laughs. "Yeah, pillows and blankets."

"So, you're taking this napping thing to a whole new level?"

"I have a feeling we're going to need to energize ourselves for that family dinner."

I laugh out loud. "You may be right."

"So noon?"

"You've got a date."

"Hey, Charlie?"

"Yeah?"

"Thanks for calling."

"My pleasure."

Suddenly, Saturday night doesn't seem so bad after all. She'll be with me, by my side, and that makes this whole thing seem much more manageable. I'm especially looking forward to our afternoon nap and snuggling with her. I smile at the thought of a couch full of pillows and blankets, movies, cupcakes, and Charlie's pretty face.

Chapter 25

♀

"Come in," I shout from the kitchen. I know it's Charlie. I left the door unlocked since I would be busy in here baking.

He walks in, and I hear the deadbolt being reset. "You shouldn't leave your door unlocked."

"I unlocked it for you."

"Maybe you should just give me a key," he says, walking into the kitchenette and waggling his eyebrows.

"You're feeling bold today."

"Are my Saturday afternoon cuddles not enough to warrant a key?" He sets a bag down on the counter just as I take the cupcakes out of the oven.

"I have no response to that," I say sarcastically, waving my free hand in the air.

"Carrot cake?"

I look over my shoulder and smile. "Yes, how did you know?"

"It smells spicy and, I don't know, carrot-y."

"Carrot-y?" I ask as I dump the cupcakes down onto the counter. I place them one by one onto the rack to cool.

I feel his chest press against my back. "Can I have one now?"

"You don't want to wait until they're frosted?"

"I'll eat one when they're frosted, too."

I hand him a particularly perfect-looking one and watch as he takes a bite. It just never gets old watching him do this. The way he pulls the wrapper down on one side, and the way his eyes close as his teeth sink into the cake —it's quite the sight.

With his mouth full, he wraps his arm around my shoulder and pulls me closer. After a kiss to my temple and a nod of approval from him over my cupcakes, I laugh.

He makes me feel warm and . . . I don't let myself finish the thought. I step out from under his arm and reach into the bag of groceries. "What beer did you bring, Charlie?"

He watches me, amused by my reaction or lack thereof. He loves that he elicits these kinds of responses from me, and I don't want to make him smugger, so I don't give him the satisfaction. My stubborn side is coming out.

He comes closer again, reaches over me, and pulls the six-pack from the bag. "Guinness."

"A dark beer."

"A man's beer."

"Ha! Guinness has less alcohol than a Budweiser."

"What? No! You're dashing my beer dreams here."

"It's true, and sorry about the dream dashing." I giggle at his pouty face.

"No matter. You ready to step up your drinking game, Ms. Barrow?"

"I can drink you under the table, Mr. Adams."

He ruffles my hair and asks, "So, I take it the challenge has been accepted?"

"Getting sloshed isn't a great idea before the dinner tonight."

"Who says I'll be sloshed?"

I nod. I can see right through his false bravado. He's nervous about tonight for sure. I am, too, but I don't want to make this about me. Not tonight, when he needs me. "You know where the glasses are."

I adjust the blanket and the pillow before sitting down on the couch. "I was thinking we could watch a documentary today?"

With two beers in his hands, he sits down next to me and passes me mine. "Cheers."

"Cheers." I sip the dark Irish beer.

"A documentary? What's it about?"

"The slaughterhouses of Montana."

He shoots me a confused look and scratches his head. "Um. Okay."

"You don't want to learn what goes into our meat products?"

His laugh mocks as he stares at the television. "Not really. Sometimes the old saying 'ignorance is bliss' is very apropos. This might be one of those times."

"Come on. It will be educational."

"It's your turn to pick, so the slaughterhouses of Montana it is."

Charlie. Sandalwood, peppermint, cedar, and coriander. "Charlie," I murmur, inhaling all that he is.

Plush lips press to my forehead and retreat too soon.

My eyes fly open to be met with his sleepy greys, the filtered afternoon light making it dark in my living room. I relax into his chest again. I fell asleep in his arms, and he won't hear any complaints from me.

"You kissed me," I whisper, just because I want to acknowledge it happened. Maybe I say it more as a confirmation since I'm still tired, hoping it wasn't a dream.

"I couldn't resist with you mumbling my name and smiling at me like that." He chuckles lightly.

"Smiling? Your name?"

"You smile in your sleep, and yep, I distinctly heard you say Charlie. Oh! I guess you could have been saying your own name, but who does that?"

I smile, too, debating if I should tell him it's because of him. I don't, though. He gets all smuggy and bigheaded when I compliment him too much. Picturing him smirking makes me giggle.

"What's so funny?" he asks. His arms are still wrapped around me, holding me tight.

"Nothing. So, how far into the movie did I make it?"

"You didn't even make it to the twenty-minute mark. I thought you wanted to watch it?"

"I thought I did, too, until we got all comfy and lay down. I blame the beer. Did you watch it?"

"I'll never eat a burger again. Thanks for that."

"So it was educational is what you're saying?"

"Repeats for you—ignorance is bliss."

I laugh against his chest, not wanting to move from this position. His fingers weave into my hair, and then drag through the length of it. I close my eyes and enjoy the sensation, the comfort it gives me.

His voice is soft as he says, "You didn't drink me under the table, Char."

"I finished the one," I say, proud as a peacock. "Are you disappointed in me?"

"So disappointed. It's tragic actually."

I scoot back so I can see his face again. "You don't want to show up at your family's house drunk, do you?"

He seems to be considering this idea. "You're right. I should be on my toes, at least in the beginning."

"You're making me nervous."

"Don't worry, pretty girl, you're safe. You're not an Adams."

"I'm a Barrow."

He laughs louder this time and taps me on the nose. "Yes, you most certainly are a Barrow."

I glance over my shoulder to see the time. "It's four. I should shower."

"Good. I didn't want to have to say anything. Ugh! That hurt. You've got bony knuckles."

"Strong ones, too." I roll all of the way off the couch, shaking the pain away from my hand from hitting him so hard, and land on my feet. "Make yourself at home." I walk toward the bedroom, leaving him there to relax.

He stretches out his legs while putting his hands behind his head. "Already am."

For some reason, I feel weird getting undressed with Charlie in the next room. Memories of that drunken night fill my thoughts and the embarrassment returns. A warm feeling overcomes my mortification, and I smile stupidly to myself, remembering how he touched me, how he felt under my hands, and that look. I close my eyes and can see that look—the one that made me feel perfect and sexy and pretty all at once.

He has the ability to make everyone feel special. It's a gift, really, but I don't mention it to him because I need to keep his ego in check. I see the way women look at him when we're out together. I also see how men compare themselves to him and stand a little straighter, as if that builds their own self-esteem.

Taking my shower, I feel hyperaware that he's in the next room and I hurry. For a split second, though, I consider inviting him to join me. But that's crazy thinking, because after giving my grand confession a second thought, I decided against telling him. I don't want to lose what we have, what we are together. We're just friends. That's all. Friends. Who cares that he frosts and compliments me? Who cares if I haven't been able to get his lower back dimples out of my head since I spied them at his apartment when his shirt rode up and his jeans hung down? Who cares, right?

"Right."

I walk into my room after drying off with a fluffy towel. I wrap another one turban-style around my head to keep my hair from dripping on the floor. There's a knock on the door as I'm digging through my drawer for undies. I jump, startled, a squeal escaping.

"Charlie?" he asks from the other side of the door.

"Yes?" I call, trying to sound normal and not like some paranoid girl in a horror movie.

"Can I use your bathroom?"

Scrambling over to the closet, I grab my robe and speak too soon. "Ummm, all right. Jus—"

The door opens, and our eyes meet. It all happens so fast. His eyes dip down, taking me in. My arms fly to cover my body, knees knock together, one arm goes over my breasts, and the other hand covers my girly parts. A scream escapes.

His gaze drops to the ground as a hand goes to shield his eyes, and he retreats backward. "I'm sorry. I thought I heard you say it was all right."

The door shuts, but I'm frozen in place.

"Charlie?" he asks, tapping on the door. "Are you okay?"

I don't know what to feel. I'm swarmed by emotions. "Hold on." I need another few seconds to put my robe on. "One minute." I grab sweatpants and a sweatshirt and pull those on over the robe. Am I dressed enough to hide the mortification I feel right now? *No.* I reach down and pull on my tall Uggs. Now I'm ready. "It's safe now. You can come in."

I rush to the far wall, farthest from the bathroom, and wait.

"Are you sure?"

The man has seen me naked, but now we're just friends so things are different . . . for now. "Yes."

"Okay, I'm coming in." The doorknob turns slowly before he pushes the door open. He peeks inside before walking all the way in. "I'm sorry. You all right?" he asks, but can't seem to look in my direction.

"Yeah, that was awkward."

"Huh." That's all he says before walking into the bathroom and closing the door.

Huh? What is "huh" supposed to mean?

"I'm done in here. I'm coming into the bedroom now."

"Okay, this is getting ridiculous. I'm dressed."

When he looks up, he looks relieved before his expression turns confused. "Why are you way over there? And why so many clothes?"

I raise my chin into the air defensively. "I didn't want to be caught off-guard again."

He stops with the doorknob in his hand. "Why are you way over there then?"

I try to play it off by shrugging and moving toward the bed casually while debating if I should lounge on it instead. I choose to sit like I'm fine, like him seeing me naked again is no big deal.

He watches me before heading out of the room in silence. I think he sees right through my act.

Just after five, I go into the living room and sit on the couch next to him.

I've been doing my hair in the next room, but I kind of missed him. Leaning into his side, I feel better just being near him. He maneuvers his arm over my shoulders, and we watch television for a few minutes.

"You can use my shower now if you'd like." I offer without taking my eyes off the television.

"You sure?"

"Positive. Hey, Charlie?"

"Mmhm?"

"Are you ever gonna look at me again?"

He laughs, which makes me laugh, and it feels so damn good to let the earlier tension out like this.

Standing to walk toward the bedroom door, he stops to say, "To tell the truth, I can't take my eyes off you."

My heart soars, and everything feels normal again. He always makes me feel so good with his sweet words. I wish I could do the same for him, but lacking time and that ability these days, instead I ask, "Do you mind if I put on my makeup while you shower?"

"No, of course not."

When he steps into the shower, he lets me know that it's safe to come into the bathroom.

I've done my eyeliner by the time he speaks. "I kind of owe you a peep show now, don't I?"

"I've think we've shared enough already."

He chuckles. "Yeah, maybe."

I move into the kitchen with my makeup bag and finish applying it in there so he can have the privacy of the bedroom to get ready. After I finish, all I'll need to do is slip my dress and shoes on, and we can leave.

When Charlie opens the door and walks out, my jaw drops. *Damn!*

"I'll take that face as a sign of approval. I look appropriate for the night's festivities?"

My throat is dry, so I swallow repeatedly to wet it before speaking. "Yeah, guess it'll have to do," I say, aiming for nonchalance.

I've seen him in a suit before, a couple of times, once at the funeral and again at the club. He looked good both times, but my mind was focused on other things. Tonight, though, with him dressed like this, he receives my full attention. He's wearing a fitted navy blue suit with white shirt and black tie, and he's killing me with his gorgeousness.

One side of his mouth quirks up in tandem with an eyebrow. "Okay, glad it's barely acceptable." He teases.

"I didn't mean it that way," I say. I then laugh as I pat him on the chest and walk back into the bedroom. "You look good, Charlie. There! You happy?"

"Sure am."

Shutting the door behind me, I make my way to the closet and pull my dress from the hanger. Stylish and fitted, professional, yet perfect for a cocktail party, I drop my emerald green dress on over my head, and then step into my favorite heels.

Moving to stand in front of the full-length mirror, I tug at the zipper on the back of my dress. I suck in my stomach and tug a little harder. "Huh!" It feels snugger than usual. It's got to be that heavy beer. Maybe that's why I'm struggling with it. After many more tries, my arm hurts from being twisted back, so I open the door to my last resort—Charlie. "Do you mind helping me with this zipper?"

"Sure." He stands and moves behind me. "Lift your hair. I don't want it to get snagged."

As the zipper rides up my back, I can feel his breath and knuckles sliding with it, lingering a bit as he goes. He releases the pull, and the palm of his hand slides to my shoulder, giving me a gentle squeeze. "You're all zipped up."

"Thank you." I turn for him. "How do I look?"

With a playful smirk, he replies, "It'll do."

I snort, then laugh because I snorted, covering my nose and mouth with my hand. Yeah, I deserved that response.

I grab my clutch and toss in my lipstick, ID, keys, and my phone. "You ready to hit this party?"

"As much as I can be."

We don't talk on the way down to the street. I can tell he's thinking of the what-might-happens, the what-ifs, and every other possible scenario to prepare himself. I take his hand and try to reassure him, hoping it helps. "It'll be all right, and if it's not, we'll leave. You and I are a team here."

I see a black Town Car parked out front, and he says, "I ordered a car."

The chauffeur holds the door open for me as we approach. "At least we can get sloshed like we talked about earlier, since we don't have to drive."

That brings a smile to his face.

I start to duck down to scoot into the car, but he stops me. "Charlie, wait."

Standing back up, he takes both of my hands in his. "You look really beautiful."

Putting a hand on my hip, I tilt my head to the side. "There you go being all charming again." His heart is pounding under my hand that now rests on his chest. Dropping my head in surprise, I watch how my hand lies over his heart and like how it looks there even more.

My eyes lift to meet his again, and for one brief second, I think he's going to kiss me.

If we were a normal couple, I know he would. But we aren't. He comes from Jim's world, and as much as I want to trust the differences between them, I can't help but remember the similarity of their backgrounds. The Town Car is just another reminder of that. I'm probably reading too much into this moment. It's just us all dressed up and the anticipation and tension of the unknown. It's the situation that makes us feel this close and makes us rely on each other like we do, like we have from the beginning. My mind races with thoughts of him and me, us, once lovers, now friends. It's all so confusing.

One thing I definitely know is that if he did kiss me, I would welcome it and kiss him back with passion. This would be me, being a romantic, and him, getting caught up in a moment. That's all.

We're just friends on the verge of something more. Two people who bonded from a bizarre situation. Although, I often wonder if we'd met under different circumstances, like on the street or in a bookstore, or if we'd hooked up that first night at the club, if we'd be where we are now. I already know the answer to that. We wouldn't. We'd be more already. We'd be a couple who are about to kiss.

Chapter 26

♂

Rubbing my thumb back and forth over my bottom lip, I continue to stare out the car window. I've been doing this for the last twenty minutes, and Charlie lets me be. She's sitting next to me looking out her window, giving me the time, the quiet she must know I need.

Tension is building, so I break the silence. "This doesn't have to be overly dramatic. It's my family, right? I mean, I love them. They love me. We're family."

Looking at me, the truth reflects back, but she remains silent, patient.

"My family." I don't know why I repeat this, but I do.

Her hand covers mine, and she agrees. "Family."

The next twenty minutes go by faster than I'd like. I felt like I had covered every angle of this dinner, played each scenario out in my head, but now I'm not so sure. I feel my nerves just under my skin itching to get out. I don't want to worry Charlie, though. It's my family. This shouldn't be a big deal. I take a deep breath, closing my eyes, and lean back against the seat.

Warmth covers my left side as she scoots next to me, resting her head on my shoulder, and says, "We're a team, okay?"

"Yeah, we're a team."

S.L. Scott

It's evening on a Saturday, so the drive to Bedford doesn't take long. We pass through the small hamlet and by the historic oak and the shops I grew up visiting almost every weekend when I was too young to stay in the city on my own.

Charlie sits up and moves toward the window again. I can see her taking it all in—the postcard beauty of the landscape, the quaint and historic downtown area, the look of money in the cars along the street and the people walking around. Her eyes are wide, the streetlamps reflecting in them as we drive underneath.

"It's visually idyllic."

She turns to look at me. "Very much."

Questions fill her eyes, and I hear them in her tone. I respond without being asked. "I didn't know the rest of the world existed. I grew up going to private schools in the city, returning to an apartment that took up an entire floor in one of the best neighborhoods of Manhattan. We'd come here on the weekends. Other family members or friends of my parents would visit." I smile at the memory. "It was always a full house filled with laughter."

I stop to pick some lint off my pants, a good momentary distraction. Those are good memories, and I haven't thought about them in years. I don't understand the sentimental feeling that's come over me.

"What happened, Charlie? Tell me." Her hand rests on top of mine again.

I turn my hand palm side up under hers and lace our fingers together.

"I grew up."

I hear a breath of disappointment escape her, and she turns back toward the window. When she looks at me again, we're pulling into the drive. I guess she realizes our time for this kind of privacy is ending.

"One day, Charlie Adams, I hope you trust me enough to let me in here," she says, tapping my temple, "and here." She places her hand flat over my heart.

I take that hand and cover it with mine. "You already are in here."

She slowly slides her hand up and rests it on my cheek. "You say the sweetest things."

The door swings open, startling us both right out of our moment, and the valet greets me. "Welcome home, Mr. Adams."

"Thank you," I reply, stepping out and offering Charlie a hand out of the vehicle.

As the car pulls away, I remain standing on the gravel driveway, staring at the mansion before me. I'm still holding her hand for no other reason than I feel the need to be close to her right now.

She tugs gently and says, "Come on. Let's go get this over with. I have four more Guinness and eleven cupcakes with our names on them at home."

I notice how she refers to her apartment as if it's both of ours, a space we share. It is when I think about it. I love any time I get to spend with her, but our Saturday afternoons mean everything to me.

We walk forward, and as the front door opens, I release her hand. I don't want to give my family any ammo. It will be hard enough that's she here witnessing my dysfunctional family first hand, so I don't want their attentions on her. She's here for me, not for their entertainment.

Hearing the clacking of her heels on the polished marble floors before I even lay eyes on her, my mother rounds the corner, arms outreached with that all-too-familiar party smile firmly in place. "Charles," she says, "I'm so glad you're here."

She opens her arms to me, and I step into her embrace, returning the hug. The hugs she gave me when she arrived home from her many trips were always my favorite thing growing up. It felt like she loved me when she embraced me that tight. "Mother, it's good to see you."

She steps back and admires me. "You're looking healthy, happy these days." With her hands still on me, she faces Charlie. "Welcome to our home. I'm happy you could join us tonight." She sounds sincere. I'll have to stay on my toes tonight.

"Charlie, you remember my mother, Emeline Adams."

"Yes, it's good to see you again, and thank you for having me. Your home is stunning."

"Well, maybe Charles can show you the rest of it while we wait for the other members of the family to arrive. What do you say, Charles?"

A server walks by with a tray of champagne, and all three of us accept a glass. "Yes, of course. You'll call us when dinner is ready to be served?"

"Yes, yes. Now run along. I've got some last-minute details to attend to."

"We should start upstairs," I say, directing Charlie to join me.

"Yes, yes, we should run along upstairs."

I'm halfway up the stairs when she says this. I turn around, crossing my arms over my chest. "Did you just mock my mother, Charlotte?"

She cocks her head to the side with a smirk and replies, "Yep, I sure did, Charles."

"I knew there was a reason we were friends." I laugh and continue up the stairs.

I give her the short tour and take her straight to my room since it's mainly guest bedrooms up here. It's weird facing the door to my past. I don't know what to expect as I stand there with my hand on the doorknob. I don't know if my parents changed it or if it's the same. So when I open the door, I'm surprised to see it just how I left it. It's a little cleaner than before, but my stuff is all here.

Charlie follows me in and shuts the door behind us, though I'm not sure why. It feels forbidden to do so, and yet necessary, just like in high school, to give me peace of mind.

"I like it," she says, walking across the room to the window and peeking out. "The gardens are pretty." She lets the drapes slide through her fingers as she walks away to explore the entertainment center. "I think this room is larger than my entire apartment."

I smile, not because it is a strange thought that a kid had a bedroom larger than an adult's home, but more that I like having her in here around my stuff.

"You have a lot of movies," she notes.

"I spent much of my teenage years holed up in here listening to music, watching movies, or playing video games." I join her and slide one of the cabinet doors open to reveal five gaming consoles and at least three hundred games.

"Wow! My friends would've loved you in high school." She works her way around the couch and to the bed. "A king-sized bed?" She laughs. "Guess I shouldn't be so surprised, considering the house I'm standing in." She sits on the bed, resting her back against the headboard, and crosses her ankles. "You were one spoiled kid, Charles. What happened?"

"Enough with the Charles bit. I hate that name."

"But you like Charlie." Not a question, but a keen observation on her part.

"Yes. It feels more me."

"So what happened, rich kid? How did you turn out so level-headed and unpretentious?"

"That's a long and boring story."

"Maybe to you, but I want to know more about the man who shares my couch every Saturday and frosts cupcakes and gets paid to write about what he sees in the world."

I sit on the other side of the bed, mimicking her position, but then she does something unexpected. She scoots down the bed and rolls onto her stomach, kicking her expensive-shoe-clad feet into the air and propping her chin on her hands.

"Tell me everything," she says. "I want to know who the real Charlie Adams is."

She looks like a schoolgirl waiting for the latest gossip, and yet, the way she's dressed and seeing her on my bed, she's a fantasy come to life. I love that she doesn't care if her dress gets wrinkled or her hair mussed up. It's exactly those things that draw me to her time and time again. It's those things that made me want to leave this privileged life. No girl I knew growing up would risk their appearance to learn more about me.

"My life is not that interesting. Trust me on this. I was living one way, and after a few years . . ." I shrug, looking around this old room. "I don't know. I just felt it was time to grow up. The partying, the people, the whole life I was living seemed pointless. There was no value in it. At the end of the day, I wasn't anywhere closer to being who I wanted to be. I found myself drinking half a bottle of Grey Goose just to get into the mood to hang out with my friends or go out. I was sloppy and careless. But one day in college, everything seemed to click into place in my head." I look back into her eyes. "You've heard all of this. Isn't this boring?"

"Never. Tell me more."

"Well, I realized I'm the only one who can make my life what I want it to be. I would never have to achieve more than a diploma to take over the family business one day. That was in the bag. I wouldn't have to make an effort for that. It would be given to me."

She sits up, sliding her legs to the side of her body. "Are you who you want to be now?"

I nod. "Yes. I'm happy with my decisions. A lot of the people from my past didn't understand and didn't respect my choices, so I left them behind. My parents cut me off until I came to my senses."

She laughs. "And have you?"

"I came to my senses years ago, but they don't see it that way. I haven't seen a dime of their money in six years."

"They'd rather you continue down that path and be unhappy rather than make a change for your well-being? Sounds destructive." She takes a deep breath and exhales with a sigh. "Well, I, for one, am glad you are who you are now. I don't think I would've liked Charles too much." She punches my arm lightly. "But I like Charlie a lot."

"Well, that makes it all worthwhile, then." We hold eye contact, a silent longing exchanged before she breaks it by looking away.

As she slips off the bed, she straightens the skirt of her dress. "We should go back downstairs. This house is so large, I'm sure we've missed the dinner bell by now."

"Your sarcasm could be considered a talent."

She curtsies then walks to the door. "You know it's all just one big cover for my insecurities."

"You've got nothing to be insecure about. You're one in a million, kid." I nudge her with my elbow as we walk back into the hall. I shut the door behind me and say, "Hey, I really do appreciate you being here. Thank you."

"You don't have to say that. I'm glad I got to see this, your room, a part of your old Charles life. So, stop thanking me so much. You're starting to make me all nervous again."

"Yeah, we wouldn't want that. Because when you're nervous, you start talking really fast and sometimes you don't make sense, but if we're lucky, we kind of get the point of the rambling. So yeah, we wouldn't want to make you nervous before dinner with the Adams family."

She narrows her eyes at me, and I can almost see the steam billowing from her ears. I like her feisty. When she's feisty and riled up, she's in top form. And that's what I need her to be in tonight—top form.

As we walk down the stairs, she turns to me and asks, "So is everyone in your family this humorous?"

"No, you just got lucky with me."

She faces forward and continues walking, but I see the small smile on her lips and hear her mutter, "I most definitely did."

Chapter 27

♀

He's been gone too long.

Charlie was summoned by a butler into a room almost forty-five minutes ago. The daunting black doors were promptly closed behind him. They're large and solid and there's no doubt that you stay out when they're closed. After Charlie went through those doors, I was led into a conservatory off the main living room.

Twenty minutes later, two others arrived. I suspect they are related to someone or everyone in the other room where the will is being read, but it would be inappropriate to ask what that relationship is. The man and woman are in their thirties, maybe mid-thirties, and dressed in designer suits. I think they might be related to each other because of their light brown hair and the shape of their eyes.

They smile when they see me looking at them, but it feels false, almost more a tactic to gauge me. I shift in my seat. "Hello," I say with a small smile.

They don't return the gesture, but the woman says, "You're here with Charles."

It's more of a statement than a question. I decide to answer anyway. "Yes." I don't see what about me indicates that I'm with Charlie, but I guess it's obvious to them.

The man stands from the sofa and walks over to the tray of martinis that were set out for us. "Would you like a drink?" He glances at the woman first, but then his eyes land on me.

"Yes. Thank you." I'm unraveling in this situation. It feels too familiar, too invasive, too much like the life I once lived with Jim. Everything is so perfectly arranged, including the people in this room.

The man hands me the glass. I sip, hoping to stave off the rising nerves inside. He sits down next to me, the loveseat not providing much room for avoidance.

"I'm Donald. That's Katherine." He holds his hand out after the introduction.

When I shake it, his palm is sweaty. He looks me over. "We're Charlie's cousins. Our mother is his mother's sister."

"Nice to meet you." That explains the sweating hand. They're anxious to find out what their mom was left from Grace. "I'm sorry for your loss. Your great-aunt sounds like she was a wonderful woman."

"That sounds like Charlie. She was a bit crazy for my tastes, hence having to wait on our inheritance until the last Saturday in July. She never made any sense." He laughs, eyeing his sister. "I guess crazy can be loveable when money's involved."

His words, his demeanor, and his sister don't bode well with me. His mocking tone is too sharp for kindness or joking, it borders closer to cruel. I don't like his assumptions of Charlie, and my defenses go up.

I look toward the entrance to the room, hoping to see Charlie walking through it, but he isn't there. Looking down at my watch, I realize it may be a while longer, though it already feels like forever.

"Today was her birthday. She wanted us to celebrate her death on her birthday." Katherine speaks up with distaste in her tone. "Charles always had a penchant for the wounded, whether it be physical or mental illness." She eyes me as if she's trying to figure out the ailment Charlie must be trying to heal in me.

I want to say they have him all wrong, to defend him against their nasty accusations, but when I think about their words, they're right. If I go by the meaning of the words instead of the tone they're said in, they are absolutely right about Charlie—he has a heart where theirs is lacking. They don't understand his motives, because they are, like so many I've met in their class of society, cold and selfish. Like the many times I reasoned out some sort of justification with Jim's family, it all came back to the same thing. They don't know any better. They live in a closed-off world where their reality is just that—*theirs*.

My reality may be different and may feel more tangible to me, but to them, it's foreign. So I brush their comments under the rug of judgment in my mind and try to give them the benefit of the doubt. From experience, I know I can blame their upbringing more than them. They are victims of their surroundings.

Katherine stands and pours herself a drink. After two long sips, she turns to face us. Her expression is annoyed as she rants. "We should be in there. We have as much right as Charles to be in there, damn it! Where the hell is Liz? If she were here, we'd be in that room knowing what the hell is going on."

"She's coming for dinner. She didn't want to waste her precious time waiting around with us," Donald replies. His tone is flat, and he seems disinterested in the topic of Liz. Turning to me, he must see what I'm thinking, because he explains the relationship. "Liz is our sister."

"She also has a very short fuse for bullshit, which is why she's not here," Katherine says. "This is so unnerving. What do you think we inherited, Donald?"

She looks at him as if the rest of her life is determined by his answer. "I have no idea how that woman's mind worked."

She looks to me, but I seem to heighten her annoyance, so she turns away and stares through the glass out into the darkness

I sit there almost revolted by the venom they spew in connection with Grace. The Grace I've been told about was nothing less than wonderful. I understand that every story has two sides, or maybe more, but I don't understand them. I know they are trying to send me a not-so-subtle message about Charlie. It's like they are saying one thing, but beneath the surface of the words lays a hostility that predates tonight. Unlike Charlie and his feelings toward his family, they seem to hate each other, and with that recognition, my heart hurts for him.

"Charlie." I turn toward my name and see Charlie standing at the door. My name slips from his mouth again, but he's eyeing his cousins, the distrust is evident. "It's time for dinner." He stretches his arm out, offering me his hand.

The three of us rise, and Donald asks, "Your name is Charlie?"

I nod, realizing I never introduced myself. The discomfort of the situation distracted me from proper etiquette.

I take Charlie's hand, and he tucks me against his side, moving me away from them. "Sorry that took so long," he whispers.

"It's all right. I was fine."

"I didn't know they were here, or I wouldn't have left you."

I stop and look up at him. "I'm okay. Are you?"

He pulls me quickly into a small corridor off the main entryway. While looking into my eyes with determination, he takes hold of my upper arms.

"Dinner might be intense. We can leave if you want." His voice is low and he glances over my shoulder quickly before returning to me.

"And you're worried? Should I be?"

His hands drop to his side, and he takes a deep breath, leaning against the wall. "Things didn't go how we thought they would. I just want you to be aware that dinner might be strained if we stay."

"Do you want to stay?" When all I want is to be here for him, to make sure he's all right, he's focused and worried about me.

"No, but I promised my mother that I would."

"And you'd break that promise?"

"Well, I think it might be awkward for an outsider to sit through this."

"I'm fine, Charlie. I don't want you to break your promise for me. And I don't want to insult your mother." I have to say that he's making me nervous. "Can we sit near each other?"

"Yes, I'll make sure we do."

He seems to relax once we step back out into the bright foyer. He looks down the short hall toward the room where the other eight members of his family are filing in. Donald and Katherine pass us, but not without giving us a curious once-over.

When we enter the dining room, the first thing I notice are the place settings with name cards. *Assigned seats.* We move closer to scope out the arrangement. Charlie is seated next to his mother at one end, and I'm farther down the other side of the table. Our eyes meet. He quickly grabs his name card and walks down to the chair across from me. He picks up that name card and says, "Katherine, you're sitting down there now."

She huffs in frustration. "And I was so looking forward to the stimulating conversation I was going to have with your friend." Her sarcasm is overstated as she walks to the other seat he left for her. Thanks to Charlie, I've dodged a bullet.

We sit down as the wine glasses are filled by two different servers working the room. I look up and see Charlie watching me. Most of the strangeness of this dinner fades away when he smiles. I smile back, moving my foot forward until my shoe is against his. That's when I notice his hand move to the top of the table and start to slide toward me, but he stops himself. A flash of disappointment covers his expression before being covered by a more aware one. Too many witnesses, too many others to judge us—to try to stuff us into some category that doesn't fit what we are or what we mean to each other.

The atmosphere is as tense as he warned me, but with each course that's served, it turns to more lighthearted talk of familial inside jokes. They tease Charles Sr. His dad seems likeable, even jovial tonight, despite whatever they were told in the other room. Or maybe he got what he wanted from Grace, which allows him the ability to enjoy dinner.

After his dad tells a boisterous joke, the group laughs, and I see that maybe they don't hate each other. Maybe it's possible for them to feel something real for each other.

I lean toward Charlie and ask, "I didn't know you were a junior?" The little fact is another key piece to the puzzle that is him.

He lets out a small laugh and opens his mouth to speak, but is interrupted by a woman standing at the door. "Charlie's not a junior. He's a fifth. Charles the Fifth. So pretentious."

The room falls silent as we all turn to watch the pretty brunette in the blood-red strapless dress enter the room without reservation or invitation. She walks confidently to the empty seat next to Charlie and sits down. Holding her glass in the air for wine service, she asks, "We're still talking to each other, so the old bat didn't screw us in the end?"

Donald says, "It's not good news, Liz, but the wine is plentiful."

So this is Liz. From Donald's comment, I surmise that they aren't happy with the will, but are happy to drink away the bad of the night.

She looks straight at me and takes a sip from her filled crystal goblet. "And who are you?"

"This is Charlie, Charles's date." His mother interjects before I have a chance.

I look down at Emeline, surprised to hear from her. When I turn back to Liz, her eyes have never left me. She's staring at me, and for a brief second as we watch each other, I feel like I've seen or met her before. There's something so familiar about her brown eyes.

She turns her attention to Charlie. "I think this is the first time you've brought a date to dinner since you discovered what a fucked-up family you have. And the girl you bring shares your name. That must make for some interesting pillow talk."

"Don't start, Liz." His tone cautions.

She glares at him a moment longer then focuses on the food that's been placed in front of her.

Charlie's mother tries to lighten the mood by talking about the floral show she's co-chairing next month, but no one seems interested in her news. They've disengaged themselves, from a family laughing, to somber individuals again as the tension returns.

I eat in silence, concentrating on my food while praying that this painful dinner comes to an end soon. I look up once, and my eyes lock on

Charlie's. I can see how much he wants to leave. Every word that he can't say aloud is visible in the grey of his eyes. More grey than blue with worry.

I move my foot forward again to bump his in an offer of comfort.

"Ow, you kicked me!" Liz looks at me, and when she sees my look of horror, she asks, "Were you trying to play footsy with my cousin?" She bursts out laughing.

"Enough!" Charlie says under his breath.

She starts laughing harder, and her dessertspoon drops and clangs against the plate, garnering everyone's attention. "Oh my God, footsy! That is so pedestrian."

Although I should be embarrassed, I'm not. Something else starts to overcome me. Watching her with her head tossed back and her dark wavy hair falling down her back behind her bare shoulders, everything clicks into place.

Jim.

Naked.

Long brown hair.

It's her.

Liz.

The other woman.

Chapter 28

♀

I don't even know if I'm breathing at this point, too stunned to notice. My thoughts are clouded, except for the realization that Liz is the woman I caught in bed with Jim. She is the one who had sex with my fiancé. She is the one who shattered my world and caused a hole in my heart the size of the Grand Canyon. I stand abruptly, the crystal glasses clinking together when my legs hit the edge of the table. My napkin falls to the ground as I stare at her in disbelief.

"*Charlie?* Are you all right?" I see Charlie in my peripheral vision, but I can't take my eyes off *her* to respond.

"What? What are you staring at?" Liz asks. The anger in her voice is evident.

I don't care about her anger. I can't. I'm too focused on my own. "You slept with my fiancé. You! You—" My tears cut off my words, choking me.

I feel the chair disappear from behind my legs then an arm wraps around me. Warm. Strong. Charlie. "Come on."

I want to throw something, anything I can get my hands on, anything that will take the pain and betrayal away in the moment. But I'm rushed out of the room.

Right before the front door closes, I hear her yell, "Wait! Jim's Charlie?"

Charlie shouts for the valet. "Get the car!"

Irrational thoughts darken my mind, and I can't wait for the car. I start to run down the rounded driveway, but gravel and high heels don't mix, and I stumble. I don't fall, catching and steadying myself.

"Charlie, don't," he calls behind me.

I can hear the crunch of the rocks under his shoes as he rushes to catch me, running to a halt in front of me. "Stop! You can't run back to Manhattan. The car is coming."

"No." I beg through tears. "I can't be here. I can't be near that house or *her*." My resolve weakens as he grabs my arms by the wrists to still me. "Please, Charlie. Let me go. I can't do this, not here where she can see, and not in front of you."

The car pulls beside us, and the driver hops out and opens the door.

Charlie's eyes reveal sympathy, and I drop my head in shame, knowing there's no other way for me to get out of here in one piece. My heart is shattered all over again, and now I'm humiliated that Charlie has to witness my breakdown. He pulls me to the car and helps me in. I'm a ragdoll, helpless and vulnerable, all my strength left in that dining room, just as I was so long ago when I first found Jim with Liz in our bed that rainy fall day, an image that has haunted my days and nights.

I hear Charlie say something to the driver who takes off running toward the house. He slides in next to me and pulls my limp body onto his lap. I'm weak, drowning in the memory.

I let Charlie hold me, needing the closeness. I'm ashamed, because he's realized that I was dumped for someone from Jim's world. There was someone who was better than me—someone made from the same cloth as him, and my ex-fiancé chose her over me. I don't fit into Jim and Charlie's world, and I never will. I'm not of their kind, not from elite breeding, or the socialite type. I'm just a Barrow from the suburbs of Chicago.

The driver returns, handing Charlie my clutch then drives us away from the Adams's mansion and away from her. As we are driven back through the center of the quaint town, I realize it's all an illusion. Charlie warned me. He said it was visually idyllic, and it is—all surface and no depth. They put on a good show for the outside world, but in my eyes, I'd rather see the ugly truth so I know what I'm getting into. This false world of happiness hides the shallow thoughts of a society that still idolizes itself above all else.

Although I knew Jim was from this world, he had convinced me, at one time, that he was different, he wasn't like them in that way. I believed he wasn't when he was with me, but once he returned to this culture that demanded his time and attention, he forgot what we had shared—real emotions were covered in a charade of perfection, much like this town.

I close my eyes against Charlie's chest. He hasn't spoken since we left, because either he knows me well enough not to, or he doesn't know what to say. I'm not sure, but I appreciate the silence all the same. Tonight, I've finally grasped how much Charlie is like Jim. Not in looks or personality, but they both escaped this superficial society only to be dragged back.

I rub my hand along his lapel and breathe him in. The realization that Charlie isn't mine to keep hurts, and even more because I was starting to open up, I was finally ready to let him in. I came tonight ready to show my heart and expose my true feelings, but I was kidding myself to think we could be more than friends. And now, we won't even be that. Maybe not today, but eventually, he will go back, just like Jim did. He will succumb to the pressure, and choose someone more worthy of his status and leave me behind.

I inhale him again, rubbing my hand over his chest, wanting to memorize his scent, to memorize him. Because one day, sooner than later, I won't get to do this again. Like Donald and Katherine, and the rest of his family, I become selfish for the remaining thirty minutes of the ride.

My thoughts dwell in the events of the night. I embarrassed him in front of his family. I revealed myself as the kind of girl someone cheats on and leaves for one of their own, someone better. I've caused a rift that Charlie will have to repair. That he will choose to repair because they are his family. I'm just the girl he bonded to in a weak moment at a funeral and pitied at another.

I adjust on his lap as his arms tighten around me. The sniffling and tears have stopped, but my throat is still tight with remorse, and jolts of pain shoot from my heart. Wrapping my arms around his shoulders, I pull myself closer to him, resting my forehead against his neck. I can't look up. I refuse to meet his eyes. I'll break down if I do, and I must be strong right now.

Greedily nuzzling against his skin, I leave one small kiss there, taking advantage of the moment, because once I'm dropped off, we're done. This friendship that has become a necessity to me, his presence in my life which has become equally expected and wanted, will be over. In retrospect, I knew about his background and wanted to believe we could be different. We can't, though, and without him in my life, the memories of us will weigh heavy on my heart.

I didn't know I'd be confronted with the feelings I tried so hard to bury deep down inside. But tonight, because of Liz, memories from the breakup with Jim resurface, wrapping around my neck and strangling the life from me.

The coffee cup was still full even though I ordered it hours earlier. I was too upset to drink it, which was strange, because I bought it thinking it would comfort me, warm my insides. The images of him and her swallowed my thoughts, making my heart ache. I remained at that table for two hours before Jim walked in and sat down across from me.

"Charlie, I'm sorry," Jim said. He reached across the table and took my hand in his, giving it a tight squeeze.

I didn't move mine, though I should have.

He looked out the window and watched as people passed. I watched him.

I watched his mouth as he said, "We should take some time apart." When he looked back at me, I didn't reply. I didn't argue. I didn't throw a fit or rant or scream or anything. I was too stunned to react properly, or even improperly, at the time. I was numb.

I looked at him as he stood up and placed a five-dollar bill down on the table to cover the coffee and walked out. The shock of what happened, of my new reality, would hit me later that night when I climbed into a foreign bed at a random hotel. The embarrassing, tearful good-bye followed the next day. I wanted to be strong, but couldn't as I packed my things and left. The only bit of solace I found was that I saw him wipe his eyes when he thought I wasn't looking.

As the memory fades, the pain still lingers, but Charlie is my savior, my life preserver in the back of this car keeping me afloat in a pool of heavy emotions and unwelcome thoughts. And yet, I'll let go. I'll give him up to try and swim again, because I know that, like Jim, Charlie will be lured back. They will get him away from me because I don't support their values, or lack thereof.

Being from Chicago is not respectable enough in their eyes, and I grew tired of this game years ago after playing it the best I could. I still lost in the end no matter what I did or said, or sacrificed, including myself.

The car pulls up to the curb in front of my apartment building and parks. We get out, and I steel myself. This is it. This is where I end it, end us.

The talk is quick, but not painless.

"No," he protests, because he's a good man. "This is not the right decision. I don't see things like that at all."

I restrain my tears, knowing they'll fall as soon as I'm inside. "Why fight to make this happen?" I wave between us. "*This* is not anything. If we end this, this is something that won't plague you a year from now or embarrass you when you attend a family event, because it's not real. This is a stage in your life when you needed someone there. Someone not from this place. *A phase.* That's all. We would have survived on our . . ." I don't bother finishing, because even I don't believe we would be as strong as we are if the other hadn't been there. But I know this is the right thing to do. This is better for him than I could ever be. Jim taught me that.

He stands up straight and walks toward me. I back away, causing a shift in his eyes; the pain is evident from my purposeful move. "You don't get to end this all on your own. You can't. I'm in here more than you're admitting to yourself," he says, pointing to his chest since I'm out of reach.

He's right, of course, but I'm more stubborn than he is.

Looking to my left, I see the strange emptiness of the sidewalk. No one is around, and I feel fortunate to not have witnesses to my cruelty. Because the one thing I need to be right now is strong, and that means saying something that will make him see the light, something that will end us once and for all. I could never hurt him publicly like that. I wouldn't. So I'm grateful the sidewalk is desolate.

"Go, Charlie! Leave me alone," I say, raising my voice. "Let me be. She's your cousin. You're her family. One thing I've learned is that no matter how far you escape, you will always be like them. I will never be able to trust you, just like I couldn't trust Jim."

His anger flares. "I'm nothing like him! You know I'm not. You don't believe what you're saying. You're lying to yourself to save your heart the trouble. You're lying to yourself as an excuse to stay holed up in that apartment feeling victimized by a rich kid you had the misfortune of falling in love with. He was never who you thought he was. He was always that person, Charlie! You were just too blind or too in love to see it."

He tentatively steps closer again. This time I remain, letting his words pierce me without a fight. I need to hear this, because they're the last words we will share.

After taking one deep breath to gather my resolve, I look into his eyes and say, "He may have been a rich kid I foolishly fell in love with, but I won't make that same mistake twice, *rich kid*. Walk away while I still don't mean anything to you."

"Too late for that. You can't push me away because you think you're saving me from heartache down the road."

"Yes, I can." I grow frustrated by his sensibility in the midst of this mess, which weakens my stance. I continue anyway, still believing that I'm right. "I'm not good. I'm not whole. Tonight, tonight proves that."

It's in that moment that the truth becomes so evident. "I can't do this with you. I still had feelings for Jim, and he died on me. I thought that maybe . . . he came over one time and begged me to take him back. I slammed the door in his face. I wanted to hurt him like he had hurt me. That was two months before his death. He died skiing in Switzerland, Charlie. How could he say he loved me that much and then go on vacation?

This won't end well for me, and I won't survive your rejection when you find someone more suitable." I'm shaking my head and walking backward, needing away from everything that hurts, everything like Jim's death and the reality that Charlie isn't mine to hold onto.

When I look up, I see tears in Charlie's eyes. His hands are reaching for me as he moves toward me again. "I'm sorry. I'm so sorry he hurt you, that he left you, but I'm not him. I wouldn't do that to you, and you know that deep dow—"

His words make me snap with a smack of reality. "But you chose Rachel, not me!" I try a final blow to end us. "I'm just a runner-up to you, someone you settled for. And for that reason alone, I could never fall in love with you." As the lies I just told swirl around my brain, I feel like I'm going to be sick.

He flinches at my words. "You know that's not what happened. You know how I felt that first night, Charlie."

"I don't know anything anymore. I don't think I even really know you."

He stares at me in disbelief. The sadness in his eyes penetrates my heart, so I turn, grabbing my stomach and blocking him and that look on his face from my sight. I won't ever forget it, and I hate that it will be the last expression I'll see on his beautiful face. All hope is left there on the pavement between us when I leave him standing there without a second glance, knowing this is right for both of us, best for us. I can't be what he needs, what he deserves, and asking him to wait around is selfish.

I wish I could throw these old feelings away and move forward, but tonight was proof that none of it, none of my life with Jim, was resolved.

Charlie probably feels this is all to spare my feelings, all for me, but it's not—it's for him. He just can't see it as clearly as I can right now. He doesn't understand yet. But he will, and then he'll agree that this was for the best.

The door shuts behind me, and I make my way up the stairs, recognizing that this has been my modus operandi with Charlie from the beginning. I never intended to let him in, and yet, the more time I spent with him, the more time I wanted to spend with him. He got to me with his charm and cute smile, his happy blues and sleepy greys.

I unlock my apartment door and step inside, avoiding the direction of the couch. If I look at that couch, our snuggle spot, I'll lose it for sure.

I leave the lights out and lock the front door. Tossing my keys and purse onto the dining table, I make my way into the bedroom. Everything is easier to face in the dark, even my own reflection, as I stand before my bathroom mirror brushing my teeth. In the dark, I don't have to see the mouth that once kissed him passionately for hours or the lips that told him lies tonight. In the dark of this small room, I don't have to see the eyes that hid the truth from him while watching his own share his every emotion. Sadly, it's the pain in them that stays with me.

I crawl into bed, pulling the covers up to my chin, and try to remember the happiness and laughs we shared. I'm hoping one day the memory of his smile will replace the harsh words exchanged tonight, and that those memories will outweigh all of the rest.

One day.

Chapter 29

♂

What the hell just happened? I stare at the door where Charlie disappeared in total shock. How did the day go from holding her on the couch this afternoon to her breaking all contact with me tonight?

My family.

My damn family and my annoying, scornful cousin Liz. That explains it all.

I should chase Charlie, or bang on her door or call her, but she seems to be in no mood for negotiation. Her mind is made up, and I don't know how to unmake it.

I stand exactly where she left me in the middle of the sidewalk. Ten, twenty, maybe even thirty minutes pass in a blur.

The driver taps me on the shoulder, startling me out of my thoughts. "Sir, can I drive you home?"

I glance up to her window. She hasn't turned on a single light in her apartment since she went upstairs. *What does that mean? Why hasn't she? What is she doing up there?*

I'm worried about her, though I know I should be feeling rejected instead. I leave, finally convinced that she needs time to sort through her thoughts and figure out what she wants. I'll give her tonight, and maybe during these remaining hours of darkness I can come up with a plan. I refuse to let her walk away from me and end us. I refuse to not have her in my life.

In the meantime, I need to talk to Liz and figure out what happened between her and Jim. Maybe if I hear her side, I can help Charlie by knowing more about the situation. I call Liz on my cell from the car.

"Charlie?" She's nervous when she answers. She should be. We were close as children, but have had a rocky relationship over the last couple of years because my ideals changed and didn't meet her expectations.

I rub my forehead, feeling a headache coming on. "Tell me what happened. Tell me everything."

"I'm sorry. I didn't know that was her. That she was Jim's—"

"Jim's Charlie? Yeah. So you knew he was engaged, and yet you still fucked him?"

"It wasn't like that—"

"What was it like, Liz?" I have no patience for this roundabout story, and I am struggling to hold in my anger. "I'm calling to hear your side. This is your one chance. Start from the beginning and tell me."

"We met at a bar down on Wall Street. It was happy hour, and I remember a sports talk show was on the big screen over the bar. I heard a group of guys nearby discussing the Giants lineup for the season. I heard Jim before I saw him—"

"I don't want the love story version. I want to know why you chose to hurt someone else by sleeping with her fiancé."

"I didn't know he was engaged or even had a girlfriend the first couple of times we hooked up. He didn't talk about her to me."

"You didn't know?" I want to give her the benefit of the doubt. I want to, but she sounds like she's holding back.

"I didn't know for sure. I saw a photo on his phone at the bar—"

"You did know, then. You knew and you still went through with it? You know no guy carries around a photo on his phone if the girl isn't important to him."

She doesn't respond. What more can she say that won't make her sound worse?

"Liz, how long before she caught you?"

"We'd been together for two months at that point."

Damn it. Charlie suspected as much or more, but never had it confirmed.

"Please don't hate me, Charlie. I'm sorry. I'll tell your friend or girlfriend, whatever she is, if you want. I feel terrible since he died and—"

"No! You won't talk to her—"

"Please forgive me. I hate when we fight."

"You hate when we fight?" I laugh. That idea is preposterous. "We'd have to be on speaking terms to fight." This whole conversation worsens my headache and makes my chest hurt for Charlie. They've damaged her, and I've been thrown into the mix for being related. I don't know why I need more details, but I do. Everything Liz has told me is what I'd expected, but I need the confirmation, and if she's smart and cares about repairing our relationship, she'll answer with the truth. "Did you continue to see him after being caught?"

She hesitates, but then answers, "Yes."

I hang the phone up and slump further down onto the seat. After being dropped off in front of my building, I go to my apartment reliving every moment of the night.

It was bad enough that she was forced to spend time with Don and Katherine alone. That's no picnic, but then to recognize Liz from one of her most painful times in life? Yeah, that's gotta hurt. She was quiet on the ride home. I thought she was trying to forget the last two hours of torture, but she wasn't. Her mind was reeling, in overdrive, and plotting her escape.

She fed me lies. All lies. I could see it in her eyes. The words were surface, a defense mechanism. Although I know deep down it's not how she feels, her comparison of me to Jim and then calling herself a runner-up . . . that hit deep.

I float through my nighttime routine, unaware if I've brushed my teeth or changed my clothes. I find myself under my covers and thinking, replaying the car ride and how she felt in my arms. I tried to take the bad away, feeling if I could have held her tight enough, it would have disappeared, and I would see her smile again. I wanted to believe that could happen. She's made it apparent that I can't protect her that way, because she's not here and we're not friends now.

I think back to the reading of Grace's will and remember the look on my family's faces, the surprise and shock on mine. It was quite the turn of events in and of itself, but to have Charlie hit with her past during dinner was even more shocking.

I wish I could take back the entire night. I wish it was four o'clock again, and we decided to blow off the dinner and stay on the couch all night. It wouldn't have changed the will. I'm so stupid for going to my parents' and for taking her, exposing her to all that.

Her couch is our safe haven, our bonding spot, our place. It's where the rest of the world doesn't exist. It's where cupcakes and beer are a perfectly acceptable lunch, and chick flicks are played after horror movies, and somehow that makes sense. It's where we aren't just friends buying groceries at the store or a platonic coffee at the corner. It's where we get to be who we want to be without having to define us to anyone else.

And that's gone now.

I toss and turn for hours. My sleep is restless, and I'm upset from the loss. I feel it deep within me, maybe more than I should considering how long we've known each other. But I don't care about that. I only care about her, so I get up and get dressed though it's just turned 5:00 a.m.

After I knock on the door just above the closed sign, it swings open, and Tony stands there smiling. I grumble. It's too early to be chipper. Tony's outlook is contagious, so I return the smile and greet him properly.

"Morning, Tony."

"Good morning to you. So, what brings our illustrious New York writer out at the wee hours of the day? Oh, wait! Let me guess." After he flips the sign over to display open, I follow him toward the counter.

The smell of hot, fresh bread fills the small shop. It's stronger than usual in the early morning. I lean against the counter, needing a strong cup of coffee to keep me on track with my mission.

Tony starts his round of guessing. "Considering it's Sunday, I'm thinking it's either some investigative, undercover-operation-type news piece, or it involves a woman."

"Am I that transparent?"

"Yes, you are. So I'm right?"

"It's the latter."

"A woman, huh? I take it by your current disposition that it's not good news in regards to this woman?"

"You'd be correct."

"Man, that's rough."

"Yeah, rough is right."

"How'd you lose the girl before I got to meet her?"

"Long story."

"They always are, my friend. Last time you told me it was a complicated story."

"That, too."

"So, what can I get you today? A bagel to melt in her mouth, or biscotti to dip in coffee, or maybe a muffin that shows how much you care?"

"The muffin."

"Ah yes, the win-them-over-with-a-muffin routine," he says with a smile.

"Are you always happy this early in the morning?"

"Pretty much. I've been baking for three hours at this point. It's just good to talk to someone other than my brother."

"I didn't know you had a brother who worked here."

"I try to keep him busy in the back. He doesn't have a sparkling personality like me."

That makes me laugh. Thank goodness something does. He hands me a coffee, because it's apparent I need one, and places two muffins in a bag. "You should be all set, and let me know if the muffin works. I have it on good authority that women can't resist my baked goods, but it's always good to hear about it."

"Will do," I reply, dropping a ten on the counter. "Keep the change, and thanks."

I head back out and down to the nearest subway station. I'm still holding onto hope, though it would be wise if I left that flighty emotion on the platform.

I'm not wise, though. I never have been when it comes to matters of the heart.

Conviction.

Once I believe in something, I have conviction. That's something more tangible to me. I can feel that emotion in my bones, deep down in my soul. I can grasp it in my hands and have it carry me forward. Conviction is what drives me now.

I step onto the train and plop down in a seat. The car is empty except for the few souls with some tedious weekend job that requires their presence before the regular workweek starts again tomorrow.

I get off at her stop and make my way up to street level. Walking the two short blocks to her building, I see the sun starting to rise in the distance. I look up at her window as I approach. It's still early, so I'm not surprised to see the curtains drawn closed.

After entering the code and walking up the four flights, I'm at a loss as I stand in front of her door. *Do I knock?* It's not even six in the morning. *Do I wait out here?* Not a well-thought-out plan overall, but the need overtook me. I wasn't sleeping anyway, so I don't regret coming over.

I slide down the wall and decide to wait before knocking. That lasts about fifteen minutes, then I give into the urge. I want to see her, and I'm hoping we can work this out. Maybe sleep has given her a new perspective.

Performing my special knock just for her, I try to determine the balance between soft enough to reflect the hour, but loud enough so she can hear it from her bedroom. Guess it worked, because I hear her walking across her wood floor and then nothing. I assume she's looking through the peephole.

She doesn't open the door.

She doesn't say anything.

Waiting and listening, I don't even know if she's still on the other side. But I'm here and I have to try. "Charlie? Please open the door and talk to me."

I lean against the door, my palm flat against the solid wood. I haven't heard her walk away, so I try again. "I brought coffee and muffins. Best in the city." I hold the bag up so she can see if she's still spying through the peephole. When I don't hear anything, I lower my voice and plead with her. "Please, talk to me."

Nothing.

I slide back down the wall and wait. *She's got to come out at some point, right?*

Sleep takes hold despite the people and the city coming to life around me. When I open my eyes an hour later, I bend my neck to the left. It's stiff from the poor sleeping conditions. I'm about to stand up when I notice a note on my legs.

I've gone out for the day. Please go home.
C.

She's very stealthy, and now I'm left wondering if she's telling me the truth or lying to get rid of me.

Standing up, I stretch, realizing how ridiculous this is. *Why am I here?* She's not going to speak to me. She's stubborn that way. So I leave the coffee and muffins there and walk down the stairs. No sense in hanging around her hallway all day if she's not home or won't come to the door.

I push the door wide open and walk to the middle of the sidewalk, looking in both directions briefly. I'm not ready to give up, but I need to give this plan some serious consideration. If she's not going to talk to me, what's the point in sleeping at her doorstep?

I glance up at her window and see the curtain fall to the side. *Charlie! That sneak!* She is home.

My first instinct is to run back up there and bang on her door until she lets me in. But my second is to let her think she's deterred me. Then I'll return tomorrow and every day after until she agrees to talk to me. I know she cares, or she wouldn't have bothered with the note and wouldn't be spying on me from her window. I leave, shoving my hands into my pockets and head toward the subway. I need more sleep and fuel to put this pester-her-until-she-talks-to-me plan into action.

I'll play to her weaknesses, and I'll get the girl back.

Chapter 30

♀

He's shadowing me. *Why?* Why can't he just get the message? I've been pretty clear that I do not want to see Charlie, and yet, it seems he's around all the time. I see him even more than before. Doesn't he have New York observations or quirks to write about? What happened to him writing a novel? What happened to all I said the other day? Was I not clear?

It's been two weeks, and I still haven't caved to my craving to hear his voice. I want to. Sometimes I call Rachel just so I don't call him. I may not be talking to him, but I sure am seeing him everywhere.

Not only that, but it's scorching outside and he's wearing T-shirts. Short-sleeved T-shirts! It's all very distracting, especially when I'm not supposed to be focusing on him at all. Some of the shirts are more fitted across his chest and some are tighter around his biceps. Has he been working out? Where did that tan come from? He's distracting. He shouldn't look this good—it's annoying.

He's been coming to my work and waiting down on the sidewalk near the building's entrance. I didn't expect to see him the first time I strolled out the lobby doors, then *bam!* There he was next to a giant potted ficus tree.

He was leaning against the potted plant like he had every right to be there, sunglasses on, worn and soft-looking T-shirt with a beer logo, jeans that fit just right, and sneakers. Cool sneakers, though, not like the ones people jog in or buy for show. Sneakers that said he cared about what he wore, but didn't put too much effort into the fact. He's just completely distracting.

Someone bumped into me as I stood frozen in my spot, reminding me to move out of the flow of pedestrian traffic. Slowly walking forward, I put my sunglasses on, and took a right down the sidewalk. I pretended I hadn't seen him, but I could feel his presence, his nearness. Risking a glance over my shoulder, I saw him about ten feet back, several people separating us.

I stopped and moved to the side, looking back once more. He came closer, tentative, until he was right there, right in front of me. He was bumped from behind, and then we were touching, just briefly, but we were. Scenarios of kissing him in the middle of the sidewalk during rush hour flitted through my head, but then I remembered we couldn't, and I sighed.

Just when I turned to leave, he said, "Don't go."

I closed my eyes and straightened my shoulders back. Taking a deep breath, I opened them and walked back into the flow of people. He stayed there until I couldn't see him any longer.

My heart was hurting, but my resolve was strong. This was the right thing to do.

An interesting thing I have discovered about Charlie is how persistent he is, even at the risk to himself. It made no sense why he showed up every day for the following two weeks. It made no sense to see him reading a book on a bench across from my apartment last Saturday. Doesn't he have anything better to do with his time, like play video games or roll around in his family's money? He makes no sense to me, and that intrigues me more than anything.

Today is the day I decided I'm going to talk to him and ask him to leave me alone. I step off the elevator and hide behind the security guard's desk in the middle of the lobby. This spot gives me a great vantage point where I can see him before he sees me. Yeah, I learned my lesson the second time he showed up. I didn't like the surprise from the previous day, which left me flustered. So I've been more prepared the last two weeks.

Every day he's leaning against the potted ficus, his shades pulled down over his eyes and his arms crossed over his chest. He sometimes crosses his ankles, which makes him more exasperatingly attractive. I see women checking him out. Every once in a while, one will stop to talk to him, but he points toward the building like he's waiting for someone, and they move along. He's not lying. He's waiting for me, and I find myself smiling from this knowledge before I internally reprimand myself for the traitorous thought.

Today, as I peer over the shoulder of the large guard, my heart sinks. He's not there.

"Can I help you, miss?" the security guard asks.

I answer without eye contact, because I'm too busy searching for Charlie. "No. I'm fine. Thanks."

"Miss, you seem to be hiding from someone. Are you all right?"

"I'm all good."

"You might want to consider filing a restraining order if you're in danger."

I look up at him, confused. "I'm not in any danger. What makes you think that?"

"Umm . . ." His eyes dart to the left and then come back to me. "Because you've been hiding from someone out there for the last two weeks."

"I'm not hiding," I state, firm in my belief. "I'm preparing."

"Preparing?"

"Yes." I gulp and readjust my handbag at my elbow. "Thank you for the help, but the police aren't necessary."

"All right." He sounds skeptical, so I walk away and head for the doors.

I still feel the disappointment in my chest that Charlie's not here. By the time I walk out into the late-afternoon sunshine, I'm mad. I can't believe he gave up on me that easily! *See?* I justify to myself, and hold my chin up. I was right about him all along and take back all the nice things I thought about him and his persistence.

Looking around once more, I finally start walking in my usual direction. My mind can't seem to figure out if the validation of being proven right is worth the disappointment that my heart feels for that same exact reason.

Turning the corner to head home, I hear, "Did ya miss me?"

Startled by the unexpected voice in my ear, I cover my heart with my hand. "You shouldn't sneak up on women like that!" I don't stop walking, and I don't give him the satisfaction of looking at him, although the wind wafts his scent in my direction, reminding me of how we used to cuddle on the couch.

"I saw you looking for me."

I refuse to give into him. I will stand firm. "I was just looking around. You know, it's good to be aware of your surroundings when living in the big city."

"I think you were looking for me." It's too easy for him to keep pace with me.

Stay strong. "I think you're being arrogant."

"Did you think I'd given up?"

"I hoped, but here you are."

"You looked disappointed."

"Disappointed that my stalker didn't show up?" I laugh at the thought. "Surely you jest." I know he's right.

"Stalker? Hmmm. I don't see it that way at all. I like to consider myself more your guardian angel." I can hear his smug smile in his words and feel it in the way he walks next to me with his arm pressed against mine.

I stop, feeling haughty. With my hands on my hips, I scoff. "Guardian angel? And how do you figure that?"

"Well, at this stage in our relationship—"

"Or lack thereof, considering we don't have a relationship," I say, correcting him.

He rolls his eyes. "Or currently lack thereof, I protect you. I've been within a few feet of you for the last two weeks on this dangerous walk home of yours. Even the subway. Stuff happens on there all the time. I'm kind of handy to have around."

"Madison Avenue isn't exactly a derelict area, and I never asked for your help or guardianshipness," I explain, holding my purse tight to my side. "Anyway, I can take care of myself and do a fine job of that every day."

"I know you can take care of yourself. I think my point is you don't have to do this all on your own. And I don't think *guardianshipness* is a word."

"Sure it is. And I don't have to do *what* all on my own? Walk home? I worked here a year before I met you and walked home all on my own just fine."

He stops walking and scratches his head. With a confused look on his face, he asks, "What are we fighting about again?"

I stop without giving it a second thought and roll my eyes. "Charlie, what are you doing here? Why are you everywhere I go?"

His eyes are set on mine, and the smile and playful tone are gone. "All kidding aside. I want our friendship back."

"Well, damn. That was just so straightforward and stuff. I didn't actually expect you to lay it out like that so easily. I thought we'd go a few more rounds before I got the full truth."

"Nope. No more beating around the ficus tree. I miss you, I want to see you again, and spend my Saturday afternoons with you."

My hands fall to my sides, catching my purse as it slides down my arm. I look back up at him and see the sincerity in his eyes, all of his truths exposed to me in his expression. My willpower starts to give. I feel it deep within, and dang it, if I'm honest with myself, I miss him, too. "Walk with me?"

He smiles, and inside I know this is the right decision for now. "My pleasure."

My mind isn't changing. I'm flattered by his dedication and persistence, and especially his honesty, but I'm not where I need to be. I stop, moving out of the pedestrian traffic.

"Charlie."

I guess it's the tone in my voice or the way I sighed when I said his name, because he says, "That doesn't sound good." He stops in front of me. "Before you make a huge mistake, because I can tell that's what you're about to do, I need to say something."

I'll give him this. A few more minutes in his presence and I'll give him anything, so I hope he's quick before I lose all of my willpower. I nod for him to continue.

"You could never be considered someone's second best." He takes my hand without permission, rubbing his thumb over the top. "Not that it means anything to you now, but I would have asked you out if I thought you had any interest in me. When you left the club so fast, I figured we weren't meant to be."

His sweet words fill my heart, and I swallow hard. Lifting up on my toes, I kiss him on the cheek and linger, whispering, "Thank you."

"It's too late, isn't it?"

"I'm not good, Charlie. I've started meeting with a counselor, but I've only had one session." A heavy silence fills the space between us as he releases my hand gently. "I'm not okay. That means *we'll* never be okay if I don't work through this." I step closer, still struggling to resist touching him again. "I'm sorry I dragged you into my mess."

"As long as you don't say 'this isn't you, it's me.' "

I smile, because I would have said that next. Instead, I remain quiet, watching him process the meaning behind my words.

His hands are shoved into his pockets, and his body leans closer as he asks, "We can't be friends anymore?"

I shake my head, not able to say the words. Tears threaten, but don't fall.

He looks to his right then up at the building behind me. I think he might be holding back his own tears. He closes his eyes, hiding them. "Is this good-bye forever, Charlie?"

I rush to answer. "I don't want it to be, but I can't make any promises either."

His breathing hardens, puffing his chest out with each intake. After a quick sniffle, he opens his eyes and clears his throat. "It hurts to be this close to you and still not be as close as I want to be. Please don't leave." I hear his own hard swallow, his nerves making his voice shake enough for me to notice his distress.

Looking down at my hands, I say what I need to. "My life has crumbled, and I can't seem to rebuild it. You were there to help me, but all we did was Band-Aid the situation instead of dealing with it—the pain, Jim's cheating, his death. I thought me moving on and forgetting about what happened was the same thing as healing. It's not, though, and I finally figured that out."

"Char—"

"Please let me say this." I sniffle and he goes quiet. "You're right. I am leaving. But it's not because of you. I hope you will believe me. I need to face my life and figure out who I am now instead of relying on who I was with *him*. I'm sorry if this hurts you. I never wanted to do that, but if I don't take ten steps back and focus on me, I'll hurt you more in the long run. I see that now."

The tears dry, because this realization is my epiphany. I know I'm making the right decision for *me,* and that's what I need. The weight burdening me for so long lifts, confirming this truly is right.

After another long pause, he says, "You have my number if you need me. I'm not going anywhere." I can hear a new lightness in his tone. He knows this is the right decision, too.

"I do, and the same goes for you. I'll be here. I'm just not your couch-cuddler anymore."

"I guess this is good-bye?"

"For now." I hate this feeling, hate the word *good-bye.*

"Hmmm. Good-bye for now then." He takes a step back.

"Hey, Charlie?"

"Yeah?"

"Good luck on the book."

"I finished it, actually, but I might need to make some tweaks to the ending."

"Well, make sure to let me know when I can buy it."

"I'll try."

"I'll be the first in line."

"Take care of yourself, Charlie." His voice is soft and kind, just the way I want to remember him, reflecting the man I know.

I can't manage another word. I know he can tell, because he turns and walks away, leaving me there. My heart aches in my chest. *Good-bye, Charlie.*

Chapter 31

♀

I've put six months into counseling, and reading. I've avoided watching movies. I cook now and don't bake. I had to because all of those things had too many memories attached to them.

I'm staring at my phone, a bad habit I've developed over the last six months. But it's not my phone that I find so intriguing, it's the photo on the display screen. The day it was taken was wonderful. I might even venture to say perfect. Charlie held my phone out in front of us as we went round and round on the carousel in Central Park. He stood beside me as I rode the pink horse with a lavender saddle. Leading up to that picture was an adventure in itself.

"Which one do you want?" He nudged me conspiratorially.

I watched the carousel make a full circle before making my final decision. "That one," I said, pointing. "The pink horse with the purple saddle and the gold hooves."

"That is so girly," he joked.

"That's the exact reason why I want it. It appeals to my inner five-year-old."

The carousel stopped, and the ticket taker opened the gate. Charlie jumped the small barrier despite the operator yelling at him for cutting in line.

He didn't care, though. Charlie stood proudly next to the horse with his hand staking claim by holding the gold pole. He cut off two kids and a mom, but no real harm was done. They wanted the green and yellow ones on the other side anyway.

When I approached, he bowed, swaying his arm in presentation. "Milady, your horse awaits."

I wanted to say something sarcastic or clever, but I couldn't. My heart was in my throat. He was so sweet and sincere in wanting to get me the exact horse I wanted. As soon as he was upright, I hugged him, hard.

That was last summer, before the infamous dinner and before I was forced to confront my past in front of his family . . . and in front of him.

I'm brought out of my daydream when Rachel calls my name. "Charlie? Earth to Charlie. Hey, it's quitting time. Go home."

I spin around in my chair and look up at her, slightly dazed. "What?"

She taps her watch and smiles. "It's five thirty. You're done for the day, unless you want to stay and help field the phone bids tonight."

We don't get to see each other as much at work since I got a promotion two months ago, but I don't miss working the phones like I had to before. Now I work them on an as-needed basis. I smile, laughing in jest. "No, thanks for the offer, but I have a book at home that I'm hoping to finish tonight."

"Sounds like a very provocative evening ahead," she says, making fun of me.

"Are you mocking how I choose to spend my Thursday night?" She teases me a lot about the changes I've made. It's not considered an exciting life for most twenty-six-year-olds, but that's okay. I've had too much excitement the last few years. I did what I needed to do for me, and it was nice in a way.

I've settled any outstanding notions regarding Jim, those lingering doubts I had. They weren't real, just like the life I led with him. I wouldn't have taken him back, because his cheating on me changed who I was on the inside. The guilt was gone. I realized this when I slammed the door on him, closing the door on that part of my life also. I just never spent the time to take note of that.

I'm okay with the breakup now. Yeah, it hurts to think about, but he wasn't who I was meant to be with. No one I was meant to be with would hurt me that way. I see that now. My thoughts drift to Charlie. I miss him and think about him every day.

"Absolutely," Rachel says, "I should have never given you that e-reader for your birthday. I don't even remember the last time you went out with us." She throws her hands in the air in a dramatic fashion before dropping them down again.

"Maybe because it's always the two of you. You and Justin. It's fine hanging out at your place, but sometimes it makes me feel like a third wheel or worse . . . lonely."

"You don't like him?"

I shake my head. "No, I don't mean it like that. You know I like him. You guys make a great couple. But that doesn't change the fact that I still have to return home to an empty apartment."

"You don't have to, Charlie. You're choosing to. There's a difference."

"I don't want to talk about this again." I turn off my computer and grab my purse out of the bottom drawer of my desk.

"We never talk about this."

"Why does it feel like we do, then?" I stand up and look at her. That's when I notice the change, notice how much she has changed. She's beautiful, more beautiful, because she's in love. Maybe it's her recent engagement, but no matter what it is, I want that, too. I want the way her skin looks brighter and her eyes shine. Even her smile appears bigger than I remember. *Did she have her teeth whitened?* Everything about her is just . . . prettier, and she looks happier.

She leans against my desk and rubs my arm. "You've gone through a lot this last year. You've given yourself the time you need to rediscover who you were before Jim, but I see the longing sometimes. I know using that word sounds cheesy, but it's there, in your eyes. You want love, and I think you're ready for it."

I look down at a file lying open on my desk, running my fingers down the text. "Maybe you're right. Maybe I'm ready to start dating again."

Standing upright, she clasps her hands together. "That's the Charlie I know. Go home and finish your book, and let's plan to go out this weekend."

"Yeah, okay. That will be fun."

She looks at her watch. "I've gotta run, but we'll make plans tomorrow morning."

I nod as she dashes around the corner.

Walking through the lobby, I push through the revolving door as I hold down the feeling of sorrow that's overcome me. It's winter, and the dark of night comes earlier. I close my eyes, absorbing the chill on this February day. The weather has been cold, colder than I remember in years past. It makes me wonder if loneliness has played a part in the forecast. I reopen my eyes, feeling self-conscious, and start walking again.

"Hey, Charlie, wait up."

I stop, looking over my shoulder, surprised to see a guy jogging toward me. It takes me a moment to place him, but then I recognize him from a night out with Rachel and Justin. "Conner? Um, hi. What are you doing here?"

I know he's Charlie's best friend, and I want to ask about him, but maybe I'm ready to call and talk to him myself. My heart still holds a place for him that I can't deny any longer.

"Hi, I came to see if you'd grab a drink with me. Just one, if you can spare the time."

"Oh. Sure. What's this about?"

"Let's get that drink." He smiles, and my defenses go down. "You can relax. I'm not going to hit on you or stalk you or anything like that."

"So I take it this isn't a social call?"

"Kind of."

"There's a place right across the street. It's dark, not fancy."

"Cool." He walks next to me and seems relaxed, but I can't help but think this is a bit of an odd visit. "How've you been?"

We cross the street as we chat. "Are we making small talk?"

"Yeah, I thought we would."

I laugh. I like his honesty. "I'm doing good."

"You look good." I raise an eyebrow, and he stammers to correct himself. "I mean you look . . ." He shrugs. "Shit! I'm screwing up here. You look good. I don't mean that in an inappropriate way, though. Happy, maybe. Are you?"

"I'm still working on happy. I have my days, just like everyone else."

He nods in understanding, which makes me wonder what Rachel or Justin, or maybe even Charlie, has said in regards to me. The place is empty except for one other occupied table at the back of the bar. He points at a table against the wall, more toward the middle.

"So, I hear you've got something of mine," he says, leaning his elbows on the table.

"What's that?"

"My lucky rabbit's foot."

"The orange one?"

"Yes, ma'am. So you do know of it?"

"Don't call me *ma'am*. I'm younger than you. And yes, I might have seen said lucky rabbit's foot."

"Feisty. Charlie said you were feisty and a lot stubborn."

"He's right on the last account. So you came to get your foot back?"

"Not exactly. I came to tell you a story."

"Well, you wanted to grab a drink, and here we are, so I think drinks are in order before we start this story. I'd like Boddington's on draft."

Conner smirks. "Coming right up, doll."

When he returns with two pints, he doesn't waste time getting to the point. "Last April, I went on vacation, an end of season skiing trip. I was only supposed to be gone for a week or so, but ended up staying three because I met this girl. Okay, that's beside the point. The point I'm trying to make is that at the time, my man Charlie was on what I'd like to call a losing streak with the ladies."

"That surprises me," I say, then sip my beer.

"He doesn't have trouble meeting them. I'm not going to lie to you, because he wouldn't. The man has a lot of opportunities. He's taken advantage of some of these opportunities before." He coughs. "But that's not who he really is. He's more a one-woman kind of guy. I admit, I didn't understand that kind of thinking before. I thought he was nuts, but to each his own."

Sitting back in my chair to get more comfortable, I can tell this isn't going to be a short story. I wave my hand for him to stop rambling and get to the point.

"So I gave him my lucky rabbit's foot and told him it would bring him luck in the love department."

I take a swig of my drink, because I think I know exactly where this story is headed. I can't resist a good love story, though, so I have to ask, "And did he? Did he find love?"

"Are you always this slow?"

I narrow my eyes at him. "Do women put up with your rudeness?"

"The truth, Charlie, and I'm not here to talk about me. Do you really not know?"

"What? What am I supposed to say here? What do you want to hear? Are you here to break the news that he's met someone and they're together and his world is perfect now?"

I start to stand, but he grabs my wrist. "Stubborn is putting it mildly. Hostile might fit better."

I roll my eyes and lean down, both hands flat on the table. "Tell me the moral of the story, Conner."

"Do you have the rabbit's foot on you now?"

He's more intuitive than I guessed for someone as shallow as he is. I sit back down, hugging my purse to me, and stare at him for a minute.

He nods his head, knowing the answer before I have to say it. "Did I hit a homer? Strike gold? Win the golden ticket?"

I drop my handbag on the table, dig inside the interior pocket, and pull out the neon orange rabbit's foot keychain. I hold it up by the little chain, and we both smile.

He pats the table with his hand twice and stands up. "I think you know deep down what the moral of this story is. If you don't, I suggest you spend some time and try to figure it out." He walks backward right past me, heading for the door. He turns around and struts with confidence, which is really annoying in a funny kind of way.

"Hey?" I yell. "Don't you want your lucky rabbit's foot back?"

He turns his back to the door and opens it with his backside. "Nope, I think you need it more than I do." And even though it's dark outside, he drops his shades down from the top of his head, covering his eyes, and walks out.

I let the chain of the rabbit's foot slide over my finger and twirl it around several times before dropping it back into my purse and leaving the bar.

Chapter 32

♀

Friday doesn't turn out the way I planned at all. Rachel knocks on my door just before ten with a mocha in hand for me. Maybe she wants to bribe me or cancel our plans for the night.

"Irene wasn't at her desk, so I came on in. Hope you don't mind?" she asks, walking into my office.

Having an assistant is nice, but sometimes I miss the casualness of the two of us talking over our cubicle walls. "You know you can walk in here, Rach. Ooh, thanks for the coffee." I take the cup from her and smile.

She remains standing, awkwardly shifting from foot to foot. My stomach sinks when she struggles to say what she came to say.

"Justin just called." She watches for my reaction as if I will shatter into a million pieces from hearing that her boyfriend called her.

"And?" I shrug, confused to why she's being so careful with her words.

She finally sits down on the other side of the desk and leans forward. Placing her hand on top of mine, she speaks in a hushed tone. "I know you're not comfortable talking about Charlie."

I'm starting to lose my patience, because she's making me nervous, especially with an opener like that. Sitting back in my chair, I cross my arms defensively across my chest and ask, "What is it, Rachel? Just say it."

"Well, we both think that Charlie might need you."

"Need me . . . how?"

I knew what I wanted to do as soon as she explained the situation. It's what I need to do for Charlie, what I know Charlie would do for me. He'd go. He'd go at the risk of being rejected. So I'll go, too, and take that same risk.

What if Charlie doesn't want to see me or doesn't want me there? What if he invites a woman or has a girlfriend?

Her face shows the sadness I feel inside. "Are you sure you want to go?" she asks.

"I do. For Charlie, I will."

She smiles, but it's soft, sympathetic. "Do you want me to go with you?"

"No," I say, shaking my head. "I'll be fine. Thank you, though."

"Call me later?"

"Okay."

I take a cab to the church, not wanting to be later than I already am. When I walk into the cathedral, I see a sign with the name *Lackey* and a guest book. I don't stop. I need to be there for Charlie, so I walk through the doors and see row after row of empty pews except for one.

Charlie.

My breath catches as I realize no one else is here. No one came to say good-bye to Veronica, except for us. I expected to see family, but didn't know her well enough to know if she had any. I expected to see friends, people who knew her, but maybe she didn't have any of those either. All of her neighbors are no-shows, except for the kindest man I know.

I take a deep breath and walk up the aisle. His head is bowed when I scoot onto the pew and sit beside him. He looks up, and our eyes meet. No words are exchanged as I slip my hand into his and weave our fingers together just like old times. I'm relieved when he doesn't move his hand away, but instead gives a very light squeeze.

The minister steps up to the podium and clears his throat before he starts into the eulogy. Charlie has his head down most of the time, but looks up at the minister every few minutes. He glances at me once, as if he doesn't believe I'm really here. At least that's how it feels to me.

He holds my hand tighter and during the short service, I realize that I don't want him to ever let it go. The feelings he's always stirred inside me flicker and spark back to life. I have my friend again, and I think I want to hold onto him forever.

The service is short and sweet, and not near enough is said about a woman who had such a vibrant attitude in life. It's clear the minister didn't know her, so I'm sure this ended up being a standard presentation.

We remain seated for a while after the minister leaves, taking in the loss of our friend, a friend I didn't have enough time with. I close my eyes, drop my head, and say a prayer for her, knowing in my heart that she's with her Johnny again.

As the minutes tick by, I wonder if Charlie might want some more time alone, so I stand. He does, too, following me into the lobby. I stop near the front doors of the church and glance around before looking back at him.

"I'm sorry," I say for lack of anything better coming to mind. He puts his hands in his pockets and just looks at me. "Veronica was a lovely lady."

"Yes, she was. Too bad more people didn't know her." He pauses and looks out the window at the traffic when a cab honks its horn, cutting off a Porsche as it drives past.

I touch his arm, because ever since our hands fell away from each other just moments ago, I miss it. "No one but us?"

He shakes his head. "She had no family in the city, and I couldn't find any distant relative information when the landlord let me into her apartment." His eyes take in my hand on his arm, but he doesn't move away. Instead, he covers my hand with his own. "I'm glad you're here. Thank you for coming."

"Justin told Rachel, but I wish you would have told me instead."

He drops his hand and walks to the basket full of programs, taking one. His back is to me. "I hope you understand why I couldn't." Turning around, he says, "I couldn't, Charlie. I'm sorry."

"No, no apologies necessary. I understand."

As he looks at me, I see a glint of determination in his grey eyes. Grey eyes equal sad, confused, or mad. I want to see the blue like when he smiles back at me. I want to hear him laugh again. I've missed his views on life, his sarcastic side, and his humor. I've missed his face and his arms wrapped around me, the way his breath hits the back of my head when we nap, and him. I just miss all of him.

Our eyes meet once again, and the urge to run into his arms and hug away the pain I've caused begins to overwhelm me. I step forward just as he turns away.

"I should go," he says, bending to pick up a messenger's bag that's on the floor. "I have a few things I need to settle with the arrangements and the cemetery."

Stepping back, I grip my hands tightly together, holding myself back. "Yes, um, I should go, too. I need to get back to work." I step backward toward the door, raising my chin and gathering myself together. "I really am sorry about Veronica. She was a wonderful woman."

He nods and looks down at his shoes. "We'd become close over this past year. I hope she liked the service and flowers."

Pushing the door ajar, the cold air hits me hard. "Can I ask you something, Charlie?"

"Anything."

I don't know if this is appropriate or not, and I have a strong suspicion already, but I need to ask. "Did you do all of this for her?"

He looks puzzled before he rubs his neck, as if the question makes him uncomfortable. "Yes. I wanted her to have the service she deserved."

"She did. I think she'd like it." I push the door open and start to walk out, but stop, not wanting to leave. I still want to know everything going on in his life, whether I have a right to or not anymore. "By the way, how's the book?"

He pulls the strap of the bag over his head and says, "Actually, I picked up my official copy from my publisher this morning."

"So it's coming out soon?" I want to ask so much more, but limit myself to this topic.

Chuckling lightly, he pulls the book from the bag and offers it to me. "You can have it, if you like."

"No." I shake my head in protest. "I couldn't. It's your copy."

"I can get more. Anyway, I have a book signing tomorrow, so I can get lots more."

"Are you sure?"

"I'd like you to have it, Charlie."

I take the book and run my hand over the cover before holding it to my chest. "Thank you." Feeling our time is done, I add, "I should go, and I know you said you have stuff to do."

I glance over my shoulder toward the street, then look back. "Take care of yourself." I want to tell him that he looks good, healthy. I can't judge his happiness, but he's living, his life has gone on after me. I remain quiet, though I'm not sure if I should offer more. We're caught in this weird state of middle ground.

"You, too, Charlie." My name crosses his lips sounding more like a good-bye.

I walk home from the funeral, in no mood to return to work. My heart isn't in it today. It's with Veronica *and* Charlie. I tuck the book into my handbag to protect it and pull my coat tighter around me as the late winter wind whips my hair into a frenzy. I wrap my scarf around my neck, bundling to keep warm. But in some weird way, this feels good, justified under the circumstances. The harsh winds make the sadness feel as real on the outside as it is on the inside.

After entering my apartment, I start a pot of coffee before I even take my coat off. I'm frozen to the bone, and I'm sniffling with a runny nose. I draw a warm bath, and five minutes later I'm soaking in bubbles, drinking my coffee, and starting to warm up.

The only thing I want to do after soaking is curl up on the couch and watch movies. It reminds me of Charlie and makes me miss him even more. Maybe seeing him this afternoon did that, and this is just compounding the feeling. I close my eyes and let the memories of snuggling with Charlie warm my heart.

The sound of an infomercial wakes me, shouting for me to *buy, buy, buy*. It's after four in the afternoon, and I bring my hand to my head. I'm hot and sweating. My head is stuffy, and my nose is clogged. After three loud and dramatic sneezes, I accept the fact that I've gone and caught myself a cold.

Needing some meds to clear my head and to unstuff my nose, I get dressed in sweats and an ultra-warm sweater, pull on my coat, scarf and hat, and head to the nearest pharmacy. I text Rachel and let her know I'm canceling for the night. After purchasing a bagful of medicines, all claiming to cure the common cold and relieve me of these symptoms, I make one last stop. I order hot and sour soup, and lo mein noodles from my favorite Chinese restaurant. I'm craving comfort food. I wish I had someone to take care of me, but since I don't have that, I'll settle for the Chinese food.

The food takes longer than I expect, and I'm tortured by the sight of couples coming and going, laughing, smiling, holding hands, and kissing.

I miss that.

I miss laughing like that.

I miss smiling like that.

I miss holding hands with someone.

I miss Charlie.

I miss him so much.

Just as tears threaten to fall, my order number is called. I grab it and dash out the door. Being sick has made me tired and overemotional. As if being sick weren't bad enough, seeing Charlie was great, but it dredged up all of those old feelings, leaving me feeling vulnerable and turning me into a sentimental fool.

I return home and slip on my favorite flannel pajamas. After eating my dinner on the isle of denial—otherwise known as my bed—my purse beckons me. I walk into the living room and grab it, bringing it back to the bedroom. The book inside draws my attention, my curiosity piquing. I pull it out and set it on my nightstand. *I shouldn't read it*, I tell myself. I feel bad enough about how everything with Charlie has turned out. The last thing I need right now is hearing his voice in my head as I read the words he wrote. I roll over, ignore it, and fall asleep.

Chapter 33

♀

The next morning, I'm feeling better, but not by much. By late afternoon, I've taken three naps and only left my bed to pay for the pizza I ordered and to refill my water glass twice. Too scared to check my appearance in the mirror, already knowing how horrible I must look, I do what I haven't done in a while—I avoid.

My phone beeps with a text message. I'm in no mood to deal with people, so I leave it. An hour later, I see Charlie's book and reach for it. I take it in hand, admiring the nice cover, and set it on the blanket next to me. I stare at it for several minutes, rereading the title several times. *My Everything.* The pull of his printed words draws me in, making me want to open the cover and read more.

Resisting the temptation, I trudge into the bathroom. Lethargy has set in from lounging around for the last twenty-four hours. As I grab some toilet paper to blow my nose, the spool flies off the holder and lands in my toilet.

"Damn it!"

Using the handle of the plunger to retrieve it, I'm struck with déjà vu.

Toothbrush.

Toilet.

Fishing it out.

All too familiar indeed. My life was so off-kilter there for a while, then it seemed to hop back on track when—

Charlie!

The thought occurs like a lightning strike. He's gone from my life, and a string of these irritating events are happening once again.

Dropping my keys down that grate outside work three months ago, the bird poop that fell on the side of my head on Christmas day, and the time I tripped in Central Park on nothing but my own feet. Yep, I'm out of whack again.

I dump the soggy toilet roll in the trash then rush to my purse to grab the orange rabbit's foot. After climbing back in bed, I glare at the book again, fighting the urge to pick it up. I reach out and my finger finds its way to the cover, and drags across his name.

Charlie Adams.

Charlie Adams.

And a third time. *Charlie Adams*.

"Damn it, I have no willpower." I pick the book up and start reading. The dedication page is simple with three words: *To My Destiny*.

A sudden lump in my throat makes me gasp for air.

Destiny.

I turn to chapter one, interested to see what kind of book he wrote with a dedication like that.

> *My Everything ~*
>
> *I want to say I fell in love at first sight. That would be the romantic version, but that's not the truth. I fell in love with the woman who would become my sun, my beacon, my compass, my everything when I sat next to her at a funeral and saw the depths of sadness and true beauty for the first time.*

My breathing is staggered, and my heart is pounding as I read until I reach the end of the first chapter. This isn't a book of New York observations. I flip through it, recognizing different passages with each word, setting and scenario. This is a book of *us* observations. *Us*. He's writing about us. This can't be. I'm being silly. This isn't us. This is fiction. We're real . . . or were.

I turn to the end, needing to know what becomes of these star-crossed lovers he so eloquently writes about. These lovers. *Lovahs*. I can hear Charlie in his bad British accent saying the word, and I giggle, remembering how happy I was that day. Even when things were sad, he gave me hope, comfort. He made me happy every day I was with him. He was the light in the dark. He was my light. *My sun. My beacon.*

> *My Everything ~*
>
> *I kissed her, exposing my past, giving her my present, and offering her a future we could share together—a kiss that would span more than a lifetime. A kiss that told her she was my forever and a day.*

The book falls from my hands as I lie back, closing my eyes, his words engulfing me in warmth and love, hope, and a future. *My compass.*

I hold the rabbit's foot in front of my face, our own past and present flashing before my eyes.

Conner.

Lucky rabbit's foot.

Charlie.

Love.

Lucky.

Destiny.

Love.

Love.

Love.

Oh my God!

Charlie gave it to me.

Charlie is in love with me.

Something inside my brain finally clicks in sync with my heart.
I'm in love with Charlie.

My Everything.

He's my everything, too.

I'm in love with Charlie!

Glancing at the time, I grab my phone ready to call Charlie, but I see a text message from Rachel instead: *Charlie has a book signing at seven. Barnes and Noble, 82nd and Broadway.* She knows. She knows that, deep down, I'm in love with Charlie.

I run through the apartment, slipping on my wellies, coat, scarf, and hat, grabbing my keys, my wallet, and the book, and then run out the door to hail a cab.

When I get inside, I give the driver the address. Glancing at my watch, I see the signing has already begun. "Hurry, please."

When the cab pulls up to the curb outside the bookstore, I'm stunned in place. Before me is a six-by-six-foot poster of Charlie's face filling one entire window. God, what a glorious face it is, too. Guess he's not my secret anymore. My heart begins racing, and I jump into action to get to that man, my man, as soon as possible.

I pay the cab driver and jump out only to be confronted with a line that is out the door. As I scan over the crowd, I notice it's all women in line. Oh, except for three guys toward the end—one very tall, one very effeminate, and the other very metrosexual. Judging by this crowd, it makes me question if they are here to support Charlie's book or to try and score a date with the author.

Walking toward the front of the line, I reach for the door. A very terse woman with small glasses stops me.

"If you're here for the signing, the book is sold out, and the line has closed."

"I'm friends with the author," I say, giving her a smile and trying to win her over with kindness.

"*Mmhm,* and I'm sure that all of these people who showed up on time for the signing can claim the same. I'm sorry, but the line has closed. Mr. Adams has been here over an hour, and we don't want him to have to sleep here."

I read the tag on her shirt. "Nancy." I smile, trying to stay calm. With my most professional, direct tone, I say, "It's imperative that I speak with Charlie."

"I'm sure it is, but it won't be here tonight. Please step away from the line or I'll call security."

I look over her shoulder and see him through the glass. He's surrounded by people with clipboards and books, as well as a giggling woman who keeps flipping her hair behind her shoulder. She's a flirter. Her body language says it all. He gives her his attention, but his smile is one of politeness only.

I turn back to Nancy and hold the book up. "I've already got a copy. I just want him to sign it for me."

A scowl covers her face. "Well, in that case," she says with a tight smile. I think she's going to let me in. That is until her tone drops and her beady eyes stare me down. "This line is for customers only." She turns her back to me, ending the discussion.

Stubbornness flames inside my chest. I walk away from the main entrance and around the corner all super-spy, ninja-like hoping the gatekeeper doesn't spot me. Taking off into a sprint to the side entrance, I yank on the handle, but it just jolts. *Damn it! It's locked.*

Defeated, I walk across the street, letting my imagination get the best of me. I'm sure he's being flattered and offered a phone number. Jealousy flares, and I back away from the door, a plan forming. I buy myself a coffee and sit at a table near the window to watch as the line begins to dwindle. When only five people remain, I stand and make my move. I watch him through the bookstore window as I cross the street again. I notice him looking around a few times, and although he always smiles to the person standing in front of him, I see he's disappointed. I just hope he's reacting that way because I'm not there.

Hope can be a dangerous emotion, and it can hurt me as much as help me. But without action, hope has no chance, so I'm going for it. I'm getting my everything.

I cross the street and head toward the side entrance, the one that was locked earlier. It's a risk, because he might leave through the front, but I'm willing to take it. I've already made several mistakes today that have cost me.

The first is leaving the house dressed like a homeless person, because honestly, there is no excuse for that other than I needed to see him. Maybe he'll see the charm in my pajamas.

The second mistake is that I left without my phone, forgetting to grab it from my bed because I was in such a hurry. Calling him would have saved me the hassle of standing on a dark side street.

When I get closer, I see a group of women with his book in hand. I sigh, frustrated that there is a crowd already gathered, and briefly wonder if these women are professional stalkers. I lift my chin and walk toward the group, wanting to get a primo spot so he'll see me. The fan-girls are serious about maintaining their current positions, though, and I discover they aren't afraid to elbow me to keep it.

"Okay, okay, I get it," I mumble, irritated. Talking to myself is something I've started doing in the last year. It's quite embarrassing, but whatever. I can't worry about that right now. I have a Charlie to track down, to stalk.

The bookstore's side door flies open, and two women walk out, directing the crowd to back away from the car. Then, like a celebrity, he walks out. *Charlie.* I hear a collective swoon, including my own.

His body language shows his discomfort in the situation. His head is down, and he's focused on the car door that's open for him.

When the crowd starts calling his name, he looks up, all shy and a lot gorgeous, and smiles.

This is it!

"Charlie! Charlie! Charlie!" I scream, trying to be the loudest of the Charliegirls.

He doesn't respond, and suddenly images of flinging myself on top of the car come to mind. *That's absurd . . . right?* Yes, I nod. *Totally ludicrous.* I need an immediate and very different tactic. I jump in the air, which isn't very high, and yell again. "Charlie! Charlie? It's me, Charlie!"

He's just about to duck into the car, but stops and looks up.

"Charlie!" I call his name one more time and hold the rabbit's foot into the air. I grip his book to my chest and pray he can see the lucky charm even if he can't see me among his fans.

Suddenly everyone goes quiet, and I hear him say, "Charlie, is that you?"

My heart stops when I hear his dulcet tones calling me. I jump up once. "That's me! I'm here."

Then, like Moses parting the Red Sea, my Charlie parts the groupies, and he's standing there with his hand out toward me and smiles. "Come here."

My body responds, and I'm there, standing in front of him in pink, cupcake-covered pajamas and smelling like pizza. Thank goodness my coat hides my unfortunate outfit choice. I pat down my hair, feeling where it's matted, but try to be as presentable as possible for my declaration.

He takes my hand and pulls me closer as he backs up toward the car. "What are you doing here?"

I can't help but feel encouraged hearing the hope in his voice.

My cheeks heat under his gaze, a gaze I can confidently call adoring. I gulp, praying my knees don't buckle. "You didn't sign the book for me."

Looking between us, he sees the book, and a look of disappointment colors his handsome face. "Oh. Yeah, I can do that." His hands drop to check his pockets, and he says, "I don't have a pen."

"And I'm sorry." I blurt the words.

His eyes crinkle at the corners in confusion. "You're sorry I don't have a pen?"

"No." I shake my head. "I mean, yes. Yes, I'm sorry about that, too, but really, Charlie, I'm sorry I'm always apologizing to you because I screw up so much. My head gets clouded and my past was holding me back, but I came here tonight with hope. I read some of your book, and you wrote about us. I was late and I was told it was sold out and I couldn't come in and then the lady with little glasses threatened to call security on me so I had to leave the line and—"

"Wait! Hold up." He throws his hands up between us, so I shush immediately. "You read some of the book, and now you're here because you want me to sign it?"

"I read some of it, the beginning. I just started reading an hour ago and . . ." I want to clear the air and start over, so I take a deep breath to calm my nerves. "I came here because you wrote about us. This is us in here. Our story," I say, tapping the book.

He nods as he backs us to the car. Considering he's giving me all his attention, the groupies lose interest and start to leave. I mentally celebrate this small victory, because I'm the last woman standing.

"Yes, it is," he says. He looks away, but when his eyes return to mine, he smiles.

"My life was off-kilter, but you got me back on track. I was dropping toothbrushes in toilets and missing my subway stop and you loved me!"

By his expression, I'm assuming he's trying to interpret my ramblings. "Off-kilter? Charlie, what are you talking about?"

"Do you still love me?" I ask.

He ponders the question, but not for long. Looking shy, his eyes meet mine, and he whispers, "Yes."

"I love you, too." The words escape me, loud and happy, as I squeeze his hand.

"You do?"

"Yes! You're *my everything*, too."

His bright eyes melt me as he quickly pulls me against him. Rubbing the back of his hand gently across my cheek, he repeats barely above a whisper, "My everything." His eyes stay on me as his hand slips to the back of my head. "I want to kiss you."

"I want that, too. I know I'm laying all of this on you at once, but I want you to kiss me so very much."

"If I kiss you, this will be real. No more running."

I lean into him, getting even closer, because this is it. This is when our future begins. "It was always real. I was just too blind to see it."

His fingers weave into the back of my hair as he draws me forward. "This is your last out. Are you sure?" he asks. His minty breath fans across my face.

"Positive. Now, seal it with a kiss." I stare straight into his eyes so he can see how much I want this, how much I'm ready for us to begin. He leans in, closing his eyes, but I stop him abruptly, "Wait!"

He jerks back, startled. Confusion and sadness appear.

"I want to kiss you, but I have a cold," I say. "I don't want to get you sick."

He chuckles. "A cold couldn't keep me from kissing you right now." Grabbing me, he kisses me with every bit of passion and every ounce of need he possesses. The kiss is intense, and our lips aren't tentative. This kiss is comforting and yet makes me tingle down to my toes, like we were always meant to do this.

Leaning back, he smiles proudly. "Come on. Let's get you to bed."

I perk up even more. "I like the sound of that."

Laughing, he takes my hand again, and leads me to the car. "I see you dressed up for my book launch." I playfully punch his arm, and he feigns pain where my fist lands. "You've still got a mean right jab, too. Have you been working out?"

"I've had some time on my hands."

We both slide into the back of the car, holding hands, fingers entwined and bonded. I'm smiling so big, because this is different. This is us, the same us as before, but better. This is us, knowing what we're getting into and going into it with open eyes and open hearts. This is love. I will cherish this. I will cherish us, because everything that's happened in our lives has led us to this true love—friends, lovers, everything, the whole heart and soul kind of love. "This is really happening, isn't it?"

"Better believe it." He's confident. "You know, Ms. Barrow, now that I have your love and your full undivided attention, I may never let you go."

I lean my head on his shoulder. A giggle escapes because I'm a girl and I'm in love, and though it's not the first time, I know it will be the last. I kiss him because I can, and then I straddle him in the back of the Town Car for that exact same reason.

I hold his face and kiss him all over—his eyelids, nose, forehead, cheeks, and his wonderfully welcoming lips.

Leaning back to look into his happy blue eyes, I say, "Oh, and I still want my book signed."

"I think I might be able to do that for you." He rubs my cheek again. "I'm craving cupcakes."

I giggle. "I might be able to help you out there." I sigh, happy. "I'm so glad I finally came to my senses, but you, you knew all along. You wrote our love story. You knew we were always meant to be, didn't you?"

He kisses me long and slow then leans back, resting his head on the back of the seat while looking at me with that smuggy smile I love so much. He easily replies, "Naturally, Charlie."

Epilogue

♂

I've often wondered over the last three years what would have happened if Jim hadn't cheated on Charlie. *Would they have gotten back together if he hadn't died? Would they have gotten married and had children?*

I realize these thoughts cross my mind because I love her so much. My life wouldn't be what it is if she wasn't in it. Without her, I wouldn't be a married man, a successful writer of love stories, or a man determined to start a family because the world needs more of her in it.

Looking across the garden, she delightfully leads a group of ten elementary students in their art lesson. She uses her hands to demonstrate how to hold the paintbrush comfortably, and how much pressure to apply to the paper in front of them. With a large flourish of her brush in the air, she smiles and tells them to start painting.

Charlie quit her job at the auction house when we got into the developmental stage of the gardens. The Creative Coalition was her concept, and I wanted her to be a part of every decision. She was thrilled and thankful to be included. I wouldn't have it any other way.

She catches me watching her, but that's nothing new. It's hard to take my eyes off her. Against a backdrop of blooming rose bushes, her cheeks turn the prettiest pale pink when she smiles and sends a small wave my direction. Her yellow dress is bright and happy, just like her. Like today, from the moment I met her, she's been my own personal sunshine, and I revel in her rays.

That kiss after my book signing was a promise. From then on, we've been together. As clichéd as it sounds, those six months we spent apart gave her the chance to finally deal with Jim's legacy of betrayal and guilt. As much as I wanted to stay by her side, I became a barrier to her in dealing with her trust issues. Without me there, she could do what I couldn't—heal her broken heart. Although it hurt my own heart to let her walk away that August, it was best for her.

I thought about her all of the time. I picked up my phone to call her at least three times every day, but I would set it down again, knowing she had to make the next move. The hard part was not knowing if she ever would.

She did. Thankfully.

Today, I sit in the garden of the nonprofit organization we started last year, which introduces the humanities to underprivileged children. The kids go on field trips to museums and the New York Public Library in Manhattan. They volunteer at local charity organizations to learn compassion, and take a variety of courses such as writing, painting, and sculpting free of charge.

Grace left me twenty-five million dollars. My family was livid that I got the bulk of her estate, but they were more shocked that she left the remainder of her money to the New York City Department of Education to be used to continue the in-school art program she supported while she was alive.

Charlie and I used eleven million of it to buy a condemned building for the land and the lot next door. It was torn down, but we utilized the existing foundation to support a smaller eco-friendly, two-story building that houses our offices and three classrooms. We turned the remainder of the land, including the vacant lot, into a large green space christened Grace's Garden. We wanted to build something beautiful among the dilapidated surroundings and I think we succeeded.

"How are you?" I ask as Charlie sits down next to me on the bench.

"I love being here." She takes a deep breath. "I love this program and the kids and the hope I see in their eyes. I love," she says, turning to look me in the eyes, "you. Thank you for loving me."

"You're thanking me for loving you?" I quirk an eyebrow.

"Yeah, I guess I am thanking you for loving me."

"The pleasure's all mine." I chuckle.

She stands and looks around. "I need to confirm the trip to MoMA for next week. Will you cover the class for me?"

Standing up, I salute her. "Consider it covered."

Walking over to the class, I think about my family and how much has changed. My mother has visited the gardens several times, even bringing my dad for a picnic once. She likes it here, and she likes Charlie. She once told me she was happy I'd found someone who loved me for me and not my money. We both knew that was as close as she would get to admitting she was wrong for pushing her social agenda on me. Deep down, I know she respects that I stood by my beliefs.

But it pleased both my parents and Charlie when I finished my degree just over a year ago. I went to school while the Coalition was being built. I have a degree now but not in business like my parents wanted. I earned my Bachelor of Arts in English. I did it for me this time.

My mom recently came to our apartment with three copies of my latest book for me to sign. She was giving them to friends and was proud that I'd made my way on my own. She didn't apologize for not supporting me years ago, but we're in a good place these days. I consider that progress in rebuilding our relationship.

Approaching the class from behind, I clap my hands together once to get their attention. "How's everyone doing on their paintings?"

"My rose looks like a turtle, Charlie." Julian is nine and bright as can be, but painting may not be his forte.

I stand behind him, analyzing the lines and overall picture. "I like the detailing, but it might look like a turtle because of the colors you chose. Close your eyes and imagine your rose in red or orange or yellow, instead of green and brown. Doesn't look like a turtle in those colors."

"So color matters? Yeah, okay. Maybe I'll add some red." He gives me a high-five and a smile. I start to move to the next student, but he stops me. "Charlie?"

"Yes?" I ask, squatting down next to him.

"I'm not really into this painting stuff, but I liked that writing class we did last month."

"Then you should take the next level. You have a way with words. I think you're a talented writer."

"My mom doesn't have much money—"

"Don't worry about that. Like the other courses, we'll cover all of the expenses for you. You just need to promise me that you'll work hard and show up on time."

"Deal," he says. His smile is huge and contagious.

I still can't believe this is real. Grace would be so proud. Mrs. Lackey would be proud of her matchmaking skills, too. Little did she know that her funeral would make the woman of my dreams a reality.

A little over one year ago, I was worried that Charlie sensed a setup. Not to discount my romantic ways, but a picnic in the middle of the workday felt like a setup even to me. The calm of today makes me laugh, remembering that special afternoon.

I secretly arranged for her to have the rest of the afternoon off from work. How would I know that her department would receive the consignment from a private collector in Maine today?

So, Charlie is anxious and a little hesitant to take me up on my lunch offer when I call her that morning. Luckily, I can be persuasive.

I show up a few minutes early and wait downstairs for her.

"Hey handsome."

"Hey pretty girl." I kiss her, having wanted to do that all morning.

"We're having a picnic?" She eyes the bag in my hands.

"Yep, seems like a very couple-y thing to do."

"It's March and kind of chilly outside for a picnic, don't you think?"

I take her hand in mine. "We have each other to keep us warm."

"Awww, I love your sappy side, Charlie," she says, poking me in the ribs. "But you're right. We do have each other." As she leans her head on my shoulder, I wrap my arm around her back, and we start walking west.

"Central Park?"

"No, the library."

I can see the excitement in her eyes, and she smiles, pleased with this idea.

Two quick subway stops later and we're there. As we climb the library steps, I move closer to her, just wanting to be near her. My heart beats faster with every step we take, and it's not from the climb.

"I want to eat over here." I lead her to the left of the front doors, past Patience the lion to the Beauty fountain.

She stands there looking a little confused, so I start talking. "I need to tell you something, Charlie, and thought this place was right for us."

"We're not here for lunch?"

"We are. We're here for lunch. Are you hungry?" She's hungry. Of course she is. Maybe I should sort the food out first. No, I can't. I need to do this, and then we can eat.

"Yes. It is lunchtime." I know she can tell something's off with me, because she's wary. I can hear it in her tone.

I kiss her cheek. "I'll try not to drag this out then." Dropping the bag to the ground, I climb up on the lowest ledge below the fountain. "I wanted to bring you here because this," I say, signaling behind me to the lavishly carved marble statue, "is considered the epitome of beauty. But she pales in comparison to you. That first day, that first contact we made on the train, changed me forever. The girl of my dreams ran right into me, and I mistakenly let her go." I sit down, and she moves closer.

"What are you doing, Charlie?" she asks. Her eyes are equally concerned and thrilled.

I take a deep breath, wanting this to be right, wanting this to be perfect, but I'm not perfect, so I stumble through my unrehearsed speech the best I can. "I made my second huge mistake that night when I let you walk out of that club. I felt the spark with you, the one that people brag about—a pull, an attraction. I knew you were the one, and I let you walk away from me again." I slip off the ledge and take her hands in mine. "I'm sorry I relied on fate instead of destiny back then."

She's shaking her head as tears fill her eyes. "We both did. I walked out of the club feeling that magic, too, and I still left. You knew after that night, when it took me so long to figure it all out. Jim was always my fate, but you, you Charlie, are my destiny."

"Today is two years to the day that I first laid eyes on the most beautiful woman I've ever seen." As her tears escape her eyes, she sniffles. I cup her face and run the pads of my thumbs over her cheeks, wiping away the tears. I want to say so much to her. I want to tell her everything I dream of in life, but she knows all that. I want her to know that I want her to be a permanent part of my life. But instead, I kiss her as passionately as I can, needing to show her how much I love her and how much I care.

I grab the bag and take her to the other side of the main library entrance.

"Where are we going now?" she asks and I can hear the excitement in her voice.

"Do you trust me?"

"Why would I not?" She smiles.

"Just checking." From the moment I kissed her after the book signing, she never held back, even at the threat to her own heart.

I lift her by the waist and set her at the base of the Truth fountain just north of the library entrance. I pull the ring out of my pocket and kneel down in front of her. After a large and rather uncomfortable gulp, I say, "Charlotte Barrow, I was attracted to you the moment I saw you on the subway. I liked you the minute we started talking at the club. But I fell in love with you the day you took a chance and went to my great-aunt's funeral with me."

She hops down from the ledge and comes to me. "Stand, please, Charlie. I need you to hold me."

"But tradition?"

"Screw tradition. Nothing we have ever done has been traditional. Why start now?"

I stand, and she throws herself into my arms. With her face tucked against me, she exclaims, "Yes! Yes, yes, a million yeses!"

I can't stop the laugh that erupts. "I haven't asked you yet!"

"I don't care," she says, leaning back and grabbing my face. A kiss, two more, and a smile. "I want to marry you. I want to share the rest of my life with you. I want to make babies with you. I want everything with you, but I would be fine with nothing else as long as I have you."

She's never been one to desire money. "You'll have everything you ever need and more, baby. I promise you that." She's crying. I kiss her forehead and hug her to me. "Will you marry me, Charlie?" I whisper into her ear, nuzzling in her hair.

She nods against my neck, struggling to speak as she cries. "I will. Thank you."

I lean back, amused by her answer. "Are you thanking me for asking you to marry me?"

She laughs as she wipes her tears away. "Yes, I guess I am."

Grinning ear to ear and feeling a bit teary-eyed myself, I slip the ring onto her finger. I worried while shopping that I would buy a ring that she would think was too showy or too plain. I needed to find balance. I thanked Jim for the inspiration on this one. Seeing that ring at the auction told me that I could buy a ring that was as classic and beautiful as she was. It wasn't about being the biggest or the flashiest one out there. It would be a ring that she loves, not one to impress others. His loss was definitely my gain and I'll be forever grateful for their breakup, which led to her being in my life.

"I love it. It's perfect," she says, then kisses me. She's right. The delicate band of diamonds is perfect on her finger.

We spend the rest of the lunch hour eating, laughing, and loving.

"You have the rest of the day off if you want it, but I know how important that consignment is to you."

"This is real. What we are, this is life, our life, and it's the most important thing to me. It's way more important than some old stuff that will still be there tomorrow."

When I finish reminiscing, one of the other teachers has arrived to take over the painting class for me, and I walk through the gardens to the office to finish some paperwork. It's a beautiful day, and it's times like these that I think of my great-aunt, and what an inspiration she was in my life. She would have loved how we spent the money. She would have loved Charlie even more. I wish they could have met. Although both Charlie and Grace have told me never to live in regret, all of those regrets led us to where we are now, and this life makes me smile.

Just over an hour later, Charlie calls from the front, "You ready?"

I shut down my computer and meet her at the door. Grinning, I grab her by the hand and pull her to me. Locking her body within my arms, I stare down into her bright blue eyes. We still play the same games we did before we were married. When her arms tighten around me just as strong, I say, teasing, "You still can't resist me."

"I can totally resist you," she says defiantly. "And you will not make me blush."

"Wanna bet?"

She gulps, her smile falters, and she challenges. "I dare you."

My lips are on hers before she has a chance to finish the phrase. I slide one hand up her back and the other into her hair as I press closer and deepen the kiss. As soon as I feel her body losing tension, I know I'll win this bet.

Three.

Two.

One.

My arms tighten as she gives in, her body putty in my hands. I love that I make her feel this way—needy, cherished, and beautiful. I lean back so I can see her face. Her cheeks are all pink and a bit flustered.

"Don't even say it. I can feel it," she says, smirking as she places one hand on her face.

Our arms drop down, but we remain holding hands.

"I wasn't going to say a thing," I reply, beaming over my skills.

She rolls her eyes. "You don't have to say anything. That haughty smile across your face says more than enough."

"Hottie? Did you just call me a hottie?"

"Haughty . . . wait, hottie? Let's just skip the semantics and get to the good stuff."

I bump her side playfully. "The semantics with you *are* the good stuff."

She faces me, stepping as close as she can until our bodies are flush. Wrapping her arms around my neck, her expression softens, and I can see the love in her eyes. "You're absolutely right. I love every semantical bet we have, and I love you. I always did, deep down, and I always will. Now, take me home and show me how much you love me."

I call her made-up words Charlie-isms, and still find them adorable, just like her. "We have to wait until we get home?" I tease her by pressing myself firmly against her.

"Well, well." Her cheeks redden as she looks around. "In that case, I think we should take a cab instead of the subway. It's faster." After hailing a taxi, we hop in the back. She winks at me then squeezes my thigh.

I lean in really close to her ear and say, "You keep teasing me like that, and I don't think I'll be able to control my urges."

"*Urges.* I like that word."

"It's a solid word, just like me."

"That is true. You are a solid guy." She places her hand in my lap, but plays coy for the driver's sake. Turning in the seat, she drapes her legs over mine. Pressing her lips to my cheek, she kisses her way to my ear and whispers, "I can't wait to feel how solid you really are."

"You're a little minx, Mrs. Adams."

"Oh, Mr. Adams, doth thou protest my wanton ways?"

"Protest? Never." I adjust beneath her, not finding any relief in the way she so blatantly taunts me with her "wanton ways."

The car pulls to the curb, and I toss a fifty over the front seat, eager to get my wife to bed. We barely have the apartment door closed before I have her pressed against the back of it. My hands tug at her sweater, and she pulls my shirt over my head. Our lips remain locked together until we have to part to rid ourselves of our clothes.

Stripped to our underwear, we stop, trying to catch our breath. I take the time to slow things down and admire her body with my eyes, hands, and my mouth. I hear her head bump as it drops back onto the heavy wood of the door. Lowering to my knees, I take the straps of her bra with me and unclasp it in the back. Her panties are next, which she steps out of and I toss behind me. Rising back up, I kiss her neck and that ticklish spot of hers just behind her ear. I make my way down her body, leaving a trail of goose bumps in my wake.

My tongue slides down the curve of her waist and across her stomach where I kiss her belly button and then move lower. Her hands secure themselves into my hair as I make love to her amazing body with my mouth.

It's not long before I feel her shivering under my touch, and I stand. "Let's move to the bedroom," I whisper against her lips.

My whole body is pulsing in anticipation as we walk to our bedroom. Sitting down on the edge of the bed, she parts her legs, and I adjust between them. Pulling down my boxer briefs, she kisses my body, causing me to moan. She scoots back onto the bed as I crawl over her, settling comfortably between her legs.

"Love me," she whispers, weaving her fingers into my hair and pulling me down to her.

"Always. I'll always love you," I reply honestly. I kiss her with all of my love while pushing into her warm and welcoming body.

Making love to her is unlike any experience I've ever had. I make love to her with my soul as much as my body, giving her all of me. She returns every emotion she feels for me within each movement and sound. Every time we're connected this way, I'm reminded of how fortunate we are to have found each other.

One month later, I'm chasing her through a field of giant sunflowers. Her voice is music that floats in the wind, a melody of laughter and sweetness to my ears. After we exit the field near the farmhouse, she drops down onto the green grass, spreading her arms and legs out, relaxed and beautiful.

I collapse next her and stare up at the wide blue skies while trying to regain my breath.

"Kansas is just as wonderful as you are, Charlie," she says, the happiness in her tone is heard in every word. "Tell me about the adventures you had here."

"I was an only child, so I daydreamed a lot. When I was here, the fields were never-ending, the flowers seemed taller, and my imagination was boundless."

I turn to look at her. Her eyes are closed, her face shadowed by her hat. The sun is starting to set, and although I know we should go inside and think about dinner, I don't want this carefree joy to end.

She suddenly stands and moves to block the sun from my eyes. All I see is an angel in a white dress and a Mets cap with a sun halo. The silhouette of her body, two curving lines from the top of her head down her sides to her feet, can be seen. "That dress is see-through, you know." I tilt my head and admire her body.

"Is there a problem with that?"

"Nope." I shake my head. "No problem here."

She looks over her shoulder toward the flowers, and with her body turned to the side, I can see the silhouette of her little baby bump. Four months along.

But I also notice other things. I sit up, resting back on my hands. "Are you wearing panties under there?"

"Wouldn't you like to know?"

"I have my ways of finding out."

She hikes her skirt up and straddles my lap. "I just bet you do."

"How much?"

She purses her lips and squints while looking up in contemplation. "I'll bet the farm on it."

"You're willing to gamble this place?"

"I am. It's kind of a win-win here. Even if I lose, you win, which technically means I win, too."

"I love those crazy thoughts of yours."

"Is that all you love?" She waggles her eyebrows at me.

I hold her in place as I lie back down. "I love everything about you. But, let's get to the important part. You can't get enough of me, can you?"

That makes her laugh as the breeze blows around us. "Never, but I'm woman enough to admit it."

"You're all woman, all right," I say, carefully rolling on top of her.

"We should go inside, Mr. Smuggy."

"You love my smugginess."

"Smugginess isn't a word."

"Wanna bet?"

"I think this is how we got into this mess in the first place," she says, squirming beneath me to tease.

"If by mess you mean love, then it's absolutely how we fell in . . . mess."

She laughs as she playfully pulls me even closer. "Less talking and more kissing."

I listen to the woman. She's very smart.

The End.